Cowgirls Do It Better
Better
Volume One:
Redemption

CONTENTS

DEDICATION

For my friend, Nicola, the best cowgirl I know.

CONTENT INFO

Please read through the below triggers warnings and take care of yourself when reading…

- Driving under the influence – resulting in fatality
- Parental death
- Incarceration
- Parental neglect / abuse
- Drink spiking
- Violence
- Grief
- Domestic violence mentions
- Underage drinking

Redemption *Noun*

The action of saving or being saved from sin, error, or evil.
"God's plans for the redemption of his world".

PROLOGUE

Jack

12 YEARS AGO
"I wish you'd never been born!"

Words every son wants to hear on their eighteenth birthday, I know, but that was how my family rolled, I guess.

It wasn't the first time I'd heard that and it wouldn't be the last either. The last time would be saved for a more special, even more perfect moment. The kind you never forget...but this time, well, those words kinda led to that moment.

"Same!" I shouted back, spit flying from my mouth in my drunken state. I stared at my mother, too young to know how to look after herself, let alone parent me. Her brown hair hung limp around her shoulders and her eyes were red-rimmed. Clearly she was as drunk as I was. My excuse though: I was celebrating.

Today I was eighteen. I'd been waiting for this day for the longest time. Ready to move out and abandon this rundown shack. For far too long I'd been dreaming of leaving this damn place, leaving behind the parents who raised me against their will and starting out on my own.

"Git the hell outta here, Jack*ass*. And don't come back!" Dad shouted, stumbling up next to my mom. Ah Jackass, the wonderful nickname they'd given me, how I wouldn't miss it.

Bitterness twisted in my gut at the way Dad wrapped his arm around Mom's shoulders, the solidarity they occasionally showed each other but never me. When my only crime was being born.

I couldn't take it anymore. I ducked past them and stumbled into my bedroom clumsily. It wasn't just the alcohol sloshing in my veins that made me clumsy. I'd always felt too big in my body. I was a little slow on the growth spurt but when it happened, it happened quick and sometimes I felt like I was still new to my own body.

I tripped over the jeans I'd dumped on the floor and fell onto the bed, rubbing my hands over the comforter to find my phone. I grabbed it and held it up in front of my face, the bright light of the screen too harsh.

"Ssh," I hissed at the screen, then laughed at myself. I tapped at it and brought up Scotty's number.

"Yo, yo, birthday bro! How's the day going?" Scotty answered. He wasn't what I would call my ride-or-die, like so many people had. But we were pals, we liked some of the same things and we could let off steam together.

"Fucking shit, as usual. I need to leave, parents are parenting hard today and I need out, man. You free?"

"Yeah, sure thing. Only my dad's borrowed my car

since his crapped out so you gotta come get me."

I sighed. "I can't man, I'm buzzed."

"Shit." Scotty clucked his tongue like a mother hen. "How buzzed?"

"Pretty buzzed, I ain't gonna lie."

"It's not far though, what like a ten-minute drive and most of it is the back road past the ranches. You could do it."

I opened my mouth to tell him I couldn't do it, but loud shouts and screaming from the living room erupted and I knew my parents were having one of their showstopping fights. I wanted to be anywhere else for that.

"I dunno, man."

"Eat some coffee grounds, splash some water on your face and you'll be fine. Besides it's late and in the middle of nowhere, no one will be out this time of night."

Scotty had a point. There was a loud smash and I turned my head towards the door. Despair hit me hard and had tears prickling the backs of my eyes. *Oh shit no, we're not doing this.* I inhaled sharply and slapped my cheek.

"Okay, gimme five and I'll leave." I ended the call and pulled my boots on. Glancing in the cracked mirror, I gave my cheeks a pinch. Several deep breaths later and I was feeling a bit more alert.

I opened my door and sped into the kitchen, wanting to avoid the firing line, and splashed some water on my face from the faucet. I dug through the cabinets but there were no coffee grounds, nothing.

"Shit," I groaned. I chugged some water and grabbed my black leather jacket from the table and went out the back, trying to avoid the *Parents of the Year.*

The keys jangled in my hand as I unlocked my pride and joy, a 1980s Ford truck. It had been ready for scrapping but I'd worked hard at my after-school job and saved up for it, hoping to restore it.

I jumped in, winding the window down to let the cool spring air inside the cab. I took a few more deep breaths and started the engine. The truck stalled and then roared to life. I revved the engine a few times to get her going, she was a slow starter in her old age.

The screen door on the porch banged open and in my rearview mirror, I saw my father come flying out, tripping over old plant pots on the porch, cussing and shouting.

"Jackass! Where the fuck do you think you're going?" He stumbled again and came after me.

I wanted to ease into the drive, still not feeling one hundred percent sober but I had to get out of there before he got hold of me. He didn't try to hit me anymore, now that I was bigger than him. When I was sixteen, he made that mistake once and never tried it again. And goddammit I still felt guilty about hitting him back and didn't wanna have to do that again, even if he was a piece of shit.

I put the truck in gear, the clutch resisting but I forced her. "Come on girl, not tonight," I groaned and then she was off. Something bounced off the bed of the truck and a glance in my mirror told me it was my dad's shoe. He was screaming after me, but I couldn't make out what he was saying, not that I even cared.

The scent of freshly cut grass and wildflowers came in through the window as I headed down my road and onto the main strip. I had to blink a few times, my eyes wouldn't focus properly when streetlights glared but I'd be good once I was out in the rolling fields and ranches where the streetlights were few and far between.

The road changed to dirt and gravel. I released a breath, knowing I was away from the most populated areas. Not long, and I would be at Scotty's and then I could sober up before the drive home. If I even decided to go back.

My phone rang in my jacket pocket, I pulled it out and saw Scotty was calling me. I fumbled to answer, my eyes flicking to the road then my phone slipped from my grip.

"Fuck!" I growled, lunging forward to grab it and knocking it under my seat.

"Jack?" I could hear Scotty's voice coming from under the seat, all muffled and a little bit Darth Vadery, or was that the alcohol making him sound like that? I patted the floor, trying to keep my eyes on the road. My fingers brushed the edge of the phone but I just needed a bit more space.

I took my eyes off the road.

For one moment.

And that was all it took.

When I straightened, phone in hand, I had a split second before the flash of blonde hair appeared and then the most sickening sound I've ever heard in my life.

Screaming. So much screaming.

It was coming from me.

CHAPTER ONE

Katarina

Can you call yourself an orphan when you're over thirty? Asking for a friend…

I stood by the old bur oak trees on our property line, having just scattered my father's ashes, hugging my four sisters to me. All of them were in various states of sobbing, but not me. I couldn't. I had to be the strong one and keep us all together. I was the oldest, so they all looked to me for guidance now Mama and Daddy were both gone. But who could I look to?

I tilted my head back, the rain tickling my face, twitching my closed eyelids. Perfect weather if you asked me. I actually loved the rain and I knew Daddy did too.

Sometimes we would sit together on the porch and watch as it poured and poured, big grins on both of our faces.

Not anymore.

I swallowed the sob that tried to heave itself from my throat but it stuck, refusing to go until finally I was granted some grace and it disappeared. The pastor of our church came over and, struggling to get to me through my siblings, just nodded at me.

"If you need anything from us, y'all just holler."

"Thank you for coming and saying a prayer, Pastor Dave," I gritted out, trying to keep the despair from my voice and struggling to rein it the fuck in.

He nodded once more before glancing at each woman in my arms then he shook his head sadly. I fought another wave of crushing misery. He finally left, taking his pity with him and it was just us, standing in the rain that trickled through the leaves, Daddy's ashes blending with Mama's in the dirt. *Now they're together again.*

I didn't know what to do next, but after a half hour, self-preservation finally kicked in.

"Come on, girls. We can't stand out here all day." I squeezed each of them in turn and they eventually lifted their heads, and turned their heartbroken, tear-stained faces to me for guidance.

But I didn't know what we did now. Except, maybe, eat?

"Let's go get some food in our bellies, we'll feel much better then." I cringed when I realized what I'd said. My youngest sister, Tilly, frowned at me, her blonde hair plastered to her head and her green eyes so bright. "Sorry Tills, you know I didn't mean it like that."

Not only was Tilly the most sensitive but she was fifteen, right in the middle of all those teenage hormone changes that made everything so much worse. I tried to bear this in mind whenever I spoke to her. Her sharp, bright stare softened slightly, and she nodded before linking our arms together. She was extra clingy with me at the moment, but I didn't mind. She was just a baby.

I turned my head towards the main house and started trudging back. We all kicked our feet in the wet grass, slipping occasionally and catching one another.

The sprawling farmhouse came into view, with its log structure and wraparound porch. We went up the porch steps and inside, the familiar scent of pine and sandalwood enveloping us.

In silence we removed our boots and lined them up on the rack by the glass double front door. The girls drifted into the kitchen, but I stayed, staring at the boots. Four sets of cowgirl boots in various colors. Daddy bought us all a pair on our sixteenth birthday, it was a rite of passage for us but now there would be no more colorful boots.

Oh God, Tilly…she won't get any. I put my fist in my mouth, biting down hard on my knuckles to stop the sob from slipping out, even as a tear ran down my cheek at the thought of Tilly never getting hers. I made a mental note to find her a pair, I had six months until her birthday.

"Kat?"

I looked up and saw Madison standing there, her thick brows dipped in as she looked between me and the row of rainbow boots. "Oh God, Tills," she moaned, and her lower lip wobbled.

"Maddy, I swear if you cry, I won't keep it together. And I need to, Mads," I croaked.

Maddy dashed her cheeks with her hands. "See, all gone, no tears." She blinked rapidly as big fat droplets leaked down her cheeks and the ridiculousness of it all actually had me fighting a smirk. Maddy smiled softly through her tears as she saw my lips twitch. She could always make me smile; it was her gift. At twenty-nine, she was the second eldest, the closest to me in age and we'd been thick as thieves growing up. Still were.

"All better." I shot her a watery smile.

"I'll help get some dinner ready. Leo will be by soon, if that's okay? Just to help out with a few things?" She twirled her honey blonde hair around her finger, not making eye contact.

"Of course that's fine, tell Leo he can stay for dinner, we'd love to have him," I said, watching as twin spots of pink appeared on her cheeks. Leo was her best friend, they'd been friends since they were at kindergarten together. I suspected that she'd been in love with him for a while now, not that she'd admit it. Leo was a great guy. Dependable, strong and such a rock for Maddy during this whole thing. He had been here for all of us.

Maddy nodded, gave my arm a squeeze and headed back to the kitchen. I followed, finding comfort in the familiar open-plan cottage-style design with its wide counter-tops. Wooden shelves and spice racks adorned the walls with potted herbs that dangled enticingly. The oak dining table was a battered piece that had been in the family for over thirty years and had various repairs made to it. It was one wrong dish placement from collapsing but we didn't have the heart to get rid of it. The wooden chairs had checkered cushion covers in all different colors, and an oak sideboard held the dishes along with various family pictures and trinkets decorating the top. It was cozy and warm, a family room, and the place where we all spent most of our time.

Daisy, my twenty-five-year-old middle sister, sat at the table flicking through a magazine with August, the fourth youngest. Tilly sat at the island, picking at her nail polish while silent tears slipped down her cheeks. I couldn't stand to see the tears, each one like a knife to my gut.

I clapped my hands together. "So, what do y'all want to eat tonight?"

It was just us; we would do the wake another time. Oh, there were plenty of folks from the town who wanted to pay their respects, but it was all so fresh right now that it felt like too much having lots of people around. It was better just the five of us, six if you counted Leo.

"Beef?" Daisy suggested.

Tilly gasped and shook her head. After working on the ranch a few times, Tilly had fallen in love with the animals and declared herself a vegan. Now the thought of eating animals, especially cute ones, was worse than death. "No beef. Trout?"

"No!" August shouted.

"How about vegetable chilli?" Maddy suggested, coming into the kitchen and looping an arm around Tilly's shoulders. Although she had a smile on her face, her eyes were red-rimmed and her nose was pink.

Was this life now? Just one or all of us constantly crying? Grief was a motherfucker.

"Sounds good to me," August said.

"With extra beans for you," I said to Tilly who nodded gratefully.

I turned away and began gathering the ingredients. Maddy started chopping vegetables next to me. Silence reigned in the kitchen, and it was awkward and horrible, but I didn't know how to fix it.

Luckily, there was Leo.

"Hot damn, it's wet out there!" His voice echoed around the house as he entered the kitchen, soaking wet, his white shirt plastered to his incredibly muscular chest. I watched the way Maddy's eyes lingered over it and smirked to myself. *Oh, she's very interested in her best friend.*

"Leo!" Tilly yelled and ran, throwing herself at him and sobbed a little.

"Are you that upset to see me?" he teased. If anyone else entered the house the way he did and made the comments he said, they would be getting shown the door, but Leo had been around us all so long that he was like a brother.

"Leo," Maddy tsked.

"What, tough girl? You should be used to this by now." He winked at Maddy.

"I never get used to you," she murmured. I cocked an eyebrow at her, and she clapped a hand over her mouth and turned back to her chopping, blushing furiously.

Leo came over and kissed her cheek, Tilly still clinging to him. He dipped a finger into the sauce I was making, swiping a taste. His mouth pulled down and his eyebrows worked overtime before he turned to me and made a face. "Delicious as always," he joked, shuddering.

I laughed despite the misery of the day. "Get outta here." I nudged him, and he chuckled before squeezing my arm and heading over to August.

"What are you reading at the moment in book club, Augs?" he asked.

"*Pride and Prejudice*," August replied.

He rolled his eyes theatrically. "That was *so* last year, it's all about *Emma* now, catch up."

She snorted at him. "Says the man who prefers Matthew Macfadyen as Mr. Darcy."

Leo pshed. "Hey, he did a good job, better than wooden Colin. The hand flex is iconic."

"Colin Firth's wet shirt is iconic!" August argued back. They continued their debate, and he managed to play and win a round of rock, paper, scissors with Daisy at the same time and the atmosphere felt lighter than it had in days.

"Lock him down, Maddy, before a buckle bunny does. I'm begging you," I said out the corner of my mouth.

She had the gall to look shocked again. "What do you mean?"

"You know what I mean."

She flicked her hazel eyes over to him, her lips quirking up in a smirk before she looked sad. "He's not interested," she replied.

"Do I need to have a word with him?"

Horror filled Maddy's expression. "God, no! You don't have to do everything Daddy would do."

I laughed at the thought of my father having a stern conversation with Leo, whom he loved like a son and let get away with all kinds of mischief. "Daddy wouldn't have said shit to Leo."

Maddy snorted. "You're right about that."

We continued cooking, watching as the dreary day finally gave up and let the night take over, the rain continuing to pour. August set the table and Daisy got the dishes ready. Tilly made everyone drinks while Leo washed up. Then we were all seated, looking towards the empty chair at the head of the table where Daddy would have been.

Leo cleared his throat and lifted his water glass. "To Charlie." He was the only one who would have been able to say the words, I just knew it.

We all raised our glasses. "To Daddy," we chorused. Tilly promptly burst into tears and Leo pulled her into a fierce hug and reached across the table for Maddy's hand. I hugged August next to me and she in turn gripped onto Daisy. When Leo raised his head there were tears in his eyes too and I felt guilty at how much we had relied on him lately when he was also grieving.

After a moment, we began eating and eventually chatter resumed. After dinner, Leo and the girls retired to the living room to watch a movie together and I excused myself to the porch with a glass of wine.

I opened the front door. As the sound of the rain intensified, peace washed over me. I inhaled the distinctive scent and listened to the patter of it on the wood. I turned and headed over to the old Adirondack chairs we had and settled down, leaning back and tucking my feet up under me.

And then I felt him sit down next to me with a deep sigh like he used to. When I looked over, the chair remained empty but I knew he was there.

"Oh Daddy, you've done it now, ain't ya," I sighed before I finally released the sob that I'd been holding back for hours. Hell, I'd been keeping it in for weeks now. "How could you leave us all alone?"

I pressed my tongue into my top lip as the tears scalded my cheeks. "I know you didn't have a choice. I bet you fought every step of the way, didn't you? At least you're with Mama now; reunited finally and you get to watch over us all."

There was no reply though I don't know what I'd been expecting exactly. Just some words of comfort, some reassurance, *something*.

The rain continued and I took that as a sign he was still here.

"Just promise me you won't stop hanging around us. Don't stop guiding us. You always knew what to do and I have no clue what we do now. I'm winging it, Daddy. Flying by the seat of my pants, which isn't good for any of us. So don't be afraid to send me signs, put me on the right path. But don't jump out at me, you know I hate that ghost shit," I joked weakly.

I sat there for hours, sipping my wine, listening to the rain and just being alone in my grief and thoughts. I didn't realize I wasn't alone until I felt a hand on my shoulder and looked up into Leo's warm brown eyes.

"You need anything, Kat?"

I covered his hand with mine. "No Leo, you've done more than enough."

He nodded. "Alrighty then, I'll be back in the morning. Just holler if you need me before then."

"Are you sure you don't wanna stay the night? I hate the thought of you heading home in the rain."

He rubbed the back of his neck, his eyes darting back towards the house. "Nah, I think it's best I go home. I'll see you in the morning though," he said and with a wave, he was running off the porch and heading over to his car which was parked next to my truck.

I sat for a moment longer before I got to my feet, my bones aching like I was sixty instead of thirty. I locked up the front door, turned out the lights and checked that none of the girls were still downstairs. They'd all gone to their rooms. Was it weird that we all still lived at home? I couldn't tell. We had all moved out at some point but ended up back at the ranch and then just settled again.

What did I do now? Did we stay? Did we sell up? My gut clenched at the thought of selling this place where we'd all grown up, where we had all the memories of our parents. I shook my head and decided these thoughts were gonna be no good when I'd had wine and was grieving.

I took myself off to bed. My room was the biggest with an adjoining bathroom. The wide wooden window sat low on the wall and looked out over the front of the ranch. I had a baby blue and white patchwork loveseat under the window where I usually found August sitting and reading; she said it was the perfect view even though she was only looking at her book.

My king-size bed called to me and I changed into pajamas and collapsed into it, sinking into a deep sleep almost immediately. I woke with a start a few hours after I drifted off. My eyes scanned the darkness but I couldn't see anything.

"It's the wine," I groaned, burying my head in my hands. I scrubbed my face then got up, opened the drapes and cracked my window a little so I could listen to the rain as I drifted off again and it felt like my Daddy was right there, watching over me.

CHAPTER TWO

Katarina

"You've got to be kidding me? We're broke?"
I cried.

The lawyer nodded solemnly and I fought the overwhelming urge to scream until my voice cracked. Because the shit news just kept coming.

It had been four weeks since we scattered my father's ashes, and his absence was still an aching chasm in all of us. We'd been just about getting by with us all pitching in and Leo helping out too but I knew we were barely keeping our heads above water. What I didn't realize is that right under that water were sharks, waiting to take chunks out of us.

Daddy had always kept me away from the business

side of the ranch, insisting that when the time came, he would take me through it all and show me the ropes. I always wondered why he was so protective of the books and now I guess I knew.

I scrubbed my hands through my hair, tugging on the pale blonde ends and the pain traveled up my scalp, grounding me. Glancing out the kitchen window, I watched as Daisy walked one of the horses back into the stables, her lasso clipped to her waist. She was a whizz at roping cattle, could out-rope any of the ranch hands and I'd wondered if she would enter rodeo events but she had other passions.

"How long?" I asked.

"Beg pardon, Miss Cartwright?" Peter Davidson, my father's lawyer, asked.

"How long until we lose the ranch?"

"Oh forgive me, I see. Well, you've got enough to get you through the next few months but unless you do something soon, likely six months, give or take a few weeks. I'm so sorry. Charlie was a good friend of mine and this is the last thing I want to be telling you girls."

I nodded, my tongue glued to the roof of my mouth. "What if we sell off some of the land? Or sell the little cabin behind the house?"

Peter didn't meet my eyes as he shook his head. "You could try and sell off some land, but it won't be enough. Charlie's been in the red for years. I'm amazed he managed to keep it going this long. He'd been borrowing. And as his beneficiary, it now falls to you."

Of course it fucking did.

"FUCK!" I shouted, unable to keep it in.

Peter twitched at my outburst.

"I apologize."

He waved a large hand. "No need, I can only imagine

the grief—" He rolled his lips inwards at my stern glare. If one more person told me that they didn't know how I was coping, I would go on a rampage.

"We're gonna lose it all," I said absently.

"You have six months." Peter tried to be positive.

I snorted. "I honestly don't have a fucking clue what I'm doing, Peter. Daddy always kept me away from the business side of the ranch. Now I know why."

"I understand. But six months is a lifetime away yet, you've got time. I'll leave you to it but let me know if you need anything." He shuffled his papers and put them back into his plain black briefcase. He drank the rest of his coffee before I showed him to the door.

"Once again, Katarina, I'm very sorry."

"Thank you, Peter. I appreciate that," I said nicely even though I wanted to scream. It wasn't everyone else's fault that they were sorry all the time.

I slammed the door, slightly harder than I meant to but, oh well. I trudged back into the kitchen and decided 11am was the perfect time to have wine. I grabbed a glass from the cabinet and the wine from the fridge, thinking I'd need to switch to box wine soon enough if we needed to start cutting costs. I pulled the cork out of the bottle with my mouth and dropped it into the sink.

The *glug glug glug* sound of the liquid pouring into the glass had always been one of my favorites and today I just let it pour. Right to the fucking top. I slurped the rim so none spilled over the side and then drank half of it down in one go, letting out a very unladylike belch but no one was around to hear it. I giggled to myself and covered my mouth. Then giggled again. A full laugh left my body, and I laughed and laughed until my stomach ached, and then I cried.

I heard noises out in the hallway and covered my

mouth, wiping at my eyes.

"Everything okay?" Maddy asked, coming into the kitchen with August right behind her.

"Sure!" I said, too loudly. Was I drunk already?

"You sure, sure?" August asked, raising her brow at my large, half-drunk wineglass.

"Is there some rule about drinking at 11am?"

"Hell no, not in this house!" Leo boomed, coming in behind them. Maddy snickered and I was pleased to see her smiling again.

"I forgot to ask, did Tills get off to school okay?" I asked, suddenly feeling like the worst big sister in the world. It was her first day back and although we were a pretty close-knit community in Reverence, kids could still be dicks.

"Yeah?" Leo looked to Maddy for confirmation.

"Yeah!" Maddy agreed and then when Leo looked away she pulled an *eh* face at me. She was probably trying to protect Leo's feelings; he'd wanted to be the one to drop Tilly off at school.

"Cool, thanks again, Leo. I'll shoot her a message at lunch and see how she's doing."

"No sweat, happy to help," Leo smirked, his dimples popping.

"How'd it go with the lawyer? He had a sad face when he left," August asked, concern dipping her auburn brows in.

Shit. I couldn't rain all over their parade and stress them out even more. They had enough to deal with. I was the oldest and Daddy trusted me to run this ranch so I would take one for the team.

"Yeah, everything's fine. Ranch is all ours. No long-lost brothers or sisters coming out of the woodwork trying to claim their inheritance," I joked weakly.

August cocked a brow at me. "Maybe leave the joking to Maddy, you're no good at it."

I stuck my tongue out at her because I'm thirty-one going on thirteen apparently...

"Somebody needs to teach you some manners." Leo hooked an arm around August's neck and pulled her into his chest, rubbing his knuckles across the top of her strawberry blonde head until she squealed.

"I'm twenty-fwo!" came August's muffled cry.

Leo looked at Maddy with mock fear. "Dang, we might be too late."

I snorted, rolling my eyes and left them to their silly games. I had shit I needed to think about.

I went to Daddy's office at the back of the house. The door had remained shut for the last few weeks. None of us wanted to go in there and disturb anything he'd left behind, we wanted to keep it just the way he had left it. However, desperate times called for desperate measures. I needed to learn everything I could about the ranch finances and how the hell I was gonna run this place.

Opening the door, his scent immediately surrounded me. Pine, like Lysol and sandalwood from his cologne. The smell brought up so many memories, in that painful and all too realistic way that scents could, and in that moment I wanted nothing more than to have a hug from my father. Just one more. I paused in the doorway, letting the grief wash over me before I pulled myself together. I had too much to do, too much to figure out and four sisters depending on me to fix this.

His wide desk was made from walnut wood and piled high with paperwork so that felt like the best place to start but when I began shifting through it all, I quickly got overwhelmed. I put the stack of papers on the *later* pile and instead focused on the filing cabinet which looked to be in better order.

The smell of mothballs enveloped me as I tugged it open, coughing from the pile of dust I'd disturbed. Rummaging through the first section of papers, I found the deed and title for the ranch, which was handy and I'd be sure to make copies of it at some point. Some legal paperwork about the cabin at the bottom of the yard which was a little rundown. Daddy had moved into it a few years ago and given us girls the main house, it was his safe haven away from the screeching, he'd said. It was old and not in the best condition, he'd been meaning to restore it for a while but just hadn't gotten around to it.

There was a ton of other stuff that I didn't understand but I guessed now was the best time to deep-dive into it. I got comfy in the leather wingback chair in the corner next to the floor to ceiling bookcase and started reading. By nightfall I had three piles: stuff I didn't understand, stuff to ask Mr. Davidson about, and stuff I kinda got.

I stood, yawning and stretching my aching back until my neck cracked. I paused for a moment, letting my muscles adjust. As soon as I hit thirty-one, it was like my body decided to break. I'd wake up after a good night's sleep and my neck cricked, I sneezed too hard and my back went out. Getting older was tough.

I ventured out into the kitchen where I could smell dinner cooking. Everyone was crowded around the dinner table which was piled with bowls of potatoes, carrots and greens and steam was rising from a beef brisket in the center. My mouth watered.

I saw Tilly, glaring at the beef brisket and guilt instantly swamped me at being a shit big sister twice today. I'd been so wrapped up in looking through Daddy's paperwork that I'd forgotten to text her to see how her first day was going.

"Hey baby girl, how was your first day back?" I asked, running my hand affectionately over her hair.

She scowled at me and ducked her head from my grip. "Fine."

I looked over at Daisy who just shook her head at me.

"Just fine?" I ventured.

"Yes. Lots of weird, pitying looks and people being far too nice like I could break any second," Tilly muttered, pushing her plate away. "I'm not hungry, may I be excused now?"

I put her attitude down to being a teenager and tried not to let it bother me. I looked around, wondering who she was talking to, but three pairs of eyes were watching me. Now Daddy was gone, I was Tilly's guardian. The role didn't bother me, I'd looked after her most of her life, so nothing had changed but now it was official parenting.

I needed to step up more than ever.

"Oh, me? Uh, yeah I guess. Um…go and…uh do your homework?" I squeaked at the end, unsure how to parent a teenager. Maddy gave me a thumbs up.

Tilly huffed and shoved away from the table before flouncing from the room and up the stairs. I waited a beat and then her door slammed shut.

"Teenagers," Daisy tutted.

"Cut her some slack, you were a nightmare at her age," August sighed.

"I was not!"

"Daisy, you were fucking horrendous and the rest of us were a dream," Maddy laughed. "You want some dinner, Kat? I made it."

I arched a brow at her. "*You* made it?"

Maddy rolled her eyes. "Fine, it was Leo."

"Then hell yes, that boy makes good food." I sat down

at the table. "Wife him up," I murmured when Maddy put a plate in front of me. She snorted but didn't say anything more than that.

I ate my food, listening to them talk about their days.

Daisy was trying to get a job in marketing and event management having just graduated from community college but pickings were slim in a small town.

August was working part time at the local library. She loved it there, amongst all those books and it gave her time to work on the ranch, looking after the horses including her beloved Marshmallow.

A couple of years ago August had been making waves as a barrel racer with Marshmallow. But there was an accident on the circuit, Marshmallow got spooked and fell, landing on August. Luckily, August only broke her hip but decided that as much as she loved it, barrel racing was too dangerous so she quit, instead choosing to spend her time here managing the horses.

Maddy was on her rest days. She was a local firefighter and she worked forty-eight hours on shift and then had forty-eight hours off. During her off days she also pitched in at the ranch.

After dinner we all hunkered down in the living room to watch a movie before one by one, the girls retired to bed. But I was too wired. My brain kept turning over everything that I needed to do and how unequipped I felt to deal with any of it. Finally, when the clock ticked over into 3am, I took myself upstairs to bed.

Sleep didn't come though, my brain wouldn't switch off, wouldn't give me a break. It was having too much fun giving me anxiety. I threw the covers back and swung my legs out of bed and went to the window, staring out at the bright moon.

"I'm looking for a sign, Daddy. Help me please?" I

murmured. Nothing came to me but just asking for help alleviated some of the noise in my brain and I eventually managed to drift off into a fitful sleep.

I awoke the next morning to a quiet house which immediately made me suspicious. I checked the time on my phone and saw it was nearly eleven. I'd overslept! With a groan, I pulled myself out of bed, grateful for the ranch hands, and knowing Maddy would be stepping in for me. After such a late night, my brain wasn't alert.

"Coffee…I need coffee," I rasped, my voice gruff from sleep. I trudged downstairs in my pajamas and found a pot that was still fairly warm.

"Thank you, Jesus." I grabbed a mug and filled it before I heard a knock on the door. In my sleep deprived state, I didn't stop to think about who could be at my front door at 11am on a Tuesday morning.

As I approached, I saw a man through the glass, with his back to the door, looking out over the land. Tall, very tall. I was five feet ten, the tallest of my sisters so I definitely appreciated a taller man. He was broad, his clothes looked a little small for him, his black leather jacket pulled tight across his back. His chestnut hair was in need of a trim and curled at the edges but he was one fine looking gentleman from behind.

Hello, sir.

When I opened the door and he turned around, my pulse thudded to a stop. I gasped, dropping the mug of coffee and spilling it all over the porch. It splashed up my bare legs but I didn't notice the sting.

He was as surprised as me, his sky-blue eyes wide. His red lips formed a stunned O. He gave me a once over, settling on breasts which I now realized were not being held prisoner by a bra as they normally would be.

He snapped out of it and cleared his throat.

"Uh, hey, Katarina." His voice was deep, too deep. Deeper than I remembered.

Rage vibrated through me, unlike anything I'd felt before.

How dare he.

How fucking *dare* he turn up here after *everything*.

The lack of sleep, the grief and the anger at seeing this asshole on my porch sent me spiralling.

"You motherfucker! I'll fucking kill you!" I screamed, right before I launched myself at him.

CHAPTER THREE

Jack

"Happy release day, dickweed," the guard grunted.

The buzzer went off and the metal-grinding, nerve-shredding, all-too-familiar sound of my cell door opening had me quaking at the knees a little.

Finally, the day was here.

It was over.

I nearly sobbed but I needed to keep it together until I was on my own, *truly* on my own for the first time in twelve years.

The guard led me down the corridor, other inmates jeered at me, but I ignored them. I never had to see them again. Never had to go through this again and that knowledge alone had me feeling on top of the fucking

33

world.

Processing took forever. Then they gave me back my possessions. The leather jacket I never thought I'd see again. The old cell phone that was probably way too out-of-date technology-wise and had died anyway. Even an old Nokia would have struggled to keep its juice for twelve years. Old jeans, t-shirt and boots. I changed, feeling weird about putting my old clothes back on, clothes that were a little too tight now and held too many bad memories, but I didn't really have a choice.

And then I was outside. The sun shone down, and I thought I would have this overwhelming moment of *FREEDOM!* Braveheart-style but I didn't. I was relieved, sure, but there was so much uncertainty about what came next. There was a bus to take me to the accommodation that the charity set up. I'd been given my allowance to tide me over until I could find some work.

I snorted at the thought. I would struggle to find work; especially in Reverence where everyone would know what I'd done. The prison sentence didn't end when the gates opened to free me. It would last a lifetime.

There was only me and one other person on the bus and I did not want to make friends. We kept to ourselves and were dropped off outside the accommodation. It was a crumbling building, not much to look at and neither was the room. From one set of four walls to another, with the same rules. No drugs, no drinking, no fighting, no women.

But I was grateful. I dumped my bag on the bed, an old box spring which creaked and looked too small for my large frame. There were some suspicious stains on the mattress which I chose to ignore.

I paced, not knowing what to do. I was out. The world was my oyster. But there was only one thing I wanted to do. Find out what happened to my friend. The one person who visited me during my time in prison. God knows my parents didn't. They abandoned me after the accident, washed their hands of me, screaming at me during my sentencing in court that they wished I'd never been born. At first I was bitter but they did me a favor.

Someone did care though, and I hadn't seen him for two months and I'd had no letters from him which worried me. I grabbed my jacket, locked up my new room and went out. I didn't have to ask permission, didn't have to check in with anyone until my parole officer tomorrow. I left the halfway house and headed straight for Redemption Ranch to see what had happened to Charlie Cartwright.

*

11 years ago…
Wyoming State Penitentiary

"Why the fuck is he here and why the fuck does he keep coming back?" I shouted, slamming a fist against the wall.

"Don't make me give you a warning," the guard, Patrick, stated at my uncharacteristic outburst. Me and Patrick had come to an understanding after my first year here. He took pity on me, knew I wasn't going to act out like other inmates and just wanted a quiet life.

"Look, you might as well see him. He's turned up every month to see you for a year. Just hear him out, it's the least you fucking owe him."

"I know that, don't you think I know that?" I growled, anger and guilt bubbling up. "I killed his fucking wife, I know I at least owe him a conversation but…" I trailed off.

"But what?" Pat asked.

I shoved a hand through my hair, tugging at the ends and pushed out a breath. "I don't think I can face him."

"What's the worst he can do? There are guards everywhere, he ain't gonna get to you."

I paced back and forth in my cell. "I'm not worried about him attacking me. I'm worried about what he'll say."

"Don't you owe it to him to find out?"

Patrick was right. I did owe it to him. I owed him the world, my life, if he'd take it and I wouldn't even blame him after what I took from him, from his girls.

"Fuck," I huffed. It was time to nut up or shut up. "Okay, I'll go."

"Thank the Lord, you've only got thirty minutes of visiting time left anyway."

Patrick radioed to get my cell door opened. I turned and faced the wall, hands raised. The grinding of metal had me shuddering, damn I couldn't stand that sound. Patrick slipped the cuffs on me and walked me out to where visiting took place.

There were a couple of inmates visiting family. I'd only ever visited my public defender here before, never anyone else. The room was depressing, all gray and navy which did not make the environment friendly or inviting. It was too cold and industrial which I guess was the point.

I sat there, my palms sweating, my heart in my throat as I waited for them to bring him in. My knee bounced up and down. I nibbled my lip so much that the cut I had there split open and blood filled my mouth. Then my pulse pounded as he was sitting down in front of me.

He looked older, his hair and beard fully white instead of peppered with gray. The lines at his eyes and around his mouth were deeper but his eyes shone bright and kind. He wore a denim jacket over a lumberjack shirt and faded blue jeans. He looked like a dad, like a grandpa.

I swallowed around the lump in my throat, so on edge, waiting for him to speak. He glanced around, assessing the room, eyes lingering on the handcuffs I had on before turning those kind eyes on me.

"It's real good to see you, son," he said, his words deep and warm and I let them wash over me.

Then I burst into tears.

*

Present Day...

I took my time on my walk. I was in a hurry to see Charlie, but it was the first long walk I'd had in twelve years. The crickets chirped incessantly. Cars passed and I was amazed at seeing how much they had changed over the last few years, how quickly technology had advanced. Hell, when I went inside, electric cars were still a myth. I'd seen them all on TV but it was different seeing them in person. Call me crazy but I still loved a beat-up old Ford truck to these Tesla's.

The trees were lush and green, the air smelled like fresh cut grass and I inhaled the shit out of it, letting it get me high. I had to take breaks and rest. You think that you get fit in prison but there's only so much distance you can go. My stamina wasn't what I thought. I'd bulked up but I wasn't fit like I used to be. The sun shone down on me, not hot but gently warm, perfect spring weather.

The closer I got to the ranch, the bigger the pit in my gut became as I got closer to the scene of the accident. Maybe it was a mistake to come here so soon; it hadn't occurred to me that I would see it, walk right past it. I hadn't been here since that night.

My steps slowed as I came around a bend in the road and I halted altogether when I saw the bench by the side of the road, surrounded by flowers. The memorial at the scene where Sherry Cartwright had met her untimely death. At my hands.

Guilt ate at me. I didn't think I could even walk over to it, but I forced myself. Made myself face what I'd done. The bench was gorgeous, carved from solid oak, soft and gently shaped, just like Sherry. The bronze plaque read *For Sherry: the light in our lives. Gone far too soon but never forgotten.*

The air fled my lungs and I hunched over, trying to ward off the panic attack. I didn't deserve to be here, not after what I'd done. I gasped, trying to get air into my lungs but also secretly hoping it never would; then this would all be over. Instead, I continued like that, placing a hand to my chest and trying to get control of my breathing.

I'm so sorry, Sherry. I'll never stop being sorry.

Eventually, I managed to get my breathing under control and I collapsed on the ground next to the bench. I didn't dare sit on it, I wasn't worthy.

I sat there for an hour, apologizing to Sherry over and over again in my mind, knowing I could never make up for what had happened and wondering how I was going to get through life like this.

Charlie.

I needed to get to Charlie.

I pulled myself to my feet, dusted the dirt from my hands and with a final look at Sherry's bench, I continued on to the ranch.

It was located off the dirt road. The log sign that arched over the gravel path read *Redemption Ranch.* The path led down to a sprawling green pasture where horses and cows grazed. There was a large farmhouse at the edge in front of the backdrop of the Teton mountains and it was so damn picturesque it stole my breath.

I headed down the pasture and towards the house. The thought of Charlie rambling around this place all on his own didn't sit right with me. Did he look after all this land himself? He was too old to be doing all this farming now.

Jogging up the porch steps, I spotted the Adirondack chairs on one side, thinking how amazing it would be to sit there in the summer evenings and watch the sun go down. I couldn't wait to watch my first sunset later.

Anticipation filled me as I raised a fist and knocked on the door. I wasn't sure why Charlie hadn't been to see me last month. For the first time in twelve years he hadn't come. My nervous energy was off the charts, I couldn't stand still, turning around and looking at the land, the little slice of heaven it was.

The door opened and I turned, ready to greet Charlie, ready to hug him without getting shouted at by guards.

But he wasn't there.

A stunning, leggy blonde with sharp navy eyes in purple kitty pajamas…and no bra…was there. Her face was familiar. It had been over a decade but I remembered her. She'd been in the year above me at school. Katarina.

When she saw who it was, her coffee mug slid from her grip and shattered on the porch. My throat closed, I hadn't prepared for this. Didn't know what to do or how to handle it, what to say.

"Uh, hey, Katarina," I said, completely inappropriately. My social skills weren't what they used to be but even still, this was not what I should have said, and clearly she agreed.

"You motherfucker! I'll fucking kill you!" she

screamed, fire in her eyes. Then she leapt at me, her fists raised.

I didn't fight back, I just let her get all her rage out.

After all, I owed her that.

I killed her mom.

CHAPTER FOUR

Jack

11 years ago…
Wyoming State Penitentiary

"Come on now, son. No tears, you hear me?" Charlie's voice was so soothing as he reached across and put his hand over mine.

"No touching!" the guard bellowed, making Charlie jump. Charlie withdrew his hand, but his gentle eyes didn't change, and I couldn't pull myself together.

I killed his wife, why was he being nice to me?

Why wasn't he trying to hit me, scream at me, anything other than this?

This was too much. I finally understood the phrase killing someone with kindness because that's what was happening right now.

"Come on, son. You can't show weakness here," Charlie murmured. He was right, I couldn't. Other inmates in here were eyeing me up. I'd already been in more fights than I could count, my last one being two days ago when I was jumped in the shower and very narrowly escaped a shiv to the kidney.

I pulled myself together, wiped my eyes, the cuffs clinking together. I sniffed and blinked a few times as I composed myself and then faced Charlie again. I still didn't understand why he was here and I told him so.

Charlie shrugged. "Wanted to see how you were doing, have a chat."

I scoffed. "You wanted to see how the guy who killed your wife is doing?"

Charlie nodded, my harsh words not piercing his façade. They weren't harsh exactly, they were the God's honest truth. "Well, it's not entirely charitable, it won't be pleasant for you. I'd like you to take me through what happened that night."

I deflated. "But you were at my sentencing, you know everything."

"I know, son, I know." God, the way he kept calling me *son* was destroying me and healing me all at the same time. How was that even possible? "But I want to hear it again, from you. Not from a police report or some fancy lawyer."

I snorted. "My lawyer wasn't fancy."

"You got that right," he chuckled. Charlie Cartwright was here, right in front of me, chuckling. I must be hallucinating.

I shook my head. "I'm so confused about why you're here? Aren't you going to scream or yell or hit me?"

Charlie cocked his head, his blue eyes piercing my soul. "Why would I do any of that?"

"You know why."

He waved a hand dismissively, all *psh*.

"Fifteen minutes left!" the guard shouted the warning. I flicked my gaze back to Charlie.

"Come on, spill." He sat back, folded his arms over his chest all casual, like he was having dinner with an old friend and not sat in a prison talking to his wife's killer.

I glanced down at my hands, my split knuckles from fighting back in that shower. And then I forced myself to look him in the eye. If he could find it in himself to come down here, every month for a year and get turned away, trying to see me, I could at least give him this.

I shrugged. "I was drunk, I drove, I didn't see her—"

"Say her name," Charlie interrupted. Not aggressively, but gently once again.

"Her name?"

"Yes, she's not Voldemort, you can say her name. I won't have my Sherry forgotten."

I almost laughed at how surreal this whole meeting was. Almost. "Sherry."

Charlie nodded, satisfied. "That's it, keep going."

"I didn't see Sherry, I swear. I was going too fast and then it was too late. I hit her, she…she died."

Tears filled Charlie's eyes and it tore me in two. I looked away, unable to face him.

"She did love to run at nighttime, said it was freeing. I told her it was dangerous but she always said, 'Nothing bad's gonna happen to me in this town'." Charlie shook his head sadly.

I swallowed past the boulder lodged in my throat. "I will never be able to apologize enough. I'm not fighting the conviction, I'm guilty, I know what I did and I will serve my sentence without complaint. But I don't think I can ever make up for taking her away from you," I swallowed again as the tears came back. "Or your girls."

"Well, you can start by talking to me. Why were you driving drunk?"

I shrugged. "It was my birthday."

Charlie frowned. "Your parents gave you that much alcohol because it was your birthday?"

"They didn't give me any. I took it from them because, well, they're…a lot to handle."

Charlie's sharp eyes pierced me again. "I saw them at your sentencing."

I shook my head. "They had me super young, frequently told me they wish they hadn't, and I think this kind of gave them a reason to abandon me."

"I'm sorry, son."

I shook my head violently. "Do not apologize to me, ever."

Charlie sucked in a breath. "So you were underage drinking to cope with shitty parents? Then what?"

"We got in a fight and I wanted to get out. I called my friend, Scotty but he didn't have a car and he convinced me...wait no, it was all my own choice. I chose to get into that truck and drive."

Charlie's jaw was getting tighter the closer I got to the climax of the story. "Then what?"

"I got in my truck and drove. Scotty called me and I tried to answer my phone but dropped it. I bent down to get it and when I looked back up, she, Sherry was there. I didn't even have time to blink. I must have swerved from the middle of the road to the bank and she was there."

Charlie didn't say anything, just glanced down at his hands.

I struggled for something to say, a way to ease him and my own guilt. "It…it was quick. She didn't suffer too long. I waited with her and held her while…the ambulance came. By the time they turned up she was…"

Charlie held up his hand, his eyes squeezed shut and I stopped talking, sensing I'd gone too far. We sat in silence for another five minutes and I prayed for the visit to end, to have this over with. Charlie folded his hands, like he was praying, his eyes closed and lips moving.

He opened them and looked at me. "Thank you for sharing that with me. I know it can't have been easy going over it again."

I shot him a pleading look, begging him not to thank me. Not to be grateful for anything I've done for him.

"Times up. Visitors say goodbye and move out," the guard called. Relief cut through me like a knife.

But Charlie didn't make a move to stand. "I'd like to come back, if that's okay with you?" he asked, shocking me.

My mouth opened and closed, floundering. "Why?"

Charlie shrugged. "Because I want to forgive you. I know that's what she would have wanted. You were a kid who did something stupid. You're stuck here for over a decade still, your family's abandoned you. I feel like you're being punished enough and I don't want any more tragedy. Something good needs to come from this."

I couldn't believe it. "You *want* to forgive me?" I asked, dumbfounded.

Charlie stood. "Well, I'm not going to say it's been easy getting to this point, but Sherry and the Lord have been guiding me on the right path and I believe this is it. I don't want any more sadness, there's been too much, and you're too young."

I couldn't speak. The guard came over to usher Charlie out and I just watched him walk away. He turned back when he was at the door.

"See you next month, son."

45

*

Present Day...

She came at me with such force that I stumbled back, taking us off the porch and falling back onto the grass. She straddled me, scrabbling to get to me, dragging her nails down my face and screaming at me the entire time.

I tried to hold her off. I grabbed one arm, leaving my body wide open for her to swing another fist which connected with my jaw. It hurt but not as much as it hurt her, her sharp intake of breath hissing in my ear. I didn't want to hurt her but I tried to restrain her. Her nails sliced my cheek again and I grunted at the pain.

"Hey, whoa!" someone shouted, and then the feisty wildcat was pulled off me. A man I didn't recognize had her around the waist but she still struggled to get to me. Her blonde hair flicking around her like pale fire whipping out, ready to attack me again.

"Easy, Kat, what the hell is going on out here?" the guy shouted over her.

Kat's eyes blazed at me and she spat in my direction, just missing me. "Get him out of here. You have the fucking *audacity* to turn up here? How dare you!" she shouted.

The guy looked from Kat to me and I held up my hands. I didn't want trouble. I'd only been out of prison for four hours and I didn't want to land back there.

"I'm sorry, I didn't realize you would be here. I shouldn't have come. I just wanted to see Charlie, I was worried and—"

Kat stopped fighting and went limp in the other guy's arms, and her face dropped. "Charlie?"

Something flickered over the guy's features and then

his expression hardened like he realized exactly who I was. His jaw clenched and he swung his gaze from me to Kat.

"You don't know, do you?" he asked. Kat swung her wide-eyed navy stare to him. She pushed away from him, her anger now focused on someone other than me.

"Leo, why are you talking like you know him?" she demanded, flinging an arm in my direction.

"Know what?" I asked, a cold shiver trekking my spine.

"I'm not surprised no one told you. It didn't occur to me either."

Kat's glare darted between the two of us. "What the fuck is going on? And why are you here to see my father, haven't you done enough?"

The man looked down at Kat before shooting me a sympathetic look. "Charlie died. About six weeks ago."

My world stopped.

CHAPTER FIVE

Katarina

I stared between Leo and Jack, observing the silent communication between them that I didn't like one bit.

Jack Drayton.

Of all people to be on my porch this morning, I never thought it would be this guy. When did he get out? Why weren't we notified? And why the hell had he turned up here?

His cheek was bleeding from my nails and a violent part of me, that hadn't existed until five minutes ago, reveled in it. I tracked the droplet as it slowly trickled down his cheek, satisfaction filling me and riling me up again.

Jack frowned at me, his light blue eyes narrowing. His stance stiffened, like he was prepared for me to launch myself at him again. I was ready to, but I knew Leo wouldn't let me and I didn't want Leo getting hurt in the fray. I turned my vicious stare away before I did something I couldn't control.

Then Leo told him that Daddy had died and Jack's entire attitude changed. He choked, his eyes bugging slightly and he spun away and bent forward, his leather jacket creaking as he hunched and rested his elbows on his knees.

Leo's stare flicked to me. I could see from the corner of my eye that he was concerned but I ignored it. As much Leo was like a brother, he could never understand how I was feeling. The agony we all experienced at losing my mother was a direct result of the man in front of me. I would not be moved by Jack's apparent distress.

Jack struggled to get his breath, I could hear it rasping from him. Was he having a panic attack? Because we told him my dad died? Leo nudged me but I didn't move. Eventually he sighed and slowly approached Jack, putting a hand on his back.

"You okay, man?"

At the touch, Jack flinched and immediately spun away from Leo. Leo held his hands up in surrender. "Sorry, that's my bad. I wasn't thinking. I just wanted to check you're okay?"

Jack swiped his hand along his top lip, his eyes red-rimmed and so sad that for a second, a split second, I felt bad for him. Until I remembered exactly who he was and squashed that feeling like a pesky bug.

Jack took a few deep, shuddering breaths then asked. "How?"

"Heart attack."

"Leo!" I hissed. I didn't want to share that information with Jack, he didn't deserve to know anything about us. He lost that privilege when he fractured our family.

Jack sighed. "So that's why he stopped visiting," he muttered, scuffing his boot in the grass.

My blood ran cold. "Excuse me?"

Jack's cool stare met mine and for a moment he looked confused before his expression blanked.

Leo plugged his hands onto his hips and nodded towards Jack. "Charlie's been visiting him."

"What!" I stared between them, hardly able to believe what I was hearing. Daddy had been visiting Jack? And Leo knew about it and didn't say anything? "For how long?"

"Once a month. For the last eleven years," Jack spoke softly, his eyes on the ground.

My sharp intake of breath drew his gaze. My heart thudded, trying to pound its way out of my chest and I pressed my hand to it, struggling with the ache. Jack stepped forward, concern pinching his chestnut brow but Leo jumped between us and shook his head.

"I think it's best if you leave, man," Leo said.

Jack nodded. "Of course. Kat, please know that I never would have turned up here if I'd known you were here. And, for what it's worth, I'm sorry about Charlie. He was a great man."

I bit my tongue to keep back the vitriol I wanted to spew at his words. How dare he talk about my father like that, like he knew him, like they were friends.

He hung his head and turned, trudging off the property and I watched, chest heaving with rage, until he was a speck in the distance.

Leo shuffled next to me and cleared his throat. He was

the closest thing I had to a brother and I loved him fiercely but I sure as shit didn't like him right now.

"I think it's best you went home," I growled.

"I get it, Kat. You're pissed that I knew but I only found out by accident, and Charlie begged me not to say anything."

"I don't want to hear this." I spun on my heel, heading back up the porch, ignoring the shattered mug and slamming the door shut. I stormed straight into the office and threw myself down in that wingback chair and put my head to my knees.

Jack Drayton was just on my front porch. Looking for my dad because they were... What? Buddies? My brain couldn't comprehend it. The fact that he would just turn up here, like he owned the fucking place. My fury burned bright at the audacity. I was already so on edge and delicate from trying to cope these last few months. Seeing that man had just tipped me right over the edge. My cheeks heated at the way I threw myself at him, attacking him. I'd never behaved like that before. I was surprised he didn't do more to defend himself.

I wasn't sure how long I sat there but then I heard chatter. Noise filled the house and I realized all the girls were home. I lifted myself out of the chair, stiff and achy once again and realized I was still in my pajamas. I scurried up the stairs to get dressed before coming back down into the kitchen.

When I came in, all the girls were sitting around the table. Leo was leaning against the counter with his arms folded over his chest and everyone went silent.

I glanced at each of their faces, wondering if they knew about Jack. "What's going on?"

Maddy looked to Leo. "Leo got a call from the school today."

My gaze drifted over to Tilly who suddenly found her nails very interesting. "What happened?"

Leo cleared his throat. "Our little Tills got into a fight with someone."

My head whipped back to Tilly. "What!" Could this day get any worse?

"They started it," Tilly insisted belligerently.

"Are you kidding me? You think that's an excuse? Why are you getting into fights in the first place, that's not acceptable, Tilly."

Leo snorted, clearly remembering my *Million-Dollar Baby* impression from this morning and I turned my glare on him. He just arched a brow at me.

Maddy looked between us. "What's going on?"

Leo resisted looking at her and just kept his stare on me. I needed to tell them. I didn't want them to randomly bump into Jack in town and feel completely blindsided. Like I was today.

"Jack Drayton has been released."

The room was so silent you could hear a pin drop. Then they all spoke at once.

"What?" Daisy gasped.

"Why did no one tell us he was getting out?" August asked.

Maddy stood up. "How do you know?"

A wave of exhaustion swept through me as they peppered me with questions.

"He came by," Leo answered.

"He did?"

Tilly held her phone up, showing us an image of Jack from an article. "He's cute."

"Tilly!" August reprimanded.

"What? Well, he is," Tilly sulked, every inch the fifteen-year-old.

"I don't think he knew you ladies were living here. He was looking for Charlie and evidently hadn't been informed that he'd died," Leo said.

Maddy looked between us. "Why would he be told that?"

Leo's stare bounced to me and I could see the plea in his eyes but I shook my head. I was mad at Leo but how I felt would be nothing compared to how betrayed Maddy would feel in a minute.

Leo sighed with resignation. "Charlie had been visiting him in prison."

Maddy's round gumdrop eyes landed back on Leo and he had the decency to look remorseful. She stepped closer to him. "You knew?" Her tone hurt.

He reached out and trailed a hand down her arm, clasping her hand. "I'm sorry Maddy, but Charlie asked me not to say anything."

She snatched her hand back. "But we tell each other everything." Her voice cracked and I knew Leo was now in for a world of hurt.

"Mads…" he began, but she dashed from the kitchen. He immediately went after her.

I turned back to Daisy, August and Tilly. "Leo's gonna be groveling for a while, I think."

Daisy snorted.

"What did Jack say, when you saw him?" Tilly asked.

"Just that he didn't know about Daddy and then I told him to leave. I just wanted to tell you girls in case you saw him around town as that's a big possibility now. I want you prepared and if anything happens just let me know."

The girls nodded but August was her usual pensive self, nibbling her lip and not making eye contact. She would only have had vague memories of Mama and of what happened, and Tilly wouldn't remember anything.

They were so young when she died.

It was a quiet evening, everyone subdued and lost in their thoughts. When Maddy dragged herself off the couch, a sadness emanated from her so strong I could barely stand it.

"He just did what Daddy asked of him," I said, surprising myself for sticking up for Leo.

Maddy sighed and turned to me. "I know that. But it doesn't change the fact that he kept this from me, something so big."

"I think he was trying to protect you."

Maddy snorted. "I'm a firefighter. He doesn't need to protect me, I'm a big girl."

I shrugged. "I think it's kinda nice he likes to look after you. Everyone needs someone."

"Right back atcha sis. Who's looking after you? When was your last date?"

I scowled at her. "That's not the point."

"Oh, it's different when the boot is on the other foot, isn't it? You came home to help Daddy raise us and we're so grateful you did but you don't have to look out for us anymore," Maddy said, then blew me a kiss and went upstairs to bed.

But she was wrong. Someone needed to sort out the ranch and starting tomorrow, that would be me.

*

I woke early and went out at sunrise to check on the cattle and greet the two ranch hands. I worked with them for a few hours before heading home. The house was in chaos as four women tried to get ready with only two bathrooms. Fights erupted but I managed to soothe everyone. Like a boss.

"Since you're suspended for the rest of the week, you can go and help August with the horses," I told Tilly. I expected her to talk back but she just rolled her eyes and traipsed off after August.

Maddy was on the day shift at the fire station and Daisy went with her just to scout out the town and see if there were any jobs on offer. And then it was just me.

I let out a big sigh, enjoying the peaceful silence before I grabbed a coffee and shut myself in Daddy's office. I glared at the big mound of paperwork I'd been avoiding before giving in and sifting through it. There were more bills which needed paying, and soon. More correspondence from local ranches, including Raleigh Spa & Guest Ranch, the closest one to us.

Duke Raleigh had taken over from his father a few years ago. Ranching was in their blood and passed down through the generations, just like us. But they acted like they owned ranching and were better than everyone because they turned theirs into a high-end guest retreat for the wealthy. I couldn't stand them. However, Duke might be able to give me a few pointers.

Reading the letter, it looked like Duke had reached out and made an offer to buy Redemption. My stomach clenched at the thought of selling the place but it might be worth knowing if Duke was still interested, purely as a last resort. I made a mental note to contact him again. As much as I despised the arrogant asshole, I needed to put my feelings aside and do what was best for our future.

I found a letter at the bottom of the pile which looked like it was meant to be sent to Mr. Davidson, the lawyer. I frowned, opening it up. I unfolded the letter and read the first few lines. It looked like it was a deed transferring ownership of the small cabin at the bottom of the property line. Daddy had signed it and when I saw the person he had transferred it to, my blood rushed in my ears.

"No, he wouldn't!"

My stomach churned and I reached for the trash can, upending it of all the papers and holding it in my lap, ready to vomit. Sweat sprung up on my brow and my limbs were shaking. He couldn't do this to us. *Why* would he do this?

Once my stomach settled, I placed the trash can on the floor and immediately reached for my phone and dialed Mr. Davidson.

There was no answer and after trying him for a half hour and pacing like a madwoman, I got in my truck, the letter on the passenger seat. I drove through town, down the main strip and parked up outside his building and just waltzed right in, blazing past his secretary and into his private office.

I slapped the document down on his desk. "Is this real? Can he do this?"

Peter pushed his glasses up his nose and picked up the letter, then scanned it, his mouth pulled into a thin, tight line.

"Well, it's in the process of transferring ownership. It hasn't been signed by the prospective owner so it's technically not completed, it's still in Charlie's name. Well, it'll all go to you now."

"So it's still mine, he can't get his hands on it?"

"Not unless he signs this document."

I breathed a sigh of relief, my entire body relaxing. I ran a shaky hand over my hair. "Okay, good. This is good."

"Hmm…" Peter said, cryptically.

"Hmm?" I asked, not liking the way he said that.

"Well, yes technically this cabin is yours." He held up

the deed. "But clearly this was your father's wish, so it's up to you what you do with that knowledge."

I frowned, not liking the implication of what Peter was saying. "I think I'll keep the cabin," I said tartly.

Peter held up his hands. "I didn't mean any disrespect. I know how much you loved your daddy and I know you wouldn't want to do anything that went against what he wanted, that's all."

"I'd sooner sell the ranch than give that *murderer* the cabin on *my* property!" I growled and snatched the letter back from Peter.

"It might come to that. Remember our chat? You need to make money, fast. Maybe you could sell it to him? Or maybe he could come and work off his debt to your family?"

I scoffed at Peter but his last words gave me pause. I considered it for half a second before scoffing again and shaking my head.

"Over my dead body."

Peter shrugged. I said goodbye, feeling slightly guilty at the way I'd spoken to him. My feelings were all over the place at the moment and it was all because of Jack.

I walked down Main Street, kicking at the concrete path as I went. I saw the neon sign for The Lonely Bison, the local bar and decided a stiff drink or twenty was exactly what I needed right now.

I pushed open the old-style saloon doors with a bison skull etched into the wood. The sun cast its shadow inside and speckles of dust danced in the shafts of light. Posters hung on the wood paneled walls along with the odd cowboy hat, pair of boots, lasso, and signs that read *cowgirls can't be tamed* and *go on, you CAN dance – love from Tequila*. A rustic sign hung above the bar read *no cussin', no spittin', no horses*.

Soft country rock music played in the background and the scent of whiskey was in the air. It was early afternoon now, not that busy but I knew it would pick up later. The Lonely Bison was the place to be: live music, dancing and a mechanical bull, not to mention the gorgeous owner who drew the crowds.

"Hey Katarina," a deep voice purred.

Speak of the devil…I turned my head to see Max Anderson walking around the bar. His dark hair long with a slight wave, his dark eyes that tilted so seductively. He was striking, no doubt about it but that brooding bad boy act didn't really do anything for me. Not to mention he was a few years younger, still only in his mid-twenties. And he was a notorious heartbreaker.

"Hey Maximillian. Gimme a whiskey, or ten?"

He laughed, a deep rumble. "Ten coming up."

I took a seat on a leather stool at the bar and put the deed I was still holding down on the bar top. I watched as Max poured me two fingers of whiskey, the silver rings on his fingers glinting in the light, his hair flopping in his eye. He brushed it back, sliding my glass over to me with a wink and for a moment I considered if maybe a little *adult company* was what I needed. Maddy was right, it had been years since I'd had a date or anything that would maybe happen after a date. There was no time for men or romance. Cowboys always thought they knew better than me about ranching and horses. They got competitive rather than seeing me as an equal and a potential partner. I just didn't have time to waste on that bullshit.

"I was sorry to hear about Charlie. I'll miss him and his buddies drinking the bar dry and hustling all the naïve young boys over pool and poker."

I snorted into my whiskey, imagining Daddy doing that and a wave of sadness had my eyes stinging.

"Thanks, Max." I glanced around, distracting myself. "How's business been?"

"Pretty good, could be better." He rubbed the back of his neck and hit me with his lopsided smile. "I need to talk to you about something though. Tilly keeps hanging around."

My drink stalled halfway to my lips. "What? She does?"

"Yeah, I send her away, don't worry, but I just thought you should know. I don't want her getting into any trouble or nothing. I've been pretty nice to her on account of what's going on but she's not getting the hint." He winced.

I giggled. "You think she's crushing on you? You think she's looking at you like you're her Prince Charming?" I teased.

He rolled his eyes and scoffed. "I knew you would get like this."

"I'm just kidding. I'll ask her to stop making moon eyes at you," I joked. But really I was worried. Fights at school, hanging around bars, I didn't like where this was headed when she was still so young. And what's worse I didn't know what to do about it. I needed to set a good example for her and didn't think with my recent brawl that I was doing a good job.

"Thanks for looking out for her," I said, downing my whiskey and hissing at the burn.

"Anything for the Cartwright sisters," he said with a wink. I rolled my eyes and demanded another whiskey. My eyes landed on the deed and just seeing the words *Jack Drayton* on it had me ordering another.

And another. And another.

And one more for luck, because I sure as shit needed it.

CHAPTER SIX

Jack

My only friend was dead.

I don't remember the walk back from Redemption Ranch, I just suddenly became aware I was outside the halfway house. Sadness like nothing I'd experienced for years had settled over me like a black cloud that refused to shift.

Over the years, Charlie and I had become close, which sounds crazy I know. I killed his wife. And not all the visits were great. Some of them I could feel his struggle with forgiveness. Sometimes he would sit in front of me and talk to God or Sherry about how he was feeling, and I just listened.

He was an astounding man, the best person that existed in Reverence. I was continually amazed by him and my respect for him was so profound that I wanted so badly to be like him. I promised myself when my life eventually restarted, I was going to be more like Charlie. Live my life in a way that he would be proud of.

Charlie told me that when I was released, he wanted me to come by the ranch. He said he had something for me. I don't know what, and he never said anything more than that. Just told me that I didn't need to worry about life once I was out, like he knew how much it stressed me out.

And now I'll never know what it was, I'll never get to make him proud of me. To make *anyone* proud of me.

I went into my room and glanced around the four walls with their chips and stains. I had nothing and no one. Except that sensation of wanting my mom, except I didn't want *my* mom, I just wanted comfort and I didn't know how to get it.

Goddamn, I was thirty now. And yet I felt like I had no clue how to *life*. I didn't know how to do this, but I knew if Charlie was by my side, guiding me, I *could* do it. Now I was bereft.

I threw myself down on my bed, the springs creaking under my weight. I stared up at the ceiling just waiting for sleep to come. Eventually I slept but was disturbed by dreams of Charlie, Sherry and the accident.

I woke up the next morning, the cloud of misery still hanging over me. I didn't know how to move on, to move forward, and didn't want to. I wanted to stay in this pit of despair a little longer. But eventually my back ached too much from lying down.

I got up, pacing my room and attempting to work out what all the ceiling stains were and trying not to dwell on Charlie's sad passing. I wanted to remember the good times with him, but the pain was too much.

I wasn't hungry. Wasn't tired. I needed a distraction. I

read my pamphlet on how to cope with being released from prison. I read the rules and regulations surrounding my accommodation here. I had a 10pm curfew. I checked the clock on the wall that ticked so loudly it was like it was shouting each agonizingly boring second. I had an hour before I was stuck here until morning.

I needed to get out.

Grabbing my leather jacket that was too small but felt like the only thing that was truly mine, I left the house and set off down the street. I just walked, again loving the feeling of being able to walk for as long and as far as I wanted, not confined to an eight by ten cell or the exercise yard.

I ran. It lasted about thirty seconds until I was so out of breath I thought I would pass out. My lungs burned and it felt good to focus on the physical pain rather than the emotional loss of Charlie.

I was thinking about the last time I saw him, two months ago. He hadn't looked as well as before but I just put it down to grief and tiredness. I wish I'd known. All the things I would have said to him if I'd known.

Thank you.

I'm so grateful.

I feel like your family.

I kept going because of you.

I love you like a father.

Grief wrapped an icy hand around my throat and my breath caught at the thoughts flooding my brain. I pushed the palms of my hand into my eyes, trying to scrub away the images behind them.

I heard a noise and looked up. I didn't realize how far I'd walked and I was back at the scene where I'd taken Sherry's life. And her bench was up ahead, with a familiar person sitting on it.

Kat.

I was going to leave, I was going to turn and run in the opposite direction. I knew how hard it must be for her to see me. It was hard for me to see her too. I swear I was going to walk away.

But then I heard her sob. It cut through me like nothing I'd known before. So full of anguish. And before I knew what was happening, I was getting closer.

Stop! Go back! What the fuck are you doing? My brain screamed and by the time I came to my senses, I was too close to leave without her noticing.

Except the closer I got, the less she seemed like herself. She was swaying slightly and muttering to herself.

"Kat?" I asked, keeping my distance in case of another altercation like yesterday morning.

Her head spun towards me but her eyes took a moment to focus. In the streetlight I could see her blue eyes were watery, like the ocean.

She scoffed. "Well, fuck. I guess thisss iss going to happen more hof…hoften, isn't it?" she slurred.

Shit, she's wasted.

She waved a piece of wet, torn paper at me. "I bet you're here for thisss, huh? Jussst typical. Breaking my family wasn't en…enough, you had to come and take our property too!"

"I have no clue what you're talking about," I said. I glanced around the street, conscious that although it wasn't a main road, anything could happen out here. I was proof of that.

"Let's get you home, I think you need to get to bed, Kat."

Her eyes crackled with fire. She stood up, stumbling slightly. "Don't you tell me what to do, don't you *dare* tell me what to do!"

I held up my hands, wanting to keep this as peaceful as possible. "Okay, I'm sorry."

"You're s...sorry," she mocked, her pretty face twisting in disgust. I probably shouldn't notice how pretty her face is. Not just her face, her entire everything. The woman was a smoke show and I was only human, and hadn't been around women for a very long time.

She stumbled back to the bench. "Goodnight, Mama," she hiccuped, pressing two fingers to her lips and tapping them to the gold plaque. My stomach twisted at the fact that she had to say goodnight to a bit of gold and wood instead of a person.

Because of me.

She straightened and headed off. I watched her go and was ready to leave myself, it had to be close to ten and I really didn't want to miss my curfew. But then she twisted her ankle and fell down.

"Shit." I approached her, unable to watch her struggle to stand. I couldn't leave her, no way was she going to make it home. There were bears and wolves out here, not to mention she could stumble into the path of an oncoming car.

"Come here," I said, wrapping my arm around her waist and pulling her to her unsteady feet. She turned her head to me slowly, confused.

"Jack?" she murmured.

She gripped me tight as we stumbled and I held her tighter, pressing her against me. I liked that I didn't have to crane my neck to look down at her, she was pretty tall for a woman. With tanned, toned legs that seemed endless. She was soft and dainty in my hands and my eyes dipped to her lips and for a brief moment I wondered what they would be like to taste.

Just as I remembered whose daughter I was holding,

she realized who I was and shoved away from me. "Don't touch me!"

"I'm sorry, I was just helping you up."

"I'm ssorry, I'm sorryyy. You can say it until the bison come home but it don't change a goddamn thing."

"I can't leave you here, Katarina. I know you don't want me here but is there someone I can call to come get you?"

She glared at me before she began digging in her purse probably for her cell. She held the device up and kept tapping at the screen. "Ugh, come on, sstupid facial recogmation."

What the hell is recogmation? I watched her keep trying and getting frustrated so I stepped in again. Not to help out really, I just needed to get back to the halfway house before my curfew. "Can I help?"

"It won't recognize my…my face." She held the device out to me. I took it, not understanding how these worked, phones were different to the one I had twelve years ago. I tapped the screen, just like I saw her do and it lit up.

"Passcode?" I asked her.

"Oh-four-oh-six-twenty-twelve," she muttered, stumbling again and I reached out to grab her, ignoring the pounding in my chest when I realized the passcode was the date her mother died.

"Come sit down, at least," I said, ushering her back to the bench. She pushed against me before shoving the bit of paper at my chest. I took it from her, cramming it in my back pocket while I sat her down and turned my attention to her phone.

"Want me to call your boyfriend to come get you?" I asked, tapping in her passcode. The phone unlocked and the home screen flashed up a picture of her mom and dad on their wedding day and I didn't think it was possible, standing here at the site where I killed her mom, but my guilt worsened.

She scrunched her face as she looked up at me. "Boyfriend?"

"The guy from earlier?"

"Yesss, call Leo," she replied.

For some reason it rankled me that he was her boyfriend. He seemed too young and too…whatever, it didn't matter.

I found his contact and called him, explaining what happened when he answered and he said he would be by in a few minutes, thankfully.

I held her phone out and she snatched it, eyeing me suspiciously. Then she wobbled and her skin turned pale and then slightly green.

"Oh no," she moaned. She leapt up, turned to the bushes and retched, her long pale hair falling into her face.

"Jesus Christ," I exhaled and went over to her, grabbing her hair in two handfuls and holding it back. I don't know when I decided that was a good move, only that I felt bad for her. Her body clenched violently and she coughed, more liquid gushing out then she tried to suck in air and flapped her hands.

I transferred her hair into one hand and patted her back. "Get it all out," I sighed. It seemed to help and she calmed a little while she continued throwing up all the alcohol she'd drunk. My pats morphed into a soft stroking motion without me realizing. I didn't notice she was done until she was snatching her hair off me, wiping her mouth with the back of her hand.

"Don't be nice to me," she grumped. I let her hair fall, the strands trailing through my fingers like silk.

"I will always be nice to you, Kat. I will do anything I can for you, forever," I said, my words surprising me but they were the God's honest truth. I owed this woman, all the women at Redemption, everything I had.

She frowned at me, her blue gaze piercing me but I didn't shy away from it. I stood taller, let her see my sincerity. Her frown deepened and she nibbled at her lip. She opened her mouth but then we were flooded by the lights of an approaching vehicle.

The truck pulled up beside us and the guy from this morning, Leo, her boyfriend, was rushing out. He wrapped an arm around her and led her towards the passenger side. Once she was inside with her seatbelt firmly in place, he turned to me.

"Thanks for calling me, man."

"Of course, least I can do."

He nodded, getting in the other side of the truck when I asked him, "What time is it?"

He glanced at his watch. "Nine-fifty."

"Shit! Thanks," I shouted then turned and started running. I couldn't miss my curfew so soon after being released. I didn't want to do anything to jeopardize my future. My lungs were burning and my legs aching when the house came into view.

The man who ran it was standing outside looking at his watch, waiting for me.

"Not a second to spare, Cinderella," he wheezed, before taking another drag on his cigarette.

I went to my room, collapsing onto the bed to try and get my breath back. The crinkling in my pants pocket had me frowning until I remembered it was the bit of paper Kat had been holding. I groaned, pulling it out and unfolding it.

It was wrinkled and had a stain on it that smelled

suspiciously like whiskey. But as I read it, I realized what she'd been talking about when I found her. And I understood what Charlie meant when he said he had something to give me once I got out.

He was going to give me the cabin at the bottom of their land. Somewhere to live. The lump in my throat increased tenfold and tears sprang to my eyes at what a wonderful man he was. That he would give me a place to go when my sentence ended. Only I hadn't signed it, it wasn't mine.

Part of me wanted to grab a pen and scribble my signature on there, just to give myself some security in an uncertain life. But I could never do that to the Cartwright sisters. It was a beautiful gesture, but the person who made it wasn't around anymore and I couldn't in good conscience take what he'd given.

It was an important document, and I knew how Kat would feel about not having it. With a sigh and a groan, I realized I was going to have to drop it off to her tomorrow.

Let's hope this time she didn't scratch my eyes out when she saw me.

CHAPTER SEVEN

Katarina

"Do you think she's alive?"

"I dunno, she doesn't smell like it..."

Their conversation filtered in through my ringing ears. My head pounded and my mouth was so dry I could hear the rasp of my tongue as it peeled itself from the roof of my mouth. *Ugh, what's that smell? What's that taste?*

A cold finger prodded my eye.

"Ow!" I shouted, batting at it wildly and the sudden action caused my stomach to lurch dramatically. "Oh no," I moaned and a moment later I was handed the small trash can from my room.

I retched for a few minutes before I managed to pull myself together. I looked up through the dank strands of my hair to see Tilly and August watching me with interest.

"Why are you looking at me like I'm the newest zoo exhibit?" I grumbled, clutching my pounding head.

"Because you are?" Tilly shoved two aspirin at me and August held out a glass of water. I took them and swallowed the pills with only a small sip of water because my stomach was already gearing up for round two.

"You *never* get wasted. It was super funny," August giggled, and I shot her a withering look.

"You sang…it was not good," Tilly snorted.

I pressed a hand to my forehead. "Okay, thank you very much Nurse Tilly and Nurse August but I can look after myself now."

Tilly shrugged. "Suit yourself."

"Might I suggest a shower?" August piped up, expression innocent.

"You might," I grumbled and reluctantly heaved myself out of bed. I wobbled to the adjoining bathroom, wondering what the hell had happened last night. Thankfully the steaming hot shower soon had me feeling like myself again.

I dressed in my raggedy overalls and The Lonely Bison tee and pulled my wet hair back into a high ponytail. I ventured downstairs to find a blissfully quiet house, poured myself a cup of coffee and took it out onto the porch. Resting the steaming mug on the porch railing, I looked out over the land.

Gorgeous green pastures with grazing cattle, the hazy sun rising in the blue sky. The lodgepole pines and bur oak trees swaying in the breeze as they guarded the land from the road. I picked up my mug and strolled down the steps and around the back of the property where I was greeted with a view of the Teton mountains off in the distance. This place was so damn picturesque and I couldn't imagine not being here.

I'd moved back from Christchurch College when it became clear that Daddy was struggling in his grief to look after the ranch and raise four young girls. My classes hadn't been going great. I was behind, and it took me longer to wrap my head around everything the way other students did so easily. I'd felt like a total failure trying to keep up with everyone else, but I was determined to push through.

However when I knew Daddy needed help, I dropped everything: my life, my dreams, gave them all up in a heartbeat to help my family. And I would again. Being at the ranch, looking at this view and knowing there was nothing else out in the world that could ever beat it, gave me the boost I needed to do something I'd been dreading.

I started to head back inside to make a call but stopped when the cabin caught my eye. It was an old log cabin that was meant to be a little getaway. One bed, one bath and a whole lot rundown. The windows needed replacing; the miniature porch had two broken steps and the gutter was hanging off. I didn't know what the inside looked like, as I had never really been in it. It was Daddy's domain.

"Oh, shit," I gasped when a flicker of memory from last night came back to me. Jack, the bench, the vomit, the *deed*!

"Shit, shit, fuck, shitting, fuck, fucker!" I chanted as I ran back towards the house, sloshing coffee everywhere. I set the mug down inside the doorway and pounded up the stairs to my bedroom. I found my discarded clothes on the floor and rummaged in the pockets of the shorts.

"No, no, noooo!" I wailed, coming up empty.

Jack had the deed.

I'd waved it in his face, a red flag to a bull and now I didn't have it. He could sign it and take what was, rightfully, his. I slumped onto the floor and buried my head in my hands. How was I going to tell the girls what happened? When he turned up and started living there and they had to face him every day? A reminder of what he'd taken from us.

My bedroom door swung open. "Hey Carrie Underwood, when's your next concert?" Maddy chuckled to herself as she came in. When she saw me, the smile slid from her face.

"What's wrong?"

I sighed, sinking into the loveseat by the window. "I guess I'd better tell you before he turns up. So you know how Daddy had been visiting Jack in prison?"

"Yes, *now* I do, apparently *some* people felt that wasn't something important that should be shared with me, their best friend," Maddy spoke through gritted teeth.

"So the part you're most angry about is that Heartthrob Leo kept it from you, rather than Dad visiting Jack?" Maddy's cheeks flushed when I used her teenage nickname for Leo.

"Don't call him that!" She shrugged. "I mean I guess it bothers me but, I also get why Daddy was seeing him. Holding onto grief and anger takes so much out of a person. He needed to move on and forgive." She paused. "Like we all do."

I reeled. "You understand why?"

"Yeah, don't you?"

No. "Well, you might not be so for it when you hear this. Daddy had a deed written up to gift the cabin to Jack when he came out of prison." I sat back, waiting for Maddy's outrage to kick in, but it never did.

"I guess that makes sense. He's not going to have

anywhere to go. You remember his family from the sentencing hearing, right? They abandoned him. He has no one."

Anger flooded me at how easily she saw the reasoning and didn't find an issue with it. "Because he killed someone, Maddy! There's a reason why!"

She shook her head at me. "He made a mistake, it was an accident. How many times have you done something stupid that could've had disastrous consequences but luckily it didn't?"

I gaped at her. "It's not the same, Mads."

But she was on a roll. "Last night, for instance. You were wasted, what if you'd walked out into the road and a car had swerved to get around you and crashed, and the driver died?"

"I feel like we're getting off topic."

"Funny how that happens when someone tells you something you don't want to hear," Maddy singsonged.

I glared at her. "Well, luckily for us, I found the deed and it hadn't been signed by Jack."

"So, make him sign it?"

I spun away from Maddy, unable to comprehend her nonchalance. "Are you for real? Why should I?"

"Because it's clearly what Daddy wanted, Kat," she said softly.

I folded my arms over my chest and sulked like a teenager, like Tilly. "I don't want him here."

"I know. But we're getting into a morally gray area here. And you don't do morally gray and you know I sure as hell don't. Morally gray is Daisy's department," she joked, weakly.

I snorted. She wasn't wrong. I knew she was talking sense but I didn't want to hear it.

"It was awful nice of him to call Leo to make sure you

got home safe last night," Maddy said, examining her cuticles.

My gut clenched as my brain flashed back to the moment I was puking and he held my hair and ran his big palm over my back. I shook my head. "It's guilt, Mads. He owes us, don't forget that."

"Maybe this is a sign from above, for us to live and let live, and move on. We've all lost so much. Let's just put good vibes out in the world." Maddy squeezed my arm and left the room.

I looked out the window, down at the land. "A sign…" I had asked Daddy for one, and then the next morning Jack had appeared on my front porch. And then I'd found the deed.

I glared up at the sky, a sinking feeling in my belly. "Not funny, Daddy."

*

That evening, we were all sat around the dinner table again. Tilly was pushing her food around her plate, not really interested in anything. She'd been withdrawn since she got suspended, she was probably missing school and her friends. Maybe she had a boyfriend and she was keeping him secret. That reminded me…

I nudged her. "I was at The Lonely Bison yesterday."

She gazed up at me, her green eyes brightening.

"I saw Max."

Twin spots of pink appeared on her cheeks. "Yeah? Did he say anything about me?"

"Yeah, he said you gotta stop hanging out there, you're gonna get him in trouble if you're underage." I tweaked her nose. "Which you are."

She hung her head and pushed some beans around on

her plate, subdued again. "I don't wanna get him in trouble. But..." she trailed off.

I only had a few moments before I was back to being her annoying big sister so I pushed. "Buuuuut?"

She shrugged. "I dunno, he's just cool, I guess. He doesn't treat me like my parents died."

A lump caught in my throat. I had just finished school when Mama died so I didn't have to deal with my trauma around other people. I couldn't imagine how hard that would be and hadn't considered it, hadn't taken into account how hard things were for Tilly at the moment. And how absent I had been when I was meant to be her guardian.

I needed to step up, no more drinking, no more fighting. I needed to be present and set a good example.

"Well, maybe in a couple of years, you can start hanging out there again. If Max says it's okay, of course."

That seemed to placate her a little. Before she could reply, there was a knock on the front door and my sisters all looked towards it before frowning at me.

I stood, smoothing my hand down my overalls. "I invited someone over and I want you all to be nice. I know he's not our favorite person but we need his help so keep your sassy comments to yourself."

I left the girls whispering and went to the front door, stomach sinking at the smug smile I saw staring back at me through the glass.

"Hi, Duke, thanks for coming," I said, opening the door and pasting a saccharine smile on my face. He came inside, all expensive clothes and fancy shoes, arrogance as intoxicating as his cologne. He ran a hand through his black hair, his gray eyes flitting over the house, taking in all the details with a slight smirk to his lips.

"My curiosity won out, what can I say?" His smooth

voice held a layer of self-satisfied condescension that immediately got my back up. I rolled my shoulders, shrugging it off, I needed this man's help.

I gestured into the kitchen and he entered, smiling wider as he took in all my sisters.

"Girls, you know Duke Raleigh?" I stared at each of them. They nodded, no one saying anything.

"And who have we here, let's see if I remember. Tilly is the youngest, still in school, right? Well not at the moment, been getting in fights my sources tell me." He chuckled to himself and I tried not to murder him on the spot. "Maddy the firefighter, that's hot. August, right, you work at the library now that you can't be a barrel racer?" he continued before his eyes landed on Daisy who refused to meet his stare. "And then there's Buttercup, is it?"

"It's Daisy," she gritted out. "You ass," came after it but she mumbled that.

"That's right, sorry. I was so thrown when you turned up at my ranch, begging for a job the other day that I couldn't remember your name, my sincerest apologies, Buttercup."

The tension between them grew so thick I didn't think a chainsaw would cut through it. Daisy's nostrils flared and she still refused to meet his stare. Judging by the smile on his slimy lips as he stared at her, Duke was loving every second of it.

I made a mental note to ask Daisy when she was calmer about the fact that she went to see him. I knew she'd been trying to get a job, and those were few and far between around here.

I turned back to Duke. "You would be lucky to have Daisy come work for you, she's just graduated with a major in marketing and event management. She knows what she's doing," I said, proud to defend Daisy.

"Took her a while to get it though from what I can remember, aren't you twenty-five?" he said to Daisy who ignored him.

My blood fired at his patronizing manner. "There were times we needed Daisy here. With only one parent who became ill, we needed help. We don't all have your good fortune of two healthy parents, Duke, I would remind you of that."

He seemed remorseful, his smug smile slipped and his eyebrows dipped in. "Of course, forgive me. Congratulations Daisy, that is quite an accomplishment."

Daisy got up from the table and began gathering the dishes, loudly crashing the china together, still refusing to look at Duke. His gaze never strayed from her for a moment.

"Shall we go and talk in my father's office?" I suggested.

"Sure, after you," he said, snapping his attention from Daisy. I led him through the house and settled him into my father's office which I'd tidied for the occasion and even stocked some whiskey in here and two tumblers.

"Whiskey?" I offered.

He nodded, looking around the room. I turned to pour and heard him murmur, "What a cozy little office." I turned back, ready to remind him of his manners but his expression was clear and he appeared sincere. I handed him his glass and he lifted it to me before taking a sip. I gestured to the other chair I'd brought in.

"I'll get down to business. I wanted to ask you about the offer you made to my father," I said when he sat, resting his ankle on the opposite knee. He cocked his head at me in surprise.

"Since he's passed, the estate has fallen to me, and I

found your correspondence."

"Ah." He balanced his whiskey on his knee, his eyebrows dipped and a softness appeared that I hadn't been ready for. "I'm sorry about your father. There aren't many people in this business who are as...gracious as Charlie Cartwright."

I inclined my head. "He was a good man."

He swallowed his whiskey, glancing in the tumbler, his expression still soft and I was taken aback by it. "Yes. He was good to me when I first started out and kind in his rejection of my offer to buy."

"Thank you," I replied. "I have to be honest here, I don't know the first thing about running a ranch and was hoping you could help me? Help us?"

I immediately knew I'd said the wrong thing. His expression hardened again, back to the cold Duke I recognized. "I don't believe in giving survival tips to my competition, even *Ramshackle* Ranch."

I was taken aback by his sudden change, flinching at his rudeness. "But—"

He downed his whiskey and sat forward. "Hear me now, Katarina. I am not going to mentor you through this. We are competition, not friends or partners. I offered to buy the ranch for my own selfish reasons."

My weakness showed for a moment and I hated it. "But I don't know how to keep it going, I don't know how to keep a roof over the girls' heads."

There was a hard glint in his eye and he bit the inside of his cheek. "Unless you wish to sell, I can't, *won't*, help you."

I swallowed, feeling alone in this whole situation once more. "Then I guess we're done here."

He stood abruptly, tugging at his cufflinks. "Thanks for the drink, although it tasted like cheap whiskey."

I nodded, not knowing what else to do. He peered down at me, then grunted and the clomp of his shoes on the wooden floor echoed around the small office. He tugged open the door, paused before he left, glanced around the room once more with something that looked like yearning before he shook himself.

He sighed, pinching the bridge of his nose. "You need to cut costs, Kat. Get rid of some of your cowboys. It'll be tough for a while. It's not nice but there's no room for nice in business. And it's a lot nicer than putting the girls on the street," he finished, before spinning on his heel and stalking towards the front door.

"See you again soon, Buttercup," I heard him purr before the front door banged closed behind him and I heard Daisy cursing. I inhaled deeply, leaning back in my seat, staring up at the ceiling.

"He's an asshole," Daisy said from the doorway.

I tilted my head forward and met her shining green eyes. "Why didn't you say you'd been to see him?"

She shrugged, tugging at the bottom of her shirt. "Because I was embarrassed. He wasn't exactly nice. His looks are his only redeeming quality," she grumbled, then clapped a hand over her mouth, her eyes wide.

I arched a brow at her. "Daisy, stay away from him. He's a creep."

Although there was something about the way he looked around the office and the yearning on his face. His cold, arrogant mask slipped for a moment. Especially with the fact that he gave some parting advice after refusing to help. Maybe he wasn't as big a douche as he seemed.

Daisy shook her head. "I was just kidding," she muttered, before leaving the room.

I drank the rest of my whiskey, thinking about Duke's

words. I needed to get rid of a couple of ranch hands, but if I did that who would help out? I needed someone to work for free because I couldn't do it all on my own. Maddy had a job and helped out when she could, Daisy was trying to work in marketing and events, August already managed the horses and Tilly was too young.

I was shit outta luck.

I needed someone with nothing to do and no other options.

CHAPTER EIGHT

Jack

"Do I look like I want to hire you?"

"I kind of wanna say, yes?" I teased, trying to charm the owner of Wake Me Up Before You Cocoa, the local chocolate shop and café in town. Her hard expression didn't change, and my stomach sank.

"Thanks for your time, ma'am," I sighed as I reluctantly left, ignoring the whispers and stares from patrons in the café. Once outside, I drew in a deep breath, mentally crossing another place of business off my list.

The visit with my parole officer had gone well. He'd asked about the cuts on my face and I just said I'd gotten too excited to see a cat for the first time in twelve years. He didn't buy it but didn't push me so I could relax until my next visit in a few weeks.

I needed a job though. I needed an income so I could move out of that damn halfway house that stank and was depressing as fuck.

I wanted to *live*. I wanted views that weren't of the neighbors or the stained ceiling. I wanted to do something active and important. I just didn't know what. Hence why I was going around town, begging someone to hire me, which wasn't working out too great.

It was surprising that these small-town business owners didn't want to take a chance on a criminal. I snorted at my own sarcasm. I couldn't blame them, most of them knew who I was and what I had done without me having to disclose it. There was talk and side-eye everywhere I went. I was getting down on myself but this was all my own doing so there was no use in whining. I just needed to get on with it.

I put on my big boy pants and continued on down the street. I headed into the library, not that I even knew what to do in a library but I was a fast learner. With so much time on my hands in prison, I did a lot of reading. I learned more than I ever could at school. I learned about plumbing, electrics, even woodwork which I was especially keen to explore. Carving something with your bare hands, knowing it was you who put the work in and seeing the results of your efforts really called to me and I was desperate to give it a try.

But you needed tools. Which cost money. Hence, the library.

I stepped inside the big colonial-style red brick building. I'd been here as a teenager doing research for school assignments and the place hadn't changed. Still had that musty smell and low lighting which led to a few romantic encounters here. I didn't know what it was about the library and horny kids but there was one section that was dubbed the make out row. Not that I really went down there, I'd only had two girlfriends and we didn't get too hot and heavy. I got to third base with one of them but that was it.

I was so lost in my thoughts that I didn't notice the petite woman who was carrying a tall stack of books in her arms and bumped straight into her.

"Oh!" she cried as the books tumbled down around her.

"I'm so sorry about that, I wasn't paying attention," I said, bending down to gather up the books. A ton of regency romance covers glanced up at me with characters in various stages of undress that had my cheeks heating like I was one of the horny teenagers disappearing into make out row.

"Uh," I cleared my throat, handing the books back to her, not knowing what to say. I met her stare: striking amber eyes behind thick framed glasses. Her strawberry blonde hair was loose and wavy down her back. Her wide-eyed stare and gaping mouth gave me pause. Actually, there was something about her face, she looked a little familiar, but not.

"Are you okay, miss?"

"Errr…" came out and faded and then it hit me.

I took a step back. "You're a Cartwright sister, aren't you?"

Her mouth snapped shut and she nodded. "I'm August, second youngest."

I suddenly felt hot all over and uncomfortable. "I'm guessing you know who I am?"

She nodded quickly, pushing her glasses back up her nose that was dusted with freckles.

"I'm sorry, I didn't mean to startle you. I'll leave." I turned, shaking my head. This was going to keep

83

happening now, I was going to bump into them and be faced with what I had done all over again.

"Wait!" she called, and I halted, turning slowly to face her. "You don't need to run from me," she said softly, almost squeaking the words out. She was a timid little thing. "I know who you are but, I also know that my father was visiting you."

I nodded solemnly. "He was. I'm sorry that he's gone. If you ever need anything…" I trailed off, shaking my head because what the hell would she, or anyone else, ever need from me?

"Thank you." She smiled softly, and I couldn't believe it. She wasn't screaming abuse at me like Kat had. She wasn't chasing me away or giving me strange looks or whispering about me. She was looking at me like I was a normal person.

"How long have you been out?" she asked, then bit her lip like she regretted it.

"Only a few days."

"How are you finding life?"

I thought about it and nodded. "Good so far. But technology scares me, when did everything become touchscreen? And why do self-checkouts exist?"

August giggled. "I know, they're infuriating."

We chuckled then lapsed into an awkward silence and I decided to leave while I could.

"Well, I'd better get back to my books." She raised her pile high and they wobbled before she gripped them tighter.

"Yeah, I should go."

"Bye, Jack," she said, with another soft smile.

"Bye." I began to walk away and then paused. "And thanks."

"For?"

"Being so kind, I guess. I know I don't deserve it."

She cocked her head. "Kindness costs nothing."

I snorted. "Neither does rudeness."

She giggled again and I gave her an awkward wave before I left the library. I mentally crossed it off my list of job prospects but felt lighter than I had in a while, from a simple social interaction with one of the five people who should hate me the most yet somehow didn't.

Thinking of the Cartwright sisters reminded me of the errand I needed to run. The one I was avoiding because it meant facing a certain tall, leggy, far too attractive, blonde's wrath. Feeling naively buoyed by my interaction with August, I decided to head in the direction of Redemption Ranch.

I set off out of town, my feet already hurting from all the walking I'd done but I kept going. I had no choice, I wasn't allowed to drive anymore. Maybe I should get a bicycle. I snorted to myself, picturing my big, bulky frame on a little bicycle.

When I got out of the town and into the countryside, the scent of the trees worked its way into my lungs. The meadowlarks' songs accompanied me the whole way, pleasant and familiar. I was suddenly hit with the urge to do *something*. To create. To work with my hands but I was at a loss with what to do exactly. I didn't know what to create, didn't have any tools to create, so the feeling eventually evaporated, leaving me confused.

I pushed it aside and made it to the ranch. Gathering my courage as I went up onto the porch, I knocked on the door. I stepped back and took a defensive stance in case she came out swinging again.

Katarina appeared at the door, in a little pink checkered dress that flirted with her knees and had my throat drying. Her pale blonde hair hung down in a straight curtain but all my lusty thoughts of imagining the strands wrapped around my hands disappeared when I saw the look on her face.

Stop lusting after Charlie's daughter, you pervert.

"What do you want?" The words whipped from her but she kept her fists and nails to herself. My mouth worked overtime trying to form words while she had that navy stare on me.

"Uh…"

"Uh?" she mocked. "If that's all you want to say then you can leave."

I shook my head. "No, I mean, I came to bring you back this. I meant to come yesterday but got sidetracked." I reached into my back pocket and pulled out the crumpled piece of paper, the deed to the cabin. I unfolded it and held it out to her.

She snatched it from me, her eyes wide and she looked around. "Thanks."

"No problem," I replied. With nothing else to say and no reason to be here, I turned on my heel, admiring the view and wondering how amazing it would be to wake up here every day. Would I be inspired to create again if I was around nature all the time? The dream had been so close, but I'd just handed it back to Kat, unsigned.

I was off the porch before she called after me. "You didn't sign it."

I just kept walking, didn't stop. "Nope," I called over my shoulder, popping the *P*.

"Jack, wait."

My name on her lips did weird things to my stomach that I would think about another time. I turned and she was coming down the porch towards me, her long, toned legs glowing in the sunshine.

"Fuck," I huffed, plugging my hands on my hips and

willing my mind not to drift to the places it wanted to. Jesus, what was the matter with me? I'd spent the last twelve years in prison but it's not like I had an active sex life before I went inside. You can't miss what you've never had.

She stopped in front of me and folded her arms over her chest, pushing her breasts together and giving me a tantalizing glimpse of cleavage that I desperately tried not to stare at.

"Why didn't you sign it?"

I shrugged.

She narrowed her eyes. "But you could have? You could have signed it and taken what's yours."

I shoved my hands in the pockets of my jeans and lifted my shoulders. "Wasn't the right thing to do."

We stared at each other in silence, assessing. She was a tough cookie, I liked that about her. There was a hard glint to her eye; she'd grown up and too quickly, taken on a lot of responsibility and burden. I knew that from Charlie, he often talked about her and she sounded like a pistol alright. I wondered what it would take to get her to smile, to relax…*to moan.*

I shook my head and when she didn't say more, I turned to leave.

"Wait, I…argh!" she huffed and kicked at the grass before turning those cold eyes on me again. "I have a deal for you."

I held up my hands. "I don't wanna take anything from you, or your sisters. I *can't.*" I hoped she saw the plea in my eyes but if she did, her expression didn't change.

"Well, it's not wholly one-sided." She exhaled. "Come with me." She didn't wait to see if I followed, just turned and headed off, detouring around the side of the house.

After a moment, I went after her, intrigued to see what she wanted. Also, half-expecting a firing squad to greet me behind the house so I was pleasantly surprised to see an old, rundown cabin. My heart leapt into my throat. This was *the* cabin. What would have been mine if Charlie was still alive.

Kat stopped in front of it. "This is it. It needs a lot of repairs, which isn't something I have time to do." She ran her eyes over me and I'd be lying if I said I didn't love every second of her perusal. "But you look like a big boy, I'm sure you can fix it up." Ignoring the way her lips moved when she said *big boy,* I blinked in confusion.

I pointed to the cabin. "Wait, you want me to fix it up?"

She shrugged. "If you want, or just live in it the way it is. Just be prepared for the bears to join you for snuggles in winter." Her lip twitched at her joke, and I swear I heard the *Hallelujah Chorus.*

"I'm confused, you want me to live here? You're giving it to me?"

She sighed again and nodded, looking at the ground. "It's what Daddy wanted, obviously." She waved the document at me. "I don't *want* you here. But I might need you, this is why it's not entirely a one-sided thing. I'll give you the cabin, let you sign this paper, if you repair it and also," she trailed off, looking away and nibbling her lip. "Also help out here at the ranch."

My mouth dropped open. She's offering me a job and a home?

"For free," she added quickly.

I stared at the cabin, unable to believe the offer, the luck I was having. I looked towards the sky, blinking in order to stop any tears from forming. I never expected this, never *deserved* this and couldn't believe that she was willing to give me this place and work. She was chattering away but I couldn't focus on anything except to say, "I'll take it. Anything you want."

Her mouth snapped shut. "You'll work for free?"

"Yes, I don't care. I'll do whatever you want, whatever you need." This was how I could make it up to her, make it up to Charlie and all the girls. It was my penance. And for a moment I thanked my lucky stars that Charlie raised such amazing women.

"Okay," was all she said before she headed around me and back up towards the house. I stared at the cabin a little while longer, not knowing if I was expected to follow her. I gazed around the land, the trees lining the back of the property, my new home and this ball of ecstasy built in my chest.

A moment later, Kat was standing in front of me again and she had a pen.

"Sign it," she grunted, shoving the paper into my chest and snatching her hand back.

I arched a brow at her, grabbing the paper. "You sure?"

She nibbled her lower lip again and my gaze followed her tongue as it swiped over her mouth and disappeared. She nodded. "Just, can we wait until next week? Give me the weekend to break the news to the girls? I don't know how they're going to feel but…it's the right thing to do. Daddy wanted you to have it and I want to uphold his wishes. And we need help around here but can't afford it." She snapped her mouth closed like she hadn't meant to share that with me.

"Sure. If it helps at all, I saw August at the library, and she seems nice."

"She is. They all are," she said, and I caught the warning in her words. *Stay away from them.* Message received loud and clear. I glanced down at the paper and hesitated for a second before signing and I handed it back to Kat.

She cleared her throat. "Okay, well, see you Monday then." Then she was gone.

I stayed for a moment, inspecting the outside of the cabin, trying to assess what needed doing and building a list in my head. Excitement fizzled in my veins like nothing I'd ever experienced.

I headed back into town and to the library.

I needed to learn how to ranch.

CHAPTER NINE

Katarina

"Thank you all for joining me this evening," I began, staring into my sisters' sweet faces.

"I already don't like what's happening right now," Maddy piped up.

"Should I be here for this?" Leo asked, glancing across the table. We sat three on each side.

Maddy clanged her cutlery down on the table. "Why? Should you be somewhere keeping more secrets?"

Leo sighed. "Mads, it was one secret."

"Two. You didn't tell me you were dating Booby Barbara," she sniped at him. "I had to find out from Insta!"

Oh shit, trouble in Best Friend Paradise.

Leo smirked. "We're not *dating*, exactly."

Maddy's mouth snapped closed and she huffed.

"Ahem," I coughed, jerking my head towards Tilly, and glaring at Leo.

He ducked his head. "Sorry."

"As I was saying, thank you for coming to Sunday dinner, which I propose to be a new family tradition by the way," I started again but my mouth dried up. I had been stalling all weekend about telling them Jack would have the cabin. I knew Maddy wasn't bothered but I didn't know how the others felt. I should have checked with them before I agreed to it but I was desperate. I'd just let go the two ranch hands that were taking care of everything and now, we were officially fucked. Jack had suddenly turned into our savior and trust me, no one hated that more than I did.

I decided bringing everyone together in a family environment would be best, that way someone would protect me from any wrath I incurred, hopefully.

"I need to tell you all something—"

"You're pregnant!" Daisy interrupted, gleefully.

"She needs to have sex to get pregnant, dummy!"

"Thanks Tilly," I rolled my eyes, cheeks flaming.

"I knew she wasn't getting any," Maddy whispered, and the girls tittered until Leo knocked his hand on the table, drawing their attention back.

"This is hard for me to say but, while going through Daddy's office I found some paperwork. Y'all know Daddy was visiting Jack Drayton? Well, it seems like they struck up a friendship and Daddy was looking out for Jack. He had the deed of the cabin transferred into Jack's name, ready for when he got outta prison." I paused, allowing time for this to sink in.

I met Maddy's eye and she smiled softly at me,

knowing that paper wasn't signed when we last spoke and something had changed.

"So, what are you saying?" Daisy asked, caution in her tone.

I swallowed. "I'm saying that, as of tomorrow, Jack will be living in the cabin behind the house."

I looked around, Leo wasn't fazed and neither was Maddy, Tilly was already on her phone again and August just nodded sagely.

Daisy however, was another story. "Like hell!" she spat.

My hands started to shake, I knew I should have talked to them about it sooner. But I'd buried my head in the sand. I couldn't help but feel I was making all the wrong decisions at the moment.

"Daisy, it's a legal thing, we can't—"

"We can and we will! I'm not having him here!" Her red ponytail flicked defiantly.

"I'm sorry, honey, but you don't have a choice." My words were firm. There was no going back. Was my butt sweating? It felt like it was sweating. Could butts sweat?

"First that damn Duke Raleigh, and now this?"

"Jack will be working at the ranch, for free, so he's helping us out."

"I hope he likes horses," August spoke softly.

"I hope he gets too close to Marshmallow and he kicks him in the balls," Daisy growled, folding her arms over her chest.

"Marshmallow would never!" August defended her beloved horse.

Leo snort laughed until I slapped the back of his head.

"I should hope it is for free, he owes us. Keep him away from me," were Daisy's final words on the matter.

"I don't see that he would have reason to speak to

you, but I'll tell him to stay away," I agreed, instantly dreading that I would now have to go out of my way to speak to him again.

"Is that all?" Maddy asked. I nodded and she added, "Then I'll leave you all to it," and shot Leo a snotty smile as she left the room. He shook his head muttering something under his breath about *women*.

Once plates were cleared of food, the girls dispersed to go watch a movie or scroll TikTok, and Leo went home. I grabbed a wine, I'd been having a lot recently, and made my way out onto the porch, sitting down in the Adirondack chair and folding my legs under me.

I sipped the wine slowly, enjoying the flavors spilling over my tongue. The night was still and peaceful. The clouds sparse and the stars bright. Owls hooted in the distance. It was a night that I would have loved sitting out here with my father. We would have sat in silence, not needing to say a word, just bonding in the peace of the moment. Then he would have come and kissed me on the head and said goodnight.

I ached to feel that moment again and the idea that it would never happen stole my breath. It had only been two months but it felt like a lifetime. There were fewer tears in the house now and I sometimes forgot to allow myself to grieve, too concerned with making sure all my sisters were okay, so that moments like this took me by surprise. Like I'd forgotten, or something.

When my legs began to ache from their crunched position, my wine was all gone, and the owls had quieted, I knew it was bedtime. I went inside, switched off all the lights and just reveled in the silence of the house before trekking upstairs.

I lay there most of the night once again, thinking about everything I needed to do. I felt guilty about not being there more for the girls. Not doing more and being present. Tilly was back in school tomorrow so I made a mental note to drive her myself and give her a pep talk on the way. Maybe find some words of love and encouragement like Daddy would have. Or a lame joke like Leo would.

Then I would figure out what to do with the ranch. Maybe we needed to sell off some livestock for the time being, just until we were in a better place financially. Or sell some land. The thought immediately stuck in my brain. I couldn't bear the thought of selling off any of our land.

I tossed and turned, slipping off to sleep only to wake two hours later when the sun came up and it was time to go outside to work on the ranch. I came in from the pasture with only ten minutes to spare until I needed to take Tilly to school.

"Crap," I hissed, running for the shower. I lingered too long under the warm water and when I was standing in a towel, wiping the condensation from the mirror I heard Tilly call out, "See you later!" from downstairs.

I threw open the bathroom door and ran down after her, stopping on the porch outside. The cool spring air tickling my still damp, bare legs.

"Tills, wait! Let me drive you?" I called after her.

She turned, her blonde hair slicked back from her head and she had thick, dark eye makeup. She looked amazing and badass and everything I wished I was but it was such a change from her normal look, I wondered what had provoked it.

"Nice towel, sis," she snorted.

I glanced down at the too short pink towel with yellow duckies on it, refusing to feel ashamed. Until I saw Jack Drayton appear in the distance. He was walking down the gravel drive, a little pep in his step compared to the way I'd seen him trudge recently.

"Ah shit," I hissed. Tilly followed my gaze and smirked when she saw Jack, who still hadn't spotted us yet, too busy gazing at the trees around him.

"If you can put some clothes on then I guess you can take me!" Tilly shouted loudly, drawing his attention. The moment he spotted us, me in my towel, his steps faltered and he tried to wipe the smirk from his face but I saw it.

"I'll get you for that," I growled at Tilly.

"Mornin'," Jack said as he drew closer, his eyes doing a lazy perusal of my legs. *Had I shaved them? Ugh, did it matter?*

"I'll be back soon, I just have to take Tilly to school." I turned and waddled back to the house, trying to pull the towel down at the back to hide my ass. I threw on some clothes and made it back a few moments later.

"Get in," I growled at a still-smirking Tilly and gestured to my Chevy truck. There was a silence as we drove, I was reluctant to break it, still feeling humiliated and embarrassed at Jack catching me in far too little clothing, but I needed to make sure Tilly was okay.

"So, how are you feeling about going back to school?" I asked, forcing some enthusiasm into my tone.

She didn't look up from her phone. "Fine."

Okay then. "I like your hair like that."

She grunted.

"Did you find that style on the clock thing?"

She hit me with an *are you stupid* stare. "You mean TikTok?"

"Yeah."

"Yeah, it has great tutorials."

"Great! You can show me some later on tonight then, I need to change up my hair."

She hit me with a sly look. "Why? For Jack?"

"Absolutely not!" I spluttered. "I hardly think dating our mother's killer is appropriate."

Although I didn't take my eyes from the road, I could sense Tilly withdraw. *Ugh, yes bring up our dead mom while you're trying to connect with her.*

"Is the eye makeup to impress anyone in particular?" I tried again. "Like a boy at school, maybe?"

Tilly snorted. "Boys are lame."

True. But I couldn't help but notice that her new look was a little bit like the type of women I'd seen Max flirting with at The Lonely Bison.

"You're not trying to impress a certain bartender who's eleven years older than you, are you?"

"Oh my God, can you not!" Tilly groaned.

"I'm just saying, he's too old for you. You can think about men when you're eighteen, and you need to let me and Leo check them out first. Maybe we need to talk about sex?"

"I think I'll take advice from someone who has it, thanks."

"I have it!" I defended myself and I don't know why, it wasn't true.

Teenagers are mean.

Tilly snorted again and before she could say more, I pulled up outside the school. She was opening the door before I even came to a stop.

"Have a great day, honey!" I called after her and she just waved without looking back at me. I watched her walk past a small group of girls who all began whispering and giggling at her. My heart constricted at the idea of my little sister being bullied. I made a mental note to talk to the principal about it when I saw Tilly give them a saccharine smile and flip them the bird, with both hands.

I had a feeling the principal would be wanting to speak to me soon enough.

*

When I got back to the house, I spotted Jack perched against our porch like he owned the damn place.

"So nice to keep bumping into you, Mr. Drayton," I gave him a smile with teeth.

"Thanks for putting on clothes," he drawled, my cheeks heating when I was sure I heard him mutter, "not that I minded."

"Something I can help you with?"

He tucked his hands into the back pockets of his jeans and his too small t-shirt pulled tight across his chest. Did he not own clothes that fit? One pec jumped under my perusal and my eyes flicked away.

"Working on the ranch? I came to see what you wanted me to do first?" His pale blue eyes twinkled in the sun, light and gentle, disarming me.

I folded my arms across my chest, I'd Googled power stances to help me feel more in control and this was a pretty good one. Now I felt like a badass bitch. "I figured you would want some time to settle in first?" When really, I needed time to get used to the idea of him being here. "Then we can start and you can shadow Gus, he can show you the ropes."

He nodded slowly. "Because this is a cattle ranch, right? The practice of raising herds of animals on large tracts of land?"

I wrinkled my nose. "You sound like you swallowed a textbook."

"I kinda have. I spent the weekend at the library." He rubbed the back of his neck, with an embarrassed expression on his face. His bicep flexed with each stroke of his neck and I was suddenly very aware of what *everyone* kept pointing out: I hadn't had sex in a while.

I shook my head. "Really? Not out partying or getting laid after twelve years of celibacy?" My comment was catty and I expected a smart remark back, not the surprised look on his face or the way his cheeks flushed.

"Uh, not quite. I wanted to get ahead of the game, that's all. I don't really have experience with this." He gestured to the ranch.

That makes two of us.

He seemed so confident that to see this uncertain side of him was...interesting.

"I'm happy if you just wanna take the week to get the cabin habitable and get settled in. Let me get you the keys. Where's your stuff?" I looked around and he had nothing with him.

That sheepish look was back on his face. "I checked out the cabin while you were waiting, the door was pretty easy to pop open, but I'll fix that."

"But you only had one shoulder bag when you arrived?"

"Funny thing about prison, you don't tend to accumulate a lot of stuff," he joked then looked around awkwardly.

I didn't know what I was expecting, just that he would have *something*. "Did your parents not keep any of your things from when you were a teen?"

"Wouldn't know, haven't spoken to them since the sentencing."

I momentarily felt some sympathy for him and that shocked me. He had no one. That must be so lonely, especially now that my father had died. The reminder of my father brought me out of my empathetic thoughts for the person who had taken my mother from me.

"How about them keys?" he asked, like he knew we'd reached our maximum politeness for the day.

I went inside and dug around in the kitchen drawer for them. When I came back out he was once again looking at the land surrounding us.

"Here you go," I held the keys out. He turned sharply, putting us closer together than I was prepared for. I noticed some freckles on his nose and a small scar that puckered his brow and wondered if it was from prison or a childhood incident. His light blue eyes shone and my stare locked on a ring of deep cobalt blue which held me captive. When he took the keys and our fingers brushed, I wasn't sure if I imagined the electric spark that leapt between us.

Clearing my throat, I stepped away, ducking my head. "I'll see you next Monday morning then?"

"Yep," he replied, jingling the keys. "And, seriously Kat, thank you. I know you didn't have to do this. Had the best reasons in the whole world not to do this, but this is a true lifeline and I'll never forget it."

His words were so earnest that I felt tears burn the backs of my eyes and decided this was enough proximity to him for one day. I went back into the house.

Later that night, as I sat in my father's office, procrastinating instead of going through more statements and past due letters, I looked out the window. Normally I wouldn't be able to see much in the dark but tonight, I could see the cabin, lit up with a warm light flickering like there were candles lit.

And then a moment later I saw a shirtless Jack wandering around.

He was tanned and toned, body built and strong, overpowering. I strained my eyes, was that chest hair I could see? Oh God, why am I staring at him? Why is he so attractive?

Just at that moment he looked up and through the window, our eyes connected. I squeaked and threw the papers I was holding in the air and ducked down onto the floor.

"Oh shit!" I couldn't believe he caught me staring at him. I wanted the ground to open up and swallow me whole.

Now I was in a pickle. I couldn't get up in case he was still there. I crawled along the floor towards the door to the office and when I was safely out of view of the window, I flicked the light off and ran upstairs to my room.

I couldn't work out if my pounding pulse was from the dash upstairs, being caught perving or who I was perving on. It was probably best for all of us if I didn't think about it too closely.

CHAPTER TEN

Jack

"Stop thinking about her, she's not for you," I growled as I paced across the floor of the cabin.

I'd felt her stare, her probing eyes on me. I couldn't see much out there in the darkness but I saw the light in that window then I saw her. That pale blonde hair and pensive expression. Then she was gone.

Why couldn't my brain, and body, be focusing on any other woman in Reverence? Why did it have to be *this* woman, the one woman I could never go there with. Not only because she wouldn't let me but because I could never do that to Charlie or Sherry. I'd done enough.

But her sass, her strength and bravery were like sparks in my veins. I didn't know why, maybe I just had a thing for sassy blondes who could verbally chew me up and spit me out. I'd be no good to her anyway. No experience, no game, no future, no money to take her any place nice.

"No money," I muttered to myself. My words were loud in the rustic, empty cabin. There wasn't much in here, just one bedroom, one bathroom, but it was enough. There was an actual bed, sure it needed some of the slats replacing so I could only sleep on one side but I was excited to fix it. There was a two-unit countertop with a hotplate so I could cook some incredibly basic food, which is just as well as my culinary skills haven't exactly been put to the test over the last twelve years.

The living area was open with a red brick fireplace that looked too dusty to use but luckily, it was late spring. A raggedy but comfy-looking dark red couch sat in the center of the room, and lining the wall was a battered bookcase with a couple of classic novels in there. The electrics weren't great so I'd resorted to using the candles dotted around the place which gave it a warm cozy glow.

There was a pile of tattered fabric in the corner which looked like it had some animal fur on it so I was kinda worried that a family of raccoons had made a bed here. I guess I'd find out soon. Charlie's scent filled the room and it was like he was here with me which gave it a homey feeling.

It was enough.

It was perfect and knowing it was Charlie's haven made it extra special to me.

But if I wanted to eat, clothe myself and grab some tools to do the maintenance the place needed and maybe try my hand at woodworking, I had to make some cash. The couple of hundred dollars I was given as I left prison wouldn't last me long. I was happy to give Kat my time during the day for free. But my evenings and weekends could be used for other jobs. In the morning, I was going to head back into the town and scout out some of the restaurants and bars to see if they would take anyone on to bus tables or wash dishes.

I stopped pacing and headed to bed to get a good night's sleep. I stripped my pants off and got under the blanket that smelled kinda musty but I wasn't fussed at this point. I continued to ignore my dick that perked up anytime thoughts of Kat popped into my head.

A low rumbling woke me up in the night, followed by a soft whine. I panicked for a moment wondering if a bear or wolf had broken into the cabin. I quietly slipped out from the sheets, grabbed the candle I left on the side and lit it. I peeked into the living room but couldn't see anything.

"You're not used to sleeping on your own," I muttered. Normally I would be surrounded by forty other men trying to sleep. I turned and went back into the bedroom but saw something move under the wooden bedframe. My heart was pounding, having no clue what to expect. I bent slowly and shone the candle underneath the frame and couldn't believe what I saw.

"Well hello there buddy. I'm not gonna hurt ya," I crooned. The dirty, matted ball of fluff had the decency to let out a gentle *woof*. The dog looked back at me with wide, uncertain eyes. I wiggled my fingers and it craned its neck, giving them a sniff before ducking back out of reach.

Maybe it belonged to one of the girls? But what would it be doing out here? The dog was dirty as hell and I didn't think the girls would let him live like that. I'd have to ask Kat about it and damn if the thought of talking to her didn't make my heart kick a little faster in my chest.

I tried to coax the dog out, but it wasn't willing to come and I needed some sleep.

"Stay under there all you want, buddy, but I'm going to bed."

I set the candle on the floor and got back under the covers before blowing it out. Sometime later in the night I woke up and felt something warm snuggled at my back. I didn't move, didn't speak, just chuckled to myself that the dog was cold enough to drop its aloof act.

In the morning, when I turned over there was nothing there but some light brown hairs dotted on the blanket. There was a chunk of wood at the bottom of the cabin door which had been hanging loose before I fixed it yesterday. Now it was loose again and I reckoned I knew how the mutt got in last night. The rags in the corner must have been its bed.

I left the cabin, breathing in that beautiful country air and letting the green grass and blue sky fill my view. Heading past the house, I couldn't help but let my gaze stray to the porch to see if Kat was there. I ignored the disappointment that hit me when I saw the space was empty.

I strolled into town, whistling to myself, swinging by Dough Re Mi bakery for a bagel and some side-eye. It seemed like everyone in town knew who I was, but I didn't recognize any of them. It was unnerving but I guess it was all part of the deal now.

After demolishing my bagel, I doubled back to ask if they needed any help, even a kitchen assistant, figuring I could do early morning baking before running back to the ranch. They practically laughed me out of the place.

I tried a few more local businesses before I stopped by the local mini mart to grab a few basics to keep me going. I walked past the pet food section and for some ridiculous reason bought a box of dog biscuits, just in case that mutt came back and was hungry.

I was threatened and forced out of the local Smokehouse bar and grill and even Tony's Pizzeria refused to give me a job and Tony had given *everyone* in Reverence their first job. Seeing how little money I had left, I was beginning to feel desperate. So when I saw the sign for The Lonely Bison, I figured I had to at least give it a try then I could say I'd asked around everywhere. With a deep sigh, I pushed open the door.

The whiskey smell immediately hit me but it wasn't unpleasant. An old jukebox was playing softly, a couple of guys were at the pool table and in the corner was a mechanical bull that some old man was currently riding.

"Can I help you, buddy?"

I turned towards the voice and saw a fairly young-looking guy with longish dark hair, dark eyes and stubble. He halted in the middle of stacking some bottles.

I cleared my throat, ready to get told to *get the fuck out* one last time. "That depends, are you needing some help here?"

He stopped stacking bottles and stared at me. "Help? From you?"

Even this guy knew who I was but he looked too young for me to know him. I shrugged, pretty done with all the shit I'd been getting today. Hell yeah I deserved it but goddammit, I was trying here.

"Yeah, your patrons don't need to look at my face. Just stick me in the back washing dishes or something."

The guy gave me a once over and sucked his teeth. "You're pretty good-looking," he stated.

I hadn't had a compliment for over a decade, if ever, and I'm not gonna lie, it felt kinda nice. "Thanks, but I'm not looking to hook up."

His mouth ticked up on one side. "It was an observation, not a come-on."

I didn't really know what else to say. He hadn't answered my question and I really didn't want to repeat myself just for his shits and giggles.

"You can work behind the bar, the ladies'll love you, and the controversy will increase my volume of customers," he said, his low voice held a hint of resignation.

It took a moment for his words to sink in. "Wait, you'll give me a job?"

He shrugged. "Why not? It'll be interesting to see what happens. Just no drinking on the job."

Since the accident, I vowed never to touch a drop of alcohol, which wasn't a biggie when I was in prison but I wanted to keep it that way. I had zero interest in drinking ever again.

"Not an issue," I replied.

The guy nodded. "Great, start Friday? Get here for seven."

I was so astounded that I'd gotten a job that I think I just stared at him for a full minute.

"Do you want a picture?" he joked, a rusty laugh leaving him.

I blinked, clearing my vision. "Sorry no. I just, really didn't expect you to say yes."

He shrugged again, a lazy lift of his shoulders. "Eh, I'm being selfish, I think you'll make me some money."

"I'm not sure I will but I won't push my luck. I really appreciate this, uh, what's your name?"

"Max," he said.

"Nice to meet you, Max. I'm Jack," I held my hand out.

"Ya don't say." He shook my hand and he had such a mischievous smile that I decided so far, I liked Max.

I left the bar and walked back towards the ranch,

feeling the crushing weight lifting from my chest. I had somewhere to stay. I had found a way to work off some of my guilt for the Cartwright family and now I had a job that would earn me a little money too.

Life was looking up.

CHAPTER ELEVEN

Katarina

"Do you need me to come to the ranch and kick his ass?" my best friend, Gertie, snarled.

I snorted, missing her and her fire. We had been friends since we were kids and had even gone to college together, living large and loving life. Two spitfires with the brains and attitude to take on the world.

But when it was clear Daddy was struggling here with the girls and managing the ranch alone, I'd quit and come home, leaving Gertie behind. I liked to think that if I had stayed, we would be traveling the world and living like queens. I'd always wanted to travel and get away but now the thought made me squirm. The idea of being away from this place for so long was painful.

"You there?" Gertie yelled and I tugged my phone away from my ear.

"Dang, girl. Yeah I'm here, you don't need to shout. And no, your offer, as gracious as it is, isn't necessary. He seems to be keeping to himself." I paced the porch watching the stars twinkle in the sky and thought I heard her sigh down the line. "But if you ever need an excuse, feel free to stop by." I tried to keep the hope out of my voice but failed miserably.

I missed Gertie. I hadn't seen her for a year now. She was married and living in Montana with some big business hotshot she met after I left college. I didn't like him personally, but he seemed to make her happy. That said, she'd been ducking my requests to visit and I didn't know if it was because me and Gary didn't get on. He was too domineering and ordered her around. Gertie wasn't herself around him.

There was a silence on the call before she spoke. "I'm sorry it's been so long; things are just so crazy here with the business and I…"

"It's fine. I didn't mean to pressure you," I hastily added, hearing the stress and anxiety in her voice.

"Soon, I promise."

"Soon," I repeated and we slipped into silence. I leaned against the railing looking up at the moon and sighing deeply.

"Whatchya thinking?" Gertie whispered. "I can tell there's more on your mind."

I *pshed*. "Just the usual: the ranch, the girls, the convict in the cabin."

Gertie snorted. "How are you feeling about everything? Now Charlie's gone, there's a lot riding on your shoulders, girl."

I scuffed my sneakered foot along the wooden porch.

"Yeah, there is. Honestly, I don't know. I think I'm hanging by a thread right now." I choked back a sob. A rare moment of vulnerability that no one could conjure in me but Gertie.

She snorted. "I'll bet. What else?"

"I asked Duke Raleigh for advice."

"Dickhead Duke? No, Kitty Kat," Gertie sighed.

I snickered at his old nickname. "Yeah, he wasn't too bad actually. He's still a douche but he showed a moment of weakness. He's, uh, kinda the reason I got Jack to start helping me out."

"What!"

I tugged the phone away from my ear again, flinching at Gertie's screech. "I need a hand here. I can't do it all on my own and I need someone who has no other choice and he's…"

I could hear the suspicion in Gertie's tone when she said, "…he's what, Kitty Kat?"

"Well, he's plenty strong and I need that here."

"Uh huh, strong huh? Like muscley?"

I felt my cheeks heat. "Yes muscley, men have muscles Gertie!" Right as I yelled that, movement at the side of the porch caught my eye and I saw Jack walking past. He briefly met my stare and I wanted the ground to swallow me whole when he smirked at me. Clearly he heard that. He dipped his head slightly, acknowledging my presence and kept on walking.

"I wasn't insinuating anything, no need to get defensive!"

"He heard me, Gertie!" I hissed when Jack was out of earshot.

"How did he hear you?"

I slapped a hand over my face, groaning. "He was walking past!"

"Uh huh," Gertie said, all kinds of meaning in her tone. "And where is he going at this time of night?"

I paused. She was right, it was six thirty in the evening. Did he have plans to meet someone for dinner?

"Maybe he's got a hot date?" Gertie teased. "Him and all those muscles. He's got a lot of pent-up sexual energy to expend I bet."

"Gerts, stop, please. You can't make those jokes after what he did."

Gertie abruptly stopped laughing. "You're right, I'm sorry Kat, I was being insensitive."

"It's fine. I just need to remember who I'm dealing with. He's got this charm that just gets under your skin, and he acts like a lost puppy and makes you forget for a second what he did and this is a good reminder."

"Do you think there's a world where he can make it up to you?"

I sat down on the porch steps. Further away, the cows lowed in the pasture. "I don't think so, Gerts."

"And there's nothing wrong with that. I just don't want you to be hanging on to so much anger. It ages you, honey, and you're too single to keep developing wrinkles at the rate you are."

I snorted. "How dare you! I look great for my age."

"I ain't disputing that I just—" She broke off as a crash sounded in the background and then a muffled shout. "Ah sugar, I gotta go Kitty Kat, kisses!" And then she was gone.

"See ya," I muttered, staring at my blank phone screen where she'd already ended the call. Talking to Gertie tonight had made me feel a little better although I couldn't deny I missed her like crazy. I made myself a promise that I would visit her soon, whether she wanted me to or not.

I stayed outside a bit longer, hearing the crazy antics going on inside the house. Clearly there was some kind of game going on, likely Pictionary judging from the loud shouts. I knew I should go inside and be with them and have fun but I didn't have the energy. I felt older than my years, bone tired, and I had no clue when it would end.

I snuck back inside the house and dragged my ass upstairs where I put my comfy pajamas on and got into bed with my Kindle. It was a Friday night and I was in bed by 7pm. Boy, did I know how to party. I was so boring. Too tired and stressed and acting like an old lady. I was no fun anymore. Sometimes I felt like fun didn't exist without Gertie.

Memories of the two of us tearing up the town and getting into so much mischief flew into my mind. The nights we came home late, drunk, my dad chewing us out for underage drinking, then making us work the ranch hard in the morning until we were throwing up in the pastures at the smell of cow shit. I shook my head, laughing, God those were the days.

Swinging my legs out of bed, I stared at myself in the full-length mirror. Who even was I? I didn't go out anymore, not even with the girls. I didn't date either. Enough jabs had been made recently about my personal life and the longer I stared at myself, in my heavy pajamas, make-up free face and bland ponytail, a fire stirred in my gut.

I stood up and flung open the bedroom door and went out into the hall. "Leo!" I bellowed over the banister.

"Kat!" he called back, not missing a beat.

"You had anything to drink?"

"Not a drop, Katarina."

"Good, can you take me to town?"

His face appeared at the bottom of the stairs, peering up at me, confused. Because I never wanted to go out. "To town?"

I nodded. "To The Lonely Bison?"

"You wanna go *drinking*?"

"Yes."

"Well shit, I ain't saying no to that!" he replied, gleefully.

"Me either!" Daisy shouted back.

"Or me!" Maddy added.

I heard a softer reply which I assumed was August.

"We can't all go!" I spluttered, annoyed at my family for crashing my party time. "Someone needs to watch Tilly."

"She's at a friend's house."

I frowned as all four faces peered up at me. "Oh."

"So, let's party!" Daisy yelled and then the girls stampeded up the stairs. I assumed they were going to run off into their rooms to get ready, but they hustled me into mine instead and pushed me onto the bed and attacked me with straighteners and make-up and clothes. I hadn't needed their help, but I was grateful nonetheless.

An hour later, Leo parked up outside the bar. The scent of our various perfumes hung heavy in the air and Daisy's bony ass was digging into my thighs as she wiggled with excitement. There weren't enough seats in the truck for all of us so we doubled up. She reached forward, pushing more bone into my soft thigh and unclicked the seatbelt around us both.

"We're here, let's tear this place up!" Daisy got out, tottering in her black heels with straps twisting up her calves, her little gold shimmery dress catching the moonlight. She looked stunning, especially with her red hair flying around like wild flames. I looked down at my strapless white top, denim short shorts and pink cowgirl boots. I looked casual in comparison but I didn't want to get fancy, I just wanted something comfortable.

We entered the packed bar which stank of alcohol, perfume and sweat. The loud music blared and giggles abounded from the women crowded in the corner with the mechanical bull. The moment they spotted Leo their shrieks escalated.

"You better go and join your buckle bunnies over there," Maddy said tartly, smoothing a hand down her white jumpsuit.

"Well they're more fun to be around right now than you," Leo teased but Maddy just pursed her lips. His smile waned slightly when he realized she wasn't kidding. "I guess I'll see you later alligator," he said. Maddy turned towards the bar, refusing to play their game of one-upmanship and reply with *in a while crocodile*.

He turned to me, and I just shrugged. "I don't know what's up with her."

"Try and get her drunk and find out." His brows dipped in. "She's freezing me out at the moment. Anyway, I'm not drinking tonight so let me know when you're all ready to head home."

I kissed his cheek. "Thank you, Leo. Appreciate you."

He smiled. "Anything for my girls. You have fun tonight, you hear?"

I nodded and turned back but everyone had disappeared except August who smiled up at me gently, looking demure in her green dress with long sleeves, the color doing amazing things for her fair complexion. I saw Daisy and Maddy had forced their way through the crowd to the bar and I followed behind them.

Maddy was still frowning and Daisy was glaring across the bar. I followed her glare and saw Duke Raleigh was on the other side, drinking with some fancy ass buddies of his.

"Shots?" I shouted, hoping that would lighten the mood. We were here to have fun after all.

I flagged Max down and requested four shots of Fireball. The patrons close enough to hear my order booed me, which normally happened. If you didn't order native Wyoming whiskey you got booed.

Max shot a nervous look over his shoulder before nodding. I didn't get the usual charming smile from him, and as he got our drinks ready and lined them up on the bar, he continued to glance over his shoulder.

"Busy tonight?" I asked, looking around.

He nodded but didn't say anything.

"More so than usual?" I tried again. Max was cute, it wouldn't hurt to try my flirting skills on him. Apparently, those skills were rusty as he just nodded again.

"How much?" I asked when he pushed them towards us and I distributed them to the girls.

"On the house," he shouted back.

I cocked my head. "How come?"

He gave me a small smile and rubbed the back of his neck, looking sheepish. "You'll see."

I was confused but I didn't question it. Free alcohol was exactly what I needed right now. I really shouldn't be out spending money, what had I been thinking?

Jesus, lighten up!

I rolled my shoulders and lifted my shot, the girls did the same. "To fun!" I shouted and threw my drink back. The girls cheered and copied me. We all gasped and choked as the burn hit our throats at the same time.

"Woo!" Maddy cheered.

"Again!" Daisy demanded and before I knew it, we were three rounds down of Fireball before we switched into other drinks.

Maddy slammed her last glass down on the bar. "We're having SO MUCH FUN!" she shouted, staring meaningfully down at the huddle of bunnies around Leo.

"Really? Desperate much?" August snorted and we all turned to her surprised. I forgot that when she'd had a few drinks she was a completely different person, so confident and vocal compared to her normal shy self.

"Let's dance!" I yelled over the music, dragging them away from the view of bunnies and Duke. Pistol Annies were singing about a sin they felt coming on and my hips were swinging before I knew it. I glanced around, the buzz of alcohol warming and mellowing me, just the way I needed and a smile bloomed.

As I danced I became aware of lots of eyes on us, flicking between us and the bar and the atmosphere seemed to cool.

"What's everyone's problem?" August said loudly and Daisy snickered at our quietest sister's rudeness.

"I don't know but they need to stop," I replied.

Then I saw the exact reason why.

Right then, he appeared, in a plain black t-shirt that hugged those muscles I'd discussed earlier with Gertie. His brown hair flopped forward on his forehead and his stubbled beard had my insides twisting.

We all saw him at the same time but this time it wasn't me who threw myself at him.

"Son of a—" Daisy screeched right before she launched herself across the bar.

CHAPTER TWELVE

Jack

This could work out.

That was the thought I had right before Daisy Cartwright pummeled into me, her slight weight knocking me backwards. My arms landed on the oak bar top, bottles crashing together. I was trying to keep myself upright as her tiny rage-filled fists beat my chest.

"Easy, Feisty Pants," a man said, tugging her off me.

"Put me down, Duke, I'm warning you!" she snarled, wriggling herself out of his grasp and shoving him off her, huffing her hair out of her face.

"Just trying to help, Buttercup," the guy said, holding his hands up in surrender.

"We don't need any more of your *help*," Daisy spat and instead of getting angry, the guy just smirked down at her before pulling at the cufflinks on his suit. He was dressed

118

super fancy for The Lonely Bison, kinda made me wanna spill beer on him just to make him fit in better. He couldn't be comfortable in that get-up. The Duke guy wandered off and Daisy's gaze followed him, searing into his back before it lasered onto me again.

"I don't want any trouble," I said, holding my hands up and my stare flickered to Kat who appeared next to her sister. She might have been dressed casually in a top that hugged her perky tits and shorts that highlighted the legs that seemed to go on forever, right before they ended with pretty pink cowgirl boots I was *not* imagining wrapped around me, but she was the most stunning woman in the room tonight.

"I don't give two cow pats whether you wanted it or not, it's found you, Drayton!" The redhead sure was feisty and she took a step towards me before Kat placed a hand on her shoulder.

"Daisy, no," her calming voice soothed. The bar was silent, everyone watching what was going on. This was probably the most exciting thing to happen in a long time, like a soap opera unfolding right in front of their eyes. Daisy's cheeks flamed red as she glanced around. She shrugged Kat off and stormed through the crowd which parted like the Red Sea to let her through.

"I'm sorry," Kat said to me, nibbling her lip and I tore my eyes away from it.

"You don't have to apologize to me, ever," I said.

"Hi Jack," August peeked around Kat, waving wildly, and smiling wide.

"Hi August," I smirked, intrigued as to where the confidence came from. This was not the quiet librarian I met last week.

"I didn't realize you worked here. I guess all our free drinks this evening make sense now," Kat said, shooting a glare past my shoulder to Max who offered a chagrined smile.

I groaned. "I'm sorry, I should have warned you, it was a new development since we last spoke."

"It's not my business. You don't owe me anything," she said before turning away and disappearing into the crowd.

But she was wrong, I owed her everything.

The onlookers eventually went back to their conversations and dancing, slyly watching me out the corners of their eyes. Max had been right; I'd drawn a crowd tonight and it made me nervous. I didn't know if they wanted to start shit or just ogle my ass like I was a new exhibit at the zoo. I kept my head down and just got on with my job.

I wasn't behind the bar serving, just cleaning and collecting glasses. Max said he'd show me how to mix drinks on Monday once the weekend rush was done. I didn't mind, it kept me busy, kept my mind preoccupied and it would put food on the table.

For some reason whenever I was out in the crowd, picking up glasses and making sure the floor was dry, I kept finding myself looking for those cute pink cowgirl boots. I found them at one point and admired the legs tucked into them before hating myself and looking away. I ventured near Kat again but the steam coming out of Daisy's nostrils when she caught sight of me had me veering off.

I didn't blame her. But it was nice that August and Maddy didn't seem to care I was hanging around. Or the youngest one, Tilly who I hadn't seen since I chased her out of here earlier after she was making goo-goo eyes at Max. I wasn't surprised that a couple of the girls harbored resentment, but I didn't know how to make it better, or if

I even could.

Finally, the Cartwrights headed home. Leo rounded them up but interestingly he had been talking to other women all night and not Kat. If she were my girl, I'd never let her out of my sight, let alone be looking at another woman. Dude didn't know how lucky he was to have her.

Eventually it was time to close up, Max flicked the deadbolts on the top and bottom of the doors and let out a low whistle. "Man, what a night."

I looked up from wiping down the bar. "Is it normally that busy?"

Max grinned. "Nope, that's all you, baby."

I chuckled. "Glad I'm good for business."

"It'll die down soon," Max rolled his shoulders. "Once everyone's got their fill of looking at you." He began flipping the barstools over and putting them on the bar. "Grab that broom out there, will ya?"

I headed into the back and found it, bringing it back out and began to sweep up but he took it from me. "It's cool, I'll do it."

I quirked a brow. "You sure?"

"Yes, it's only sweeping," he said, but he avoided my stare.

"Okay then. What else would you like me to do?"

"You can talk if you like. How's life going since you got out?"

Ugh, I hated talking about myself. But Max had done me a favor hiring me when no one else had so I guess I owed him.

I started tidying up beer mats so I didn't have to look at him. "Uh, fine I guess."

"Fine? That it? Come on man. I'm not just trying to grill you for information. You're an employee and I wanna make sure you're okay."

"You're cute," I teased. He flipped me off and I laughed. "Of course shit's tough. I don't know where I would be right now if I didn't have the cabin, starting work on the ranch and this job too."

"Working on the ranch, eh? That'll be tough," Max sighed, banging the broom against the side of the bar to get the remaining dust off it.

"Yeah but I think it'll be good tough. Plus, I get to pay back a little bit of the huge debt I owe to the Cartwrights. Trying to redeem myself, you know?"

"I get it. Charlie used to talk about you, at the poker games."

I left the beer mats in the corner of the bar and leant against it, folding my arms over my chest. "Poker games?"

"There's an afterhours poker game every Sunday, real hardcore stuff. Charlie used to own it each week, he'd swindle everyone out of their money. Men turned up friends and left enemies by the end of it. But they'd shoot the shit while they played. Goddamn he was proud of you," Max said, lifting his head and looking at me.

A tightness clenched my chest at his words, and I ducked my head. "He was a good man."

"I think that's why everyone came here to see you tonight. Some of 'em were curious why Charlie cared about you so much after, you know, everything."

I'd just about hit my limit of talking about Charlie without sobbing like a baby when Max changed the subject. "I know things are real tough for you right now and I'm just some random guy you don't know who's now your boss. But I'm a good listener and I don't baby people so if you wanna talk or just have a beer, that's cool with me."

Was I making a friend? I hadn't done this since I was a kid, I didn't know how to do it as an adult. Max seemed like a pretty cool guy that I could banter with so I tried and felt like I was gonna shit my pants.

"If you wanna be friends Max, just say you wanna be friends."

Max laughed, the sound rusty. "Let's be friends, I know you got room for one."

"Tell me how you came to own a bar at twenty-six?" I asked, curious about my new friend.

"It was my grandpa's bar; he went into a home recently and left it to me. My parents are alcoholics, so I had mixed feelings about it but when something like this gets dropped into your lap, you don't squander it." Max put the broom back and then together we emptied and restacked the dishwasher.

"Sorry to hear about your pops. Alcoholic parents, huh? I think mine were probably the same. Do you still see yours?"

Max shook his head. "Nah, I try to avoid it. Sometimes they turn up looking for some money and I stupidly give it to them. I can't say no, you know?"

I didn't say anything. I wasn't in a position to give anyone advice on dealing with their parents when I hadn't seen mine in twelve years. I knew they'd moved out of Reverence but I didn't know where they'd gone.

Good riddance, I say.

"So now I live upstairs and I spend my life here, all alone."

"No lady?"

We finished with the glasses and then Max was cashing out the register.

"Nope, ain't got time for that really. I'm not boyfriend material so I just hook up when I need it. What about

123

you? You didn't make any female pen pals, like the ones who fall for men in prison?"

I laughed. "Nope, unlucky."

"Well now you're out and have fresh pick of the ladies in town. Is there anyone you've got your eye on?"

I hesitated as a pair of pink cowgirl boots flitted through my mind. "Nah."

Max snorted. "Well, that's a lie."

"No one I *should* be thinking about, that's for sure."

"Kat then?"

I actually blushed. "What? How did you know?" I spluttered, not smooth at all.

"It was obvious from how much you were staring at her tonight. It won't be smooth sailing with that one I tell ya, given your history."

I shook my head vehemently. "I would never make a move. Jesus, could you imagine?"

"I dunno. She's been single a while, she might be desperate enough," Max laughed.

I paused. "I thought she was with that Leo guy?"

Max counted out some dollar bills to one side in a little stack. "Leo? Mr. Rodeo?" He waved his hand dismissively. "He's like a brother to the girls. They're not a thing."

Interesting...wait, no that wasn't interesting. I meant what I said to Max, I would never do that to Kat. To put her in that position would be overstepping beyond belief.

"That's yours," Max gestured to the little stack of bills.

"Mine?"

"Yeah, tips for tonight and a little extra to keep you going until your next paycheck is due."

I didn't know what to say. "Max, you don't have to do that."

"Well, you earned those tips and everyone needs help

sometimes. Just take it and don't make things awkward."

I hesitated a moment then took the money. "I won't forget this, thank you."

"So how do you think you're gonna avoid Kat when you're going to work with her?" he asked, closing the register, disappearing into the back to store the money in the safe.

I rubbed the back of my neck and sighed. "I have no idea."

Max appeared again and headed towards the door, flicking the bar lights off. "I guess it's a good thing you've got a new friend to vent to when the working day is done then."

"I guess it is," I smirked at him then unbolted the doors. We locked up and said goodbye. I watched as Max disappeared around the side of the bar to the staircase that must lead to the apartment above. I looked up at the sky, the moon and stars bright, shining on me all the way home.

As I got up to the ranch, I glanced up at the windows facing out front and could have sworn I saw Kat's outline in one of them. I shook my head and trudged around to the cabin, to home.

I opened the door and breathed a big sigh of relief. First shift done. Second shift tomorrow and then a free day, Sunday, before starting ranch work on Monday. I trudged my tired old ass into the bedroom, stopping dead when I saw that mutt laying on the bed, not intimidated by me one bit.

We sized each other up, the dog tilting its head from side to side as it watched me. I ducked my head back out and saw it had eaten the food I'd put out. I glanced back and its tail wagged a little, not much but I saw it.

I sighed. "Well scoot over then, there's room for both

of us," I grumbled at my new dog, and we settled down for a good night's sleep.

*

I was up before the sun fully rose on Monday morning, dressed in my jeans, new black t-shirt from the local thrift store and boots. I'd gone over the weekend with the money I'd earned Friday night and grabbed myself a few basic clothing items to tide me over. I'd bought new boxers from an actual store and couldn't believe how much they cost.

I hadn't actually spoken to Kat to find out what time she wanted me to start but I assumed it would be early. I hung around on the porch of the main house until it was six and then I knocked on the front door. I waited a beat as silence followed and then the door opened and August popped her head out.

"Oh, hello Jack," she smiled softly.

"Morning August," I said, smiling back.

"I think Kat's just getting out of the shower, then she'll need coffee before she's any use."

I chuckled. "Good to know."

August peered behind her before she whispered, "Would you like a cup of coffee?"

I thought about it and was about to decline but when I realized I was probably gonna need it just as much as Kat would.

"Sure, that's very kind of you," I replied.

"I'll bring it out to you, Daisy's in the kitchen," she hissed. I nodded, agreeing it was best if I stayed out of Daisy's sight. I sat back down on the porch and a moment later the front door eased open again and a mug of coffee was pushed through the gap. I laughed to myself at the difference between Sober August and Tipsy August.

I sat on the porch step and inhaled the coffee, the strong scent waking me up like nothing else. I nearly groaned as I drank it. About ten minutes later, Kat appeared looking fresh and stunning in a white tank top and jeans with rips in the knees and thighs, just teasing me with a hint of tanned, smooth skin.

"I'm sorry Jack, I should have mentioned a time," she said, not looking me in the eye.

I stood up. "No need to apologize, I'm ready when you are."

"Six is fine each day."

"Great," I replied. She was busy pulling her damp hair into a knot at the top of her head and still hadn't looked at me. "What shall I do with…" I trailed off, waving the mug around, not wanting to go inside the house but also not wanting to leave it dumped on the porch.

Kat finally looked my way, her navy stare frowning when she spotted the mug.

"August," I said by way of explanation. Kat's lips pulled into a thin line of displeasure before she took it from me and put it back inside the house. When she returned, she jogged past me down the porch steps.

"This way," she called over her shoulder.

I met Gus at the stables, and Kat shared that he would be around for a couple more weeks until he retired. Chatting to him briefly, I learned he had worked on ranches for thirty years. He was pretty old, had a few teeth missing and more hair on his face than he did on his head but he seemed like a nice guy.

"We gotta clean everyone out today so grab that wheelbarrow and start shovelling," Gus rasped.

The stable block was large with six individual stalls and

a tack room. Five of the stalls were filled with horses that had plaques above them with their names. Marshmallow was a white thoroughbred stallion who was mischievous and playfully head-butted me. Fitzwilliam was all black with white splotches on his ears and seemed pretty standoffish. Pickles was white with gray flecks over her coat and kept whinnying at the horse in the stall next to her, who was called Sunshine and was a beautiful caramel-colored mare. Finally there was Chester, a chestnut stallion who had the biggest stall and huffed anytime someone walked past him.

"Don't get behind them," Gus called over to me. "Best way to get yourself kicked and we don't want that."

Kat shot me a look that suggested she wouldn't mind if I did. I got to work, Kat helped me to start with. She was efficient and detail-oriented, and minded the horses, speaking to them every now and then. It was wrong to enjoy the baby voice she used but sue me. After helping with two of them she left me to it.

By the time the fourth one was completed, I was sweating buckets and my whole body ached like a son of a bitch. I hurt but it was kinda nice. I knew I was working hard and putting my body to use in a way I hadn't been able to in...ever.

August appeared at one point and crooned at Marshmallow who was apparently her horse and a very good boy. "You're doing a great job," August whispered as I trudged past her with another wheelbarrow piled with horse shit.

I smiled. "Thanks, August." It was nice to have someone rooting for me.

Kat glared at me as I walked past, and I wiped the smile from my face. My throat dried as I took in the damp column of her neck, pale blonde strands clinging to the skin.

"When you're done here, we need some help in the pasture."

By the time the evening kicked in, my feet were dragging but I was trying not to show any fatigue. Kat still looked amazing, not tired at all, she was glowing.

"We're finished for the day, Jack," she said.

God, is it fucked up that I loved how she said my name?

"Sure thing," I replied, trying to sound casual and not seconds from collapsing. I needed to get fitter and stronger, quickly. She turned and began heading back to the house. I followed behind her, not trying to walk with her, she was too quick for me. Instead I got to watch her round ass bounce along with each furious step she took.

I growled internally and forced my gaze away.

"Have a good evening," I called when she was on the porch. She turned and nodded her head in acknowledgement but didn't respond.

I rounded the house and sighed with relief when I saw the cabin. I wished there was a bathtub, but a semi warm shower would do. I stripped the second I got in the door and stood under the shower, letting the warm water wash away the mud, shit, and hay. My muscles ached and I groaned as I dug a hand into the hard knot in my shoulder.

I wrapped a towel around my waist, not bothering to put more clothes on. I was only going to quickly eat something then crash out in bed for the night. I stroked the dog, who I'd now discovered was a boy. His tail thumped wildly from his place on the couch and had me smiling at how at home he'd made himself. It was nice to come home to someone.

I was heating some beef and potato soup on the stove,

trying to keep my eyes open when I felt something prickle the back of my neck. I looked around the room but didn't see anything. Then I cast my gaze out the window and I once again locked onto that navy stare that was driving me crazy.

Kat was watching me from the main house.

She didn't move, I think she thought I couldn't see her. I stood up straight, interested in her boldness.

"What game are you playing, sweetheart?" I murmured as I moved closer to the window. She didn't move, it was like she was in a trance. My dick stirred underneath my towel, begging for some one-on-one time but I ignored him.

Kat continued to stare and I raised my hand and waved. Whatever spell she'd been under snapped and she jolted, then quickly closed the drapes and the light went out. The moment was gone. I continued to stand there, staring out the window after her and it wasn't until I heard the soup boil over that I started.

"Shit," I huffed. I pulled the soup off the stove and turned the burner off. I wiped down the spill and didn't bother with a bowl, just grabbed the wooden spoon and sat on the couch, eating away. It hit the spot like nothing else did. When I couldn't resist it any longer, I collapsed into bed and was out like a light.

CHAPTER THIRTEEN

Katarina

I needed to get laid. Soon.

I had failed when we went to the bar last weekend but I needed to try again and quickly.

Too many times I'd been distracted by the pull of Jack's shoulders when he hauled hay. The corded muscles running along his forearm as he gripped the shovel tight. The way the sweat had his shirt clinging to him so obscenely it had me panting.

It was official. I was a horrible human being. I was lusting after the man who killed my mother. Which is why I needed to get laid and bad.

I couldn't talk to anyone about it. I couldn't even admit it to myself properly. And don't get me started on the number of times the man had caught me staring at him. It was getting embarrassing.

My cheeks flushed with shame. "What would Mama think of you fantasizing about her killer like that? Or Daddy?" I scolded myself as I brushed my hair out of its ponytail.

Yesterday, I'd opened up the dating app I was half-assing. I needed to full-ass it. I'd matched with a couple of guys and was talking to one of them who seemed kinda nice, Jeremy.

We were going out tonight. It was pretty soon, less than a day of talking, but I needed to move quickly. Which is why I'd invited him for a late drink at the bar. At least that way if he was a dud then we wouldn't have the whole evening to kill.

I put on my denim dress that had buttons all the way down the middle, and I curled the ends of my hair. I went for the natural look with my makeup and decided my cowgirl boots would be good enough, once I brushed off some of the mud and shit.

The fact that I was driving to the bar said it all. I wasn't planning on drinking more than one and although I'd made some effort with my appearance, I hadn't pulled out all the stops and there wasn't a single flutter of excited butterflies in my belly.

Parking up outside the bar, I checked my teeth in the rearview mirror and sighed. "You'll hit it off and those butterflies will come," I tried to tell myself as I fluffed my hair one more time before going inside.

It was another busy Friday night at the bar, packed with locals and Leo was in the corner again entertaining the buckle bunnies. I waved at him when I entered and his eyes turned hopeful as he mouthed *save me*. I shook my head laughing. He was a big boy, and he knew what he was doing.

I took a seat at the bar, glancing around for Jeremy but he wasn't here yet. I leaned across the bar, looking for Max, eager for another free drink after the shenanigans from last week. I could see a dark head bobbing around beneath the bar.

"Hey, loser," I said, ruffling the hair of the bobbing head. "What's it take to get service around here?" *Damn, what conditioner is he using, so soft.*

My breath snagged in my throat when the head turned into a full body. The body I'd not been able to stop drooling over all week. My cheeks flamed when I realized I'd been tousling Jack's soft, soft hair.

"Oh uh…" I trailed off, not knowing what to say. "You're not Max."

He grinned at me. "I'm not, although that felt nice, feel free to do it again." My heart pounded and he visibly cringed. "I'm sorry, that was out of line."

We just stared at each other, not saying anything and the awkward tension mounted with each moment. He scrubbed the back of his neck, his sleeve riding up his bicep and my eyes glued to the muscle flexing there.

"Katrina?"

I turned towards the voice, broken out of my stupor and found a vaguely familiar-looking man standing there. I stared at him for a moment before I remembered I was here to meet him.

"It's Katarina. Hi Jeremy," I said, holding out a hand to shake as he went in for a cheek kiss. "Oh uh…" *Is that all you're capable of saying tonight?*

"Pleased to meet you, Katarina," he said, his voice soft.

"Call me Kat," I said, assessing him. I wouldn't say I'd been catfished, but Jeremy was not five ten. I'm five ten and he wasn't quite coming up to my shoulder. His blonde hair was cropped short and he was wearing a smart business suit. He gave me a smile which had a much creepier feel to it than it had in his pictures.

"What would you like to drink, Kat?" he said. "My treat."

I'm all for paying my way, I don't expect men to pay for anything. But the way he said *my treat* was patronizing as hell. "Thanks Jer, can I get a gin and tonic?"

"It's Jeremy," he replied with that icky smile.

"Sorry Jeremy."

"No problem, you grab us a table and I'll bring the drinks over."

I could feel Jack's eyes on me and refused to meet them as I hopped down from the barstool and went searching for a table a little quieter and out of the way. I managed to snag one and I wiped it down, not wanting Jeremy to get his nice suit all wet from whatever the hell was on the table.

When Jeremy came over he sat right next to me instead of on the opposite chair which felt a little awkward. I turned in my seat, taking a sip from my drink and we were practically nose to nose. He immediately slurped from his beer and placed a hand on my knee.

"So what's a pretty little thing like you doing still single, Kitty?" He was trying to be charming but my vagina began sewing itself shut.

"It's Kat. Well I look after the ranch with my four sisters so there hasn't been too much time for dating, I guess. What about you?" I asked, trying to switch the conversation back to him and pushing his hand off my knee.

"It's been hard trying to meet someone ever since the wife left me."

He definitely hadn't put that he was married before on his profile. Jeremy was sinking further and further down in my estimation. "Oh, you've been married?"

"Still am. She'll probably try and take everything in the divorce so I'm waiting until I meet someone worth taking that leap for." He nodded and ran his eyes over me in a way that suggested he was probably picturing me naked.

I scooted my chair back, putting some more space between us and took a big gulp of my gin, trying to tell myself to stop being so judgy.

"Any kids?" I asked, hoping there wasn't another surprise waiting for me.

"Christ, no," he snorted. "You?"

"Not yet," I said, trying to give off the vibe that I wouldn't be opposed to it. "So what do you do for a living?" I took another big gulp of my gin, I'd nearly drank it all and needed to slow down.

"I'm a lawyer." He banged down his beer bottle on the table, suds flying but he didn't bat an eyelid.

"What kind of law?" I asked, downing the rest of my gin, needing something to distract myself from how shit a conversationalist Jeremy was. How did he even get a wife to not divorce in the first place?

"Criminal mostly. It's getting busy now, you're lucky I managed to fit this drink in." He smirked like he was joking but I knew he wasn't. *Oh Jer...*

"How long have you been practicing law?" *Seriously, give me something.*

He shrugged. "Ten years now. I'll get us a couple more drinks, you really nailed that one."

I looked at the gin glass in my hand that was empty and my vision swam a little. Damn I had drunk it so fast it had gone to my head a bit.

"No, it's fine."

"Nonsense, one more can't hurt, can it?" He smiled again and then he was gone. I shouted after him that I only wanted a lemonade but I don't think he heard me. My ears started ringing and I kept having to blink to clear my vision. I watched the people on the dance floor who started to blur and the music pitch seemed to deepen.

A loud noise and a crash drew my attention back towards the bar. There were fewer people now that it was getting later, and I could see Jack and Jeremy facing off. *Oh shit.*

I stood up but the room started spinning and I closed my eyes, clasping my forehead as a splitting headache began. How was I so drunk? I only had one. I had been planning to drive but there was no way I could now.

"Where's Kat?" I heard Jack demand. "And where the fuck is Max!"

I stumbled towards the bar but my vision wasn't clearing and neither was the blinding headache. A shadow appeared in front of me and then an arm came around my back.

"Kat? Are you okay?"

I looked up into Jack's concerned blue gaze. "Jack?" I slurred.

"Come on, I'm getting you out of here," he said, his voice angry and he started steering me towards the door.

"No, where's Leo?" I demanded.

"He left already. Everyone's either gone home or drunk. It's just me."

I snorted. "You're the sober one for once."

His arm stiffened around me at my words. The warmth from his body flowed through me, thawing my fuzzy head.

"I'm sorry I didn't—"

"It's fine," he gritted out.

I didn't know what was wrong with me but I suddenly did not feel very good at all. "I wanna go home," I whimpered. The cool evening air kissed my skin as he took me outside.

"I know, sweetheart. I'm sorry I can't get you there quicker."

"What do you mean?"

"I can't drive you. I'm not allowed to drive."

"Oh," was all my fuzzy brain could muster. The bright lights from the street all bled into one and I groaned. "I wanna get home, Jack. I don't feel good at all. What's wrong with me?" His arm around me tightened and pulled me closer into the wall of his chest as we stumbled down the street together.

"I know you don't. Your damn date's a fucking asshole!" he growled. "I caught him putting something in your drink. I'm only sorry I didn't see him do it the first time."

"Oh my God," I cried, clinging tightly to Jack's arm.

"I wanted to beat the crap outta him but I can't risk it."

I looked up at him, his mouth pinched tight, his expression unreadable. "Because you'll go back to prison?" I whispered.

He nodded sharply. He didn't say anything more after that and I didn't ask. I didn't know how far we'd walked but I was tired, absolutely exhausted and I started stumbling. My legs wouldn't work and my vision was blurry. The fourth time I stumbled, he swore to himself and then he was hefting me into his arms.

"What are you doing?" I mumbled, pushing against his chest but my hands were just pressing against a block of granite, it was futile.

"You can't walk, Kat. We're nearly home, then you

can get into bed. After you vomit because that's probably gonna happen."

I groaned, scrubbing a hand down my face before resting my head against his shoulder, my arms circling his neck. The slightly curled ends of his hair were tickling my fingers and I longed to curl my fist in the soft strands. His scent invaded my nostrils in a tantalizing way and I groaned.

"You gonna hurl?" he asked, pausing his steps.

"Not right now. God, why do you always find me when I'm hurling?" I grumbled and a deep laugh shook his chest, bouncing my head.

I think I dozed off at some point and woke when the ranch came into view. "Please don't tell my sisters," I whispered.

He grunted. "Sorry sweetheart, I gotta tell someone so they can look after you."

"No, please, I don't want them to worry about me. Just put me in my room and then go."

He shifted me in his arms. I'm not a small woman, I can't have been light but he was easily carrying me. "I can't. What if you choke on your vomit in the night? Someone needs to watch over you until morning."

I'm going to blame it on my altered state, that can only be the reason why I suggested what I did. "Put me in the cabin then, you can stay with me. Please, I don't want to worry the girls, they've had so much to worry about recently. I won't be one more thing."

We got closer to the house, the ground lit up from the lights on the porch and I saw the look of indecision flash across his far too handsome features.

"Please Jack? I'm sorry I'm inconveniencing you but please help me out?"

He swore again, he did that a lot. "I told you I'd do

anything you asked," he murmured, looking down at me and something dark passed behind his eyes. Neither of us said anything, we just stared at each other as he took me past the house and towards the cabin.

CHAPTER FOURTEEN

Jack

God, the way she looked up at me from under her lashes, all naked vulnerability.

I bit the inside of my cheek. *Jesus Christ, she's* actually *vulnerable right now, stop.*

I managed to get us both to the cabin and into the bedroom. The dog looked up at me from his place on the bed and I clicked my fingers. "Down, boy."

She snorted, her eyes rolling slightly in her head from the effort. "Where did the dog come from?"

"I don't know, I woke up one morning and it wasn't only me in the bed," I replied, softly placing her down on the lumpy mattress.

"I bet it's not the only morning you've woken up with someone else in bed with you," she muttered, rolling onto her side.

"Actually it is," I replied and disappeared into the kitchen to get her some water. My hands were still shaking from rage about what that asshole had done to her.

I'd caught him slipping something in her drink and the second I got in his face and questioned him, he started practically crying and saying how he just wanted her to loosen up so they'd have sex. My stomach churned at the thought of what could have happened if I hadn't caught him, annoyed at myself for not spotting him doing it to her first drink.

The restraint I'd exercised by not smashing the fuck out of his face should go down in some kind of Hall of Fame. The guy took off the second Max put a hand on my shoulder. With the dude long gone, I'd asked Max if I could take off to make sure Kat got home okay.

I filled the glass and brought it back to her. She'd managed to pull herself into a sitting position on the bed. My eyes dropped to her thighs where the dress had ridden up. The dress I'd immediately imagined unbuttoning the second I saw it. I could just picture her staring down at me as I started from the bottom and—

"Here you go, drink this," I said, shoving the glass towards her. Her eyes were still dazed and her movements slow. Hopefully over the next couple of hours, the drug would wear off and she'd just feel like she had one hell of a hangover.

I grabbed one of her ankles and her gaze flicked to me, heating. I swallowed, pulse pounding with desire. The next few hours were going to be hell. I pulled off her boots and put them by the side of the bed and then tossed the comforter over her, shielding her legs from my stare, not wanting to make her feel any more uncomfortable.

Silence enveloped us, growing heavier by the moment.

She sipped her water. "What's the dog's name?" she asked quietly.

I glanced at said dog who was lying in the corner on a pile of my clothes, watching us.

I shrugged. "Right now? Dog."

"You haven't named him?" she gasped.

A smile slipped onto my face at her outrage. "Nah not yet. I didn't know if I was cut out for looking after a dog but he's kinda forced himself on me."

"Dogs choose you, you don't choose them." She nodded at me sagely, cute as a damn button.

"Wise words," I smirked down at her. A curl dropped over her face, tangling in her long lashes and I brushed it back, the lock winding round my finger like it didn't want to let me go.

"Name it," she demanded.

"You name it," I shot back.

Her face twisted in thought, her nose wrinkling adorably. "Sebastian."

I pulled a face. "No."

"Carlisle?"

I raised a brow. "Like from Twilight?"

She reared back. "Excuse me? You know about Twilight?"

I shrugged. "Watched it in prison. And read it."

She gasped at me, and I laughed at her horror.

She tapped her chin, thinking. "Hmm, okay how about Teddy?"

I pretended to think it over, looking at the dog. His head tilted to one side as he stared at me. He did kinda look like a bear. "Okay fine, Teddy it is."

"Yay, I did something right, for once." Her voice held

a hint of defeat.

I frowned as she focused intently on the water glass. "Hey, what do you mean?"

She shrugged and pushed out a breath, her hair flailing. "Oh just, everything's going to shit. I can't even have a simple date, I miss my best friend, we're gonna lose the ranch, my sisters will be out on their asses and it's all my fault."

Whoa. "What? What's happening with the ranch?"

She looked up at me, resignation in the depths of her navy stare and nibbled her lip. "We owe money, we're not making any and I've got no clue what to do about it."

"Well, what do your sisters say?"

"I haven't told them, I don't want to worry them."

"It's their home too, they have a right to worry about it. They might be able to help?" I couldn't believe she was carrying this burden all herself on those dainty shoulders. No wonder she always seemed so tightly wound. Although who could blame her after everything she'd had to deal with. And now this too?

"They've got enough going on, they don't need this."

I knew it wasn't my place to get involved. I needed to stay out of this family, I'd done enough damage, but I couldn't help myself. I wanted to help ease the burden on Kat as much as possible. "But they could—"

"No, Jack!" she yelled, then immediately groaned and clasped a hand to her forehead, her eyes squeezing shut. I leaned across and placed my hand to her forehead, her skin was hot and clammy to the touch. I smoothed my thumb over the spot between her brows and slowly they fell away from each other, her expression clearing. Her body went lax against the bed and she moaned briefly, the sound flying out of her and hitting me low in the gut, my stomach clenching.

Her eyes popped open. "What are you doing?" she demanded, and I realized I had just touched her, like it was totally my right to do so. Like it was as natural as breathing to ease her discomfort.

I dropped my hand. "Uh, sorry about that." That awkward silence hit us again and not even the sound of Teddy investigating his belly fur made things less awkward. "So, uh, where did you meet that guy?"

She scoffed. "Dating app. I'll need to report him." She began looking around for her phone.

"Don't worry, we can do it tomorrow and let the police know as well. I can take you to the hospital if you'd like to get checked over?"

She just nodded and then buried her face in her hands. "I'm so stupid," she sobbed.

My heart twisted in my chest at the sight of those blue eyes watering. I grabbed her hands where she scrubbed at her face. "Hey, no you're not, he was a fucking asshole. I'm sorry about tonight. I know that spending time with me was the last thing you wanted to be doing."

"I was trying to avoid you," she grumbled.

The words hurt. I kept forgetting the nature of our relationship when we had moments like this. I wanted like hell to forget and hope for a future where something could happen but it couldn't.

"I should have taken longer to get to know him, but I was so desperate to stop thinking about yo—uh," She cut herself off, her eyes darting away.

Surely I hadn't heard that right? Surely she wasn't trying to forget about…*me*?

No, that would be ridiculous. She hated me, had every reason to. I wasn't going to push her on it no matter how much it killed me, because I would not do this to her.

"Oh no," she wailed, clutching her stomach.

I leapt up. "You think you can make it to the bathroom?"

She scrabbled to get the blankets off her. "No!"

I snagged the metal trash can, tipping it up to get all the debris out and had it in her hands just in time. She retched, her hair falling forward. She choked as she heaved, the force of it contracting her body painfully. I sat beside her on the bed and rubbed her back like I'd done a few weeks ago when we were by the side of the road.

She continued retching and I managed to get the trash can off her to empty it. I made her sip some more water before the next round started.

"Come on sweetheart, get it all out," I said, internally panicking at how pale and shivery she was getting.

"I th-think I'm d-done," she shivered.

"I think I should call someone," I said, pulling out my phone.

"No, please. I just want to lie here and sleep." Another shiver wracked her and I pulled her closer, keeping the can nearby and tilted the glass of water towards her dry lips again. She sipped slowly and I rubbed her back and arms, tugging the blanket around her to keep her warm. She snuggled against me, fitting right into the crook of my arm, my chin resting on her head.

"Tell me about prison?" she asked quietly.

I swallowed thickly. I didn't like talking about it for obvious reasons, but she needed distracting and I'd never deny her anything. I stayed away from the darker parts and focused on the good.

"My first year was tough, just like you'd expect. It's lonely. I didn't want to make friends and guilt was eating me alive. Charlie visited me every month in that first year and I refused to see him. I didn't think I could look him in the eye, and I figured he just wanted to abuse me. I'd taken away his love and the mother of his kids," I began. She trembled beside me, and I thought this might be tough for her to hear but she was staring at me with rapt attention, sleep forgotten.

"I finally gave in and the first time I saw him, he said to me, '*Hey son*', and I just burst into tears like a big baby. How was it possible to feel more affection from him in those two words than from my own parents?"

"Did your parents ever visit you?" she asked.

"Nope, I've not seen them since I was sentenced."

"I'm sorry," she said sadly, and it hit me right in the chest that *she* was sorry for *me*. That I hadn't seen my parents when I'd taken one of hers away.

"Don't be. Anyway, it became obvious that Charlie wanted to keep coming back and at first, the visits were hard. I think I cried almost every time, and some visits were tough on him too. He was a good man and wanted to forgive but sometimes it was hard for him."

"I don't know how he did it…"

Her words were another punch to the gut. It reminded me that she would never forgive me. But she didn't have to, she didn't owe me anything.

"Then we built a relationship, he became a surrogate father figure. We talked about the outside world, he kept me up to date on current events and talked about you girls. I know all about Casper," I teased, trying to lighten the mood.

She groaned and covered her face. "Jesus, he told you about my imaginary boyfriend from when I was a kid?"

I laughed and she pinched me in the rib. "Hey, it's not my fault you watched Casper the movie and then immediately made up a boyfriend."

"Well I had to, none of the other boys would go out

with me. I was *too tall*," she mimicked and huffed.

"No such thing," I replied. She stifled a yawn. "Come on, sweetheart, enough about this. Get some sleep, you've had one hell of a night."

"But I like hearing the stories about my dad, he had a whole life with you that I know nothing about," she complained.

"I'll tell you whenever you ask me. But your body needs rest," I soothed. I was reluctant to encourage her to sleep because I was enjoying our time far too much. I knew that tomorrow, when the drugs were all flushed out of her system, we wouldn't talk like this. I wanted to savor this moment but I wanted her to be well, too.

She fidgeted next to me and snuggled in closer, like she couldn't burrow in deep enough. After a while her breathing slowed and just before she fell asleep, she said something that slayed me:

"I like it when you call me sweetheart."

*

Kat was gone when I awoke in the morning. The blankets tucked up around me, Teddy had resumed his position on the bed and the trash can was clean and dry next to me.

I tugged my phone out of the pocket of my jeans, a fifth hand iPhone that had cost most of the money I had. Seeing it was late morning, I stretched lazily and relaxed back into the bed. I didn't need to do anything until later tonight when I had another shift at the bar. Teddy ended up kicking me in the back which made me grumble and decide to get out of bed.

I showered and dressed before going outside to take a deep breath of crisp mountain air. I'd been cooped up in a stuffy prison for too long and breathing the fresh air in, feeling it hit my lungs, was such a high.

The longer I stood there, breathing deep and sun shining, the more I felt rejuvenated. It had nothing to do with the stunning leggy blonde I'd spent all night watching until I finally slipped off to sleep. Nothing to do with being needed by someone and feeling a physical closeness to a woman for the first time ever. Definitely nothing to do with being touched by another. Nope, my happy mood today had nothing to do with that.

I remembered that I'd been so busy getting Kat out of the bar last night that I hadn't collected my tips, which I needed today to buy some basic tools and wood. I went back inside and said goodbye to Teddy who hadn't moved from the bed and began the walk to town.

Swinging by the bar, I had a quick chat with Max before grabbing my tips, amazed to see there was more than I expected. Then I found the local hardware store and managed to get the most basic toolkit available: it consisted of one hammer, two screwdrivers and a drill. Not much but it was the best I could do right now. I picked up a saw, a box of miscellaneous screws and nails before checking out all the sexy timber they had. The smell of the wood seduced me more than the feel of those natural grooves.

There were suddenly loads of things I wanted to try building. I just wanted to grab a huge chunk of wood and see what I could make with it. Instead I settled for a couple of sheets of plywood.

I was at the checkout, getting eyeballed hard by the clerk, when I spotted a hand planer in the clearance bin. I grabbed it, mentally counting out how much this was going to cost.

"You need help carrying this out to your vehicle?" the

clerk offered reluctantly.

My brain began spinning. "Uh…" How was I gonna get all this home? I couldn't carry it. Sure, I was strong but these were awkward to hold and it wasn't a short journey. Then I had a lightbulb moment. "Can you just hang onto them for like ten minutes?"

The clerk shrugged at me and once I paid, I ran back to the bar. "You got any of those dollies for carting around kegs?" I asked when I spotted Max.

He frowned at me. "Dollies?"

"Yeah, like one of those hand cart things. A dolly?" I'd said dolly so many times the word didn't make sense anymore and Max continued to stare at me like I was crazy. "For carrying heavy shit around? It's on wheels?"

"Oh yeah, in the back. Why?" he replied.

"Can I borrow it? I need to get some stuff home and then I'll bring it back tonight."

Max shrugged. "Weird but okay."

"Thanks man, I owe you!" I headed in the back and found it buried under a ton of crap that I shifted to one side. I went back to the hardware store and piled it up with all my goodies and walked out with a big ass smile on my face. I practically skipped all the way home, practically because it's hard to do with a piled high dolly, especially when it came to the gravel and grass.

I unpacked the cart and looked at my new stuff, deciding immediately to fix the front door to the cabin. It needed rehanging which was why it was so damn drafty.

After fighting with the door for thirty minutes under the hot sun, I stripped off my damp shirt, tucking it into the back pocket of my jeans. I'd banged my thumbnail too many times to count, used a bunch of swear words I knew even Charlie would frown at, but I felt *good*.

I started working on the porch, fixing some of the

broken planks. Teddy eventually came out to investigate all the noise and his high-pitched bark drew my attention.

I felt her stare on me. Just like when I would catch her watching me from Charlie's office. We both pretended she wasn't watching. It was a game I was happy to continue playing because I sure as hell didn't hate the way her eyes devoured my skin.

The back of my neck prickled and I turned to face her. The sun shone behind her, casting a halo around her straight blonde hair which was gently blowing in the breeze. She was barefoot, an anklet that was usually hidden by her cowgirl boots gleaming in the sun. Her long legs bare all the way up to the white denim cutoffs she was wearing. The oversized red lumberjack shirt had jealousy coursing through me at the thought of it being from another man.

"Hey," I said, wiping the sawdust and sweat from my chest. Her eyes immediately dropped to my torso and lingered before she shook her head. I tried not to smirk and failed.

"Hey," Kat replied.

"How are you feeling today?" I watched as Teddy went over and sat next to her whining. Why did my dog love her more than me?

She shrugged, reaching one hand down to stroke Teddy's head, the other still clasped behind her back. "Stomach feels a little funny. I just feel a bit hungover and don't really remember a lot."

My stomach clenched at the thought of her not remembering our time together. We talked about incredibly personal things, and I felt like our relationship was changing, like she was starting to like me a bit. Which is crazy considering our history but I *needed* this woman to like me.

I don't know when things changed, only that they had and I couldn't stop how I was starting to feel about her.

I swallowed. "Well, I'm glad you're okay."

She flicked her gaze from Teddy to me. "I am, thanks to you. I might not remember a lot but I remember you looked after me and I…appreciate that."

"Of course, anyone would do the same." I shrugged, like it was nothing. Hoping she wouldn't see the way my heart was pounding out of my bare chest at just being around her.

"If you say so." She pulled her hand out from behind her back and was holding a red dog collar. "I uh, got you something to say thank you." She bent down and secured it around Teddy's neck. "If you hate it obviously you don't need to keep it, I just remembered this from last night. I think he needs to be claimed."

The second Teddy had his new collar on he bounded over to show me. I bent down and took in the soft red leather, and the gold bone-shaped tag that had *Teddy* engraved in it and the address of the ranch on the back. I swallowed the lump forming in my throat as I stroked my thumb over the metal.

"You didn't have to do that," my voice was rough. Goddamn why was I emotional over this?

"I know, but I wanted to say thanks. A lot of people wouldn't have noticed what happened last night. You didn't have to look after me and you did. So, thanks." She spoke softly and smiled at me, and it honestly felt like the first time anyone had ever smiled at me. I nodded in lieu of saying anything and making a fool of myself. I expected her to leave but she lingered and looked around like she didn't know what to say.

Why wasn't she leaving? Our conversation was done. Back to regularly scheduled avoidance of each other.

But she didn't go. Did she *want* to be here? Talking to me?

She tucked her hands in the pockets of her shorts. "Fixing stuff?" She huffed to herself and shook her head afterwards. "Obviously," she muttered under her breath, but I heard her and tried not to laugh.

"Uh yeah. I thought I'd do the cabin up now that I've got a little bit of money. I read a lot of books while I was in…yeah and I really liked the sound of woodwork. Crafting something with your bare hands, felt like a good outlet."

Her eyes dropped to my hands, and she cleared her throat, nodding. "What you gonna make?"

I glanced back at the cabin. "Well, you've seen my huge selection of furniture, I don't have much room for anything else," I joked and she snorted adorably. "I thought I'd try my hand at a dresser after I fix this porch."

Her eyes lit up. "Oh yeah? Any design in mind?"

I winced. "I hadn't gotten that far. I was just gonna start cutting and see what happened."

"A man with a plan, I like it," she mused, folding her arms over her chest and pushing her breasts up. I tried to keep my eyes off them, I really did. I'd been so good at not staring at certain parts of her anatomy, but I was a weak man at the end of the day. My eyes slipped briefly before flicking away.

We both saw it.

We both knew it happened and then just stood there in the awkwardness of it.

"I'm sor—"

"I'll see you Monday morning," she interrupted and turned, heading back to the house.

"Idiot," I chastised myself when she was out of view.

"Why can't I be normal?" I asked Teddy who lay at my feet, staring up at me and panting with a big smile on his face. "That collar looks good on you, boy," I said, and he barked at me.

I turned back to the porch and when I hammered too hard and put a hole in the bottom of it, I decided to take a break. My first attempt was enough for now. Besides no one was good at something on their first try.

All evening through my shift at the bar my thoughts plagued me, thinking about Kat and the closeness I'd felt between us. That she'd bought my dog a collar and come to give it to me. That she clearly wanted to talk until I ruined the moment. Every time the door to the bar opened I looked up, hoping to see her but she didn't come in.

When I made it back to the ranch in the early hours—who knew Sunday was such a popular night at the bar—I couldn't help but stare up at the windows of the house, hoping for a glimpse at Kat. The room was dark, she was nowhere to be seen and disappointment rocked me.

Dodging the porch hole I needed to fix, I let myself into the cabin. Pride bolstered me when the door didn't creak as it opened, ecstatic with the results of my first project.

I showered, walking around in just my boxers, thinking no one would see me this late. I quickly grabbed something to eat and stood inspecting the fireplace.

Then I felt it.

Those telltale prickles on the back of my neck that had goosebumps spreading over my flesh. I knew what it meant.

It was her.

I looked out the cabin window towards Charlie's office, where I'd seen her so many times before. It was pitch black, no light on inside but I knew. I knew she was there.

Stepping closer to the window, I took a bite of the apple, swiping my tongue across my lip to catch a drop of juice. Almost like I could feel her eyes on my mouth, my dick hardened in my boxers. I couldn't see her but I knew she was watching. I wanted her to watch me. I wanted to see her. I wanted to know if she felt this pull between us too. This pull that was surely headed for disaster.

Maybe she didn't care, just like I didn't. But there was a reason she did it in the darkness. She didn't want to admit to this, whatever this was. That was fine with me, I'd take her stares any way I could get them.

I finished my apple, staring out into the dark but knowing I was looking at her. Then I nodded once, goodnight, and went to bed.

CHAPTER FIFTEEN

Katarina

He knew I watched him. And I couldn't help it. Couldn't stop it.

He knew and he watched me too. He let me. In the dark of night when everything felt secret and safe. I couldn't explain why I was so obsessed with him. I shouldn't be, God knows I shouldn't be. Any man but him, literally, but I couldn't help it.

Something changed when he looked after me the other night. I was safe with him.

Protected.

Yes, I knew how that sounded, I was safe with my mother's killer. But I found something calming about him. I loved watching how he moved, the way his big

155

body adapted to life outside and in the tiny cabin. How his muscles flexed, his veins moved, and flesh shifted.

It got me off.

He was like a wet dream, like *my* wet dream. I couldn't stop staring at him and I hated myself for it.

I couldn't sleep last night, my thoughts running on overtime of what could have happened with Jeremy if Jack hadn't intervened. I was an independent woman and I prided myself on being able to look after myself. It hurt that I needed to rely on someone.

Then I told Jack about the problems with the ranch, that I wasn't handling *shit* right now. I hated that I remembered so much about the other night. How he took care of me, called me sweetheart, the words a plea each time he spoke them. I'd woken up next to him, so warm, comfortable and rested. Not bolting upright in the morning thinking about the long list of stuff going on and riddled with anxiety.

I'd mapped his face as the sun rose, the faint lines fanning from the corners of his eyes, laugh lines that he hadn't had a chance to really earn. His dark brows twitched with his dreams, drawing my attention. The creases between his brows. The chin dip, slightly hidden by the brown stubble dotting his jaw. I wanted to run my finger down the straight edge of his nose and dabble at the cupids bow on his soft upper lip. I forced myself away from him and left without a backwards glance.

Except I did something stupid: I got that damn dog collar. Which meant then I had to give it to him. And I had to watch him all shirtless and sweaty, doing manly things with hammers and drills and bits of wood that made my lady parts do a little dance, *beg* to make a little love, let alone get down tonight.

I even lingered to *talk* to him. I wanted to learn more

about him and that was dangerous. The moment I realized what I was doing, I hightailed it out of there.

Then last night, I'd hidden in my father's study and watched him. His strong thighs, the unsurprisingly big bulge in his boxers that made my mouth water.

And he'd stared right back. I knew he couldn't see me, yet he knew I was there. He even nodded goodnight, the smug bastard. I couldn't even be mad that he assumed I was there watching him because I was.

"No more," I promised myself as I made it downstairs, exhausted from being up so late. I stumbled into the kitchen which was already alive with feminine buzz and chatter. I blindly reached for coffee, needing it before speaking to anyone.

"I don't know, I've not heard anything, and you know ladies be bragging about *that* ride," Maddy snorted.

"Maybe he's just doing it with everyone, twelve years is a lot of time to make up for," Tilly said, taking a big bite of toast.

"Tilly, please!" August chastised. "You're too young to get involved in this conversation. Besides, I think you're muddying his character. I think he's a virgin, he doesn't seem like the promiscuous type."

"Girl, you're reaching! He's not some stuffy eighteenth century British twit in your romance novels," Maddy replied and August sulked.

Once that first sip of coffee hit, I felt myself becoming more human. "Who're you talking about?"

"Jack," they all replied.

Immediately my cheeks flushed, and my body grew warm thinking about him running his big hands over me. The grunts he would make as he thrust deep, those bewitching eyes demanding my body to give in to his.

"Stop talking about him, ugh. I don't want to hear his

name, let alone wonder how many women he's slept with since he got out," Daisy said.

Maddy propped her elbows on the table, leaning in. "Leo said women watch him at the bar all the time, but he doesn't pay attention."

"Ooh *Leo said*, huh? You're talking to him again then?" Daisy teased.

Maddy flipped her off and there was a knock at the door.

"That better not be who I think it is," Daisy growled.

"I'll get it!" Tilly yelled, running from the kitchen.

I heard his deep voice, my insides trembled, and I discreetly grabbed onto the kitchen counter. Why did he affect me so much, was I in heat? Could women go into heat like dogs? Is it my period? That must be it.

Tilly stuck her head around the kitchen entranceway. "Jack's here," she sang.

"I'll be a minute." I tried to get a hold of myself. "Tilly, get your ass to school and don't start a fight with anyone."

Tilly pouted then disappeared.

"I'll just take him this, he must be thirsty," August said, heading past with a steaming mug of coffee.

"Make sure you spit in it," Daisy shouted, too loudly.

"Daisy, stop it!" I hissed, feeling a sudden, bizarre need to defend Jack. She just shrugged unapologetically. I downed my coffee, burning my tongue then left the kitchen. In the hallway I began tugging on my boots, sensing him in my periphery but refusing to look at him. Eventually I stood and saw him wearing a light gray tee that hugged his chest far too tightly and black denim jeans with old scuffed black boots.

"Damn." It was gonna be hard to keep my eyes off him today.

But I needed to.

"Morning," he called, waving. "Sleep well?" The way he said it and the glint in his eye told me he *definitely* knew I was watching.

"No," I growled, extra grumpy this morning. I hurried off the porch and practically ran to the stables, his heavy footfalls coming up behind me. We began mucking out the stalls and I made sure to stay away from him. I didn't want to see any muscle flexing or damp sweaty skin that I knew would taste like salt and sin.

Later that day, after successfully avoiding him, he found me.

"What's your number?" he asked, holding his phone out.

"Why?" I ducked around him, but he followed me.

"Because if you're in one pasture and I need something back here then I can just message you or call you and vice versa."

I stopped. That was actually sensible. Especially if someone had an accident or got stuck. I turned and took his phone, our fingers brushing. I ignored the tingles that rocketed up my arm. The way his hand twitched suggested he felt them too.

"What is this phone, it's a brick," I said, turning it over.

"It's the best that hardly any money can buy," he chuckled, and I snorted. I hated how he got under my skin with his little self-deprecating jokes.

I typed my number in and pressed the save button and it immediately took me to the contacts tab and I saw that other than me it only had Max's number in there and another under "parole officer". There wasn't anyone else and that made me think two things. One, I felt sad for him that he didn't have anyone else, not even his mom and dad but after what he told me, I wasn't surprised. And two, there were no other women. Thinking back to the girls chat this morning, maybe he wasn't seeing anyone. Every time I had looked into the cabin, he'd been alone.

"I'll message you then you've got my number too," he said then smiled, his eyes crinkling at the corners.

"Cool," I replied and then walked off. I avoided him for the rest of the day until it was time to finish. The sun was low as I waved him in from the pasture but I ran into the house before we could talk.

That night as I got into bed, my phone pinged.

Unknown Number: It's Jack.

The smile that pulled at my lips was dangerous.

He was dangerous.

I didn't reply.

*

"Good morning," Jack called, heading around the side of the house. I ignored his smile. I'd ignored most things about him these last couple of weeks. I had to. I took to getting ready and out of the house early to avoid lingering near him, not wanting to spend more time in his company than necessary.

I'm sure he thought I was rude.

That I hated him.

That I wanted to be anywhere but around him.

If only that were true.

At least I'd managed to avoid him catching me staring at him again. Now I did it in the dark, like an absolute creeper.

Was I ashamed? Absofuckinglutely.

Could I stop myself? No. I'd tried. A lot.

I ignored the way his red plaid shirt stretched across his chest, practically ripping at the seams. Ignored the way the blue jeans shrink-wrapped themselves to thighs I wanted to sink my teeth into. I ignored that my body was already pulsing and wet at just the sight of my mother's killer. That thought alone doused the arousal.

But not enough.

And that's what worried me.

"Morning," I grunted, shoving my pink Stetson onto my head, feeling the uncomfortable knock against my ponytail but we had a busy day today and I needed to not have my hair flying around.

"It's moving day," he called.

I cut him a sideways glance. "What?"

"The cattle, we need to move them into the south pasture, don't we?"

I hated that he knew that. That he was a quick learner and listened and understood life here. I wanted him to be bad at this. I wanted to be able to kick him to the curb, once we got the ranch profitable again, of course. But I needed him here. He was actually good. He was a hard worker and eager, willing to do whatever was necessary. And now that August had taught him how to ride? Shit. That man on a horse was a sight to see.

"That's right," I replied, heading towards the stables to get the horses saddled.

He kept pace beside me and I inched away as our shoulders brushed, the heat too much. "Why do we need to herd the cattle into a new pasture?" he asked.

I knew he knew the answer to that, he was just trying to make conversation. Because he was friendly, dammit. I stopped abruptly and he kept walking before he noticed and frowned at me. "What's up?"

"Why are you doing that?

He tucked his hands into his pockets and shrugged. "Doing what?"

"Pretending you don't know?"

He nibbled his bottom lip but didn't say anything.

"Is it to talk to me?"

"Kat," he sighed.

"Is that it, you want us to be friends, Jack?"

He fixed me with a sharp look, an angry gleam in his eye. "Is it so hard to be civil? A bit friendly?"

The wind kicked up and I clamped a hand down on my Stetson to keep it from blowing away. I shook my head. "I don't need friendly, not from you."

"I get it, and I know why, I just thought…" He trailed off, looking around. But he didn't get it, he didn't know why. He thought he did, but he didn't.

"Come on," I grunted, marching on, irritated at myself for starting this non-fight fight and feeling sorry for him. He looked like a kicked puppy and I was Cruella De Vil.

I raced into the stables and immediately got annoyed when I saw August there, brushing Marshmallow with two other horses saddled and ready. I'd wanted to do it myself.

"We got here early and did it as a surprise," August piped up, smiling at Jack. At least he had one friend.

"Surprise," he said, weakly.

"And you chose that horse?" I nodded to the chestnut stallion, Chester, who had been my father's.

August frowned. "Yes. He needs to be ridden, Kat. And I think Daddy would like it if it was Jack."

"Damn," Jack muttered. "I didn't realize, I can take another horse."

"No, it's fine," I snapped because August annoyingly was right.

I took Sunshine's reins and headed out of the stables.

Once outside, I swung myself up into the saddle and took a deep breath as I settled myself, ready for a long-ass, busy day to wear me out. A moment later, Jack appeared next to me, looking like a natural in the saddle, his hips rocking forward as Chester trotted over.

"Ready?" I asked, pulling lightly on the reins as Sunshine nodded her head. I tried to fight my smirk. "I didn't mean you," I whispered to her, nudging her with my calves.

"Sure thing," Jack replied. I clicked my tongue and Sunshine set off at a canter before speeding up to a gallop. The wind whipped past us as I clamped down on my Stetson once again. We headed towards the north pasture and Jack rode beside me. I tried not to glance over at him but my eyes had a mind of their own. My stomach clenched at the wide smile stretched across his face, his eyes squeezed shut. My own smile tried to tug at my lips but I resisted, instead glancing at the pasture in front of us.

We were on the small side for a ranch. Only three hundred cattle right now. We used to have more but Daddy had started selling them off. I pulled to a stop and Jack shot straight past me before he realized and turned Chester around. The cattle had grazed the north pasture for long enough and it was time to treat them to something new and freshly grown. The only problem was they were scattered all over.

"They're real spread out," Jack commented as he looked around.

"Yep, this'll be fun," I replied, already knowing it would be painful to do with Jack. I'd only done it a handful of times myself, helping Daddy years ago. I'd been the one leading the herd and he had been at the back, corralling them. I pictured us doing it together and a lump formed in my throat.

"Where do you want me?" Jack asked, snapping me out of my memories. Unfortunately, they must have been written all over my face. "Hey, you okay, sweetheart?" his voice gentled, and the way he uttered that endearment had me fighting a shiver.

"You lead the front, I'll handle the back. Let's round 'em up." Urging Sunshine forward, I shouted over the wind, "You start off that way!" and pointed towards the east of the pasture.

Something about herding cattle calmed me. I liked the idea of getting all the cows together and pushing them into one group away from the cliques they'd formed. It was like a puzzle that needed solving and was immensely satisfying when it worked.

I rode around the edge of the pasture, herding the strays towards the middle, zig-zagging and redirecting them when they stepped out of line. I gestured every now and then to Jack, but what amazed me was that he knew exactly what to do. We did it all in sync. He led from the front, watching every move I made and anticipating the way the herd shifted. I got ready to shout out what to do when the front began to veer away, but snapped my mouth shut when Jack immediately began to apply pressure at the side to get them back in.

Eventually they all headed into the south pasture and Jack was waiting for me at the gate when the last of the cattle trotted inside. Once they all began to spread out, taking in the luscious new grass they could graze, burying their snouts in it, I breathed a sigh of relief. The puzzle was solved, everything was done.

I wiped a hand across my forehead, brushing away the sweat that had formed in the warm sun.

"Can I ask a question I don't know the answer to?"

Jack asked, leaning forward in the saddle and resting his forearms on his thick thighs.

I swallowed, my throat parched. Not just from his mouthwatering thighs. "Sure."

"Why do you do it on horseback? I read about doing it with vehicles, ATVs, even dirt bikes?"

I shrugged. "All those things are too loud. On horseback it's lower stress for the animals and quieter. The cows kinda think the horse is another cow and just go along with it. It's more efficient and safer, not to mention better for the environment."

He squinted at me in the sun, his nose wrinkling. "You love it, don't you?"

My cheeks heated at his teasing tone, and I fought a smile. "Me and Daddy used to do it together and it was such a rush, watching him work."

"I know how you feel," he said meaningfully, that gleam back in his eye.

"We should get back," I sighed, feeling far too comfortable in his warm stare. We trotted the horses out of the pasture and I jumped down to pull the gate closed, keeping the cows in.

We headed back but neither of us spoke as we trotted next to each other. I wasn't really in a hurry to get back but I hated that I enjoyed spending time with him. That I actually felt a tiny bit at peace, maybe because he knew things I hadn't told the girls. That I didn't have to be strong for him or hide the truth of things.

I could just be me.

"Huh."

He glanced over. "What?"

I shook my head. "Nothing just…thinking."

"I've heard that's dangerous, you know?" he teased. When I didn't say more he added, "Thinking about how to save this place?"

Guilt churned in my gut. Because I hadn't been. I'd been thinking about him instead when I should have been focusing on what to do about the girls' livelihood. Coming up with ways to save the ranch, and how to pay off the debts I'd discovered. Instead, I brooded in the office and watched Jack in the dark.

"Yeah," was all I said. I'd been too busy working the ranch with Jack and Gus too in his final few days before retirement. I'd not been focused on the business side of things, too scared to acknowledge that I was floundering, just like I had at college.

"I'm always up for a brainstorming session, if you need one?"

I glanced over at him, the late afternoon sun caressing his features. His skin had taken on a healthy sun-kissed glow from all his time outside and he'd lost that haunted look from his eyes. He seemed happy. And it made me happy to think that Daddy would be pleased Jack was doing well.

"You know how to save the ranch?"

He laughed at my clear skepticism. "Well, no. But I'm available to bounce some ideas off. I'm free in the evenings."

"Aren't you working at the bar?"

"Sure, but not every night."

"Don't you have plans though? I don't know, dates?" I don't know why I said it, only that I'm a jealous fool.

"Kinda hard to date when no one in town likes you," he said in a stage whisper.

That guilt hit again, that he must be lonely and all I did was grunt and snap at him when he tried to be nice and talk to me.

"No girlfriends then?"

"No boyfriends then?" he shot back and then I saw him frown and look away, like he hadn't meant to say that.

We rode the rest of the way in silence but it was heavy, expectant, not comforting like it had been before and I didn't know what to do with that.

CHAPTER SIXTEEN

Jack

It was the crack of dawn when I heard the mooing.

I snuffled in my sleep, confused about what was happening until I heard another moo, then another.

"What the?" I grumbled, squinting. I lifted up on one arm, peering around the blankets on the bed and dislodging Teddy.

I got out of bed, heading for the window but cracked my knee on the new dresser I'd built. I wasn't used to it being there although I was damn proud of my work. I rubbed the sore joint and brushed aside the drapes to look out the window and came face to face with a cow.

I yelped and the cow mooed in response.

"What the fuck?" I exhaled. I ran from the room and

to the front door, tossing it open and took in the view.

Multiple cows were dotted around the cabin and the house, just munching on all the luscious green grass and swishing their tails, flicking their ears nonchalantly. I was struck dumb for a moment before I pulled myself together and headed to the house.

I jogged up the porch and banged on the door. It was a Saturday morning so I didn't expect anyone to be up this early except Kat. I knocked a few more times but there was no answer. I stepped back off the porch and cupped my hands around my mouth.

"Wake up ladies!" I yelled, before knocking on the door again. The cows just watched me, stalks of grass dangling from their lips as long, gross tongues slipped out and snaked them back into their mouths. I shuddered and turned back to the door, raising my fist to knock again but it swung open.

Daisy and Tilly greeted me. One was happy, one was not.

"What the hell do you want?" Daisy glared at me.

"Do you see the cows?" I asked, jerking a thumb over my shoulder.

"Yeah, I'm not blind," she snapped back then she realized. "Ohhhh…."

"Where's Kat?"

"I'm here," a sleepy voice sighed, and I looked over Daisy's shoulder, ignoring that Tilly hadn't removed her stare from my bare chest. Kat's blonde hair was tangled around her and her face creased from her sheets. She rubbed her eyes and she looked so damn fuckable in all her sleep-rumpled sexiness that I lost my breath.

She glanced up and saw me, her eyes lingering on my chest and I swear I *accidentally* bounced my pecs. It's just my body's reaction to her and I can't help it.

She folded her hands across her white tank top but not before I was treated to the view of her hard nipples and my senses crumpled.

"What's going on?" she asked.

I pointed over my shoulder. "I know I'm new to all this, only a month in now, but I feel like these shouldn't be here?"

Her blue eyes widened and her mouth dropped open as she took in the cattle. She pushed past her sisters and nearly body-checked me on her way out to the porch.

"What the hell?" she yelped, her eyes running over the cows dotted around the grounds. Then she whirled on me, her finger poking me in the chest.

"You didn't shut the gate properly, did you?" she accused. I wrap my hand around hers, not moving it, just holding her steady as her eyes threw fire at me.

"Actually no, sweetheart, it was *you* who didn't shut the gate properly," I replied.

She scoffed. "Me? The experienced cattle herder? The one who's grown up ranching? Can't shut a simple gate?"

I tugged her closer and her eyes heated. "That's right, Katarina. The experienced one fucked up, not me," I teased, loving how fired up she was and wanting more.

"How dare you!" she spat, stepping closer, putting us nearly chest-to-heaving-braless-chest. I was desperate for that touch. *Starving* for that touch. "I don't believe that for one second. It was you."

"Whatever you say, sweetheart."

"Stop calling me that!" she snapped.

I was wrapped up in our banter and tugged her closer, dropping my voice. "But you like it."

The sparks flamed between us and I wanted them to devour us. My eyes dropped to her rosy lips and I was thirsty. Or hungry. Or something. God I just wanted to slam my mouth into hers and take all that anger, all that fire and heat, and swallow it down, replacing it with moans and groans instead.

She wrenched her hand back and I knew I'd fucked up. Again.

"Let me get dressed and then we'll go and fix it. If you can manage that simple task?"

She threw the challenge at me and I accepted, gladly. "Sure thing," I smirked and her frown deepened.

She rushed past me and I turned to watch her go and suddenly came up against a wall of sisters and Leo. I'd forgotten we weren't alone. Daisy looked ready to throttle me but the rest were watching us with interest. Leo chuckled and shook his head. Everyone disbanded and I was still rooted to the spot, watching Kat disappear.

Leo whistled, coming down off the porch. "Man, you like danger, don't you?"

"I don't know what you mean," I replied, not sounding one bit convincing.

He rubbed a hand across his jaw. "Sure you don't. Look, don't make me give you one of those big brother speeches about if you hurt her, I'll kill you, yada yada." He waved his hand in a bored fashion.

"I thought you were just a friend?"

"I am, but I'm also family. I'm like their surrogate brother." The humor fell from his face and a seriousness overtook it that actually gave me pause. "So, if you fuck with my family, I fuck with you, you got that?"

"I hear ya, sparky. I don't have any intentions with anyone," I replied, holding my hands up.

He laughed. "Again, if you say so." He glanced behind him. "I shouldn't say this but Kat needs a *man*. A strong man because she's a strong woman. If you can be that man, great. But if not, leave her alone."

I shook my head. "You know I can't be that man. We've got history and I'm lucky that she and all the girls are letting me be where I am."

"Sounds like you've been thinking about it. I think any mountain can be climbed," Leo said cryptically.

"Why are *you* here this morning, anyway? You're not usually," I changed the subject. I'd seen the way he watched Maddy at the bar and the way she glared at the buckle bunnies that draped themselves over him. Yeah they were best friends but there was something more there too.

"I fell asleep on the couch last night," he shrugged. "Happens a lot."

"I'll bet it does. Did I see Maddy get back late last night?" I prodded. "Come to think of it, did Maddy have a date? I bet you just wanted to make sure she got home safe…and alone, didn't you?"

Leo's face remained still, except for a slight tic under his eye.

I chuckled to myself. "Sounds like you've got your own mountain to climb, buddy." I slapped him on the shoulder and turned, heading back to the cabin to change and wash my face before tackling the cow situation.

Leo's words rang in my ears as I brushed my teeth. I liked him, he seemed like a decent guy, but he was talking shit. This mountain was unclimbable no matter how much I wanted to.

I met Kat out in front of the house, tearing my gaze from her long legs stuffed into those cute cowgirl boots and an oversized sweatshirt thrown on over her white denim shorts. Her face scrubbed free of makeup as usual and her long hair dragged back into a ponytail. She always looked stunning, kissable, lickable, beddable. *Everythingable.*

"August ran ahead to saddle the horses for us. It's gonna be a long day, you good to do this? I know you're not supposed to help on the weekends." There was a vulnerability in her voice that raked its claws over my heart.

"Like I've said before, I'll do anything you ask me," I replied.

She nodded once. "Thanks," she muttered before taking off at a run to the stables.

I kept pace with her, my fitness improving now that I had room to run and exercise. We mounted the horses in sync and headed back down to the house, strategizing how to get the cattle together. I would lead again and she would herd from the back. The cattle were spread so far apart, it would be tough with the house and trees in the way.

I watched her work, gesturing to her when a cow got a mind of its own and stepped away from the herd. I put pressure from the front and sides and led them backwards, up and away from the house and together we worked to get them back to the south pasture. It was harder than yesterday, it took more effort. Like their night of freedom had them acting like rebellious teenagers.

When we approached, I could see the gate was shut, which was odd. How the hell did they get out? I raised my arm, waving to Kat and signaled for her to slow down so I could ride ahead and open the gate. When the last of the cattle trotted through, Kat joined me.

"The gate was closed?" Her brow furrowed.

"The gate was closed," I confirmed, feeling kinda smug that she was wrong about me. "Guess it wasn't either of us."

"Hmm," she replied, her frown still in place. "Just means there was another way out. Come on." She clicked her tongue and pulled on the reins and set off at a trot, riding the perimeter of the pasture, along the fence. I followed suit, wondering what she was checking for.

"There!" she shouted back over her shoulder, pointing across into the bottom corner. We rode over and dismounted. I followed her and saw immediately that the fence was broken and had been partially trampled into the mud.

"Fuck!" she shouted.

"Hey, it's okay, we can fix it."

"We're gonna have to!" she snapped back.

I took a breath, not wanting to get riled up and have a repeat of earlier. Especially when I should be staying away from her. "What do you need me to do?"

"We need tools but I left them back at the ranch."

"I'll go get them, just don't touch anything," I said and mounted Chester, urging him back the way we came. I rode fast back to the house, enjoying the rush of wind, the scent of nature, the freedom. I wasn't sure where she kept hers so I grabbed what I could from my cabin and headed back, cursing softly when I saw she had in fact, touched the fence.

"What did I say?" I grumbled as I leapt off Chester, my ass only a little saddle sore. She was in a crouch, tugging the fence up out of the mud. Her arms flexed tightly as she pulled with all her might but it didn't budge.

"I touched it, I know, but I was worried the cows would see it again and try a second prison break," she huffed, her cheeks pink with her exertion. "Help me!"

I surveyed what she was doing and unfortunately the only way to help was to get in behind her. I locked my knees behind hers and reached around her, gripping the fence on either side of her hands.

Her hair tickled my cheeks, her cherry blossom scent

invaded my senses and I willed my dick not to get hard when her ass was practically riding it. Okay that was stupid to think because immediately I was thinking about her riding me, reverse cowgirl style and it was definitely getting hard.

"Ready?" she asked softly, turning slightly and our cheeks nearly brushed.

Damn, it was hard being this close to her, I wanted to throw her down to the ground and fuck her into the dirt. What the hell was wrong with me?

"Uh, huh," was all I could respond. We both pulled and nothing happened.

"Harder!" she cried and fuck that was the wrong thing to say, but it sure as hell gave me the burst of adrenaline I needed.

I tugged harder and there was a wet sounding *slurp* before the fence eventually moved. It was slow, but then released with a pop and sent us flying back. She landed against me, cradled between my legs, sprawled half over me and my arms wrapped around her instinctively.

She glanced up at me from under her thick lashes, our faces close together, our breath panting and our stares locked. Neither of us moved away; if anything, she sank into me deeper. My eyes dropped to those lips that I needed more than my next breath. I tucked a stray strand of hair behind her ear and lingered there, my fingers stroking the delicate shell before trailing down the column of her slender neck.

Her breath caught, her hard façade dropped and her flash of vulnerability made me greedy.

Made me want to take.

I wet my lips, ready for a taste and she leaned forward. My heart pounded in my ears, adrenaline riding me hard and my need roared for this woman who I wanted so much and couldn't have, like some cruel joke from fate to punish me even more.

I closed my eyes and tilted her chin slightly, ready to fit our lips together. I already knew it would be the perfect fit, the perfect pressure, the perfect taste.

Just before they touched, her breath caressing my skin eagerly, Charlie's face flashed in my mind and I froze. After everything I'd taken from him, would he really want me in this position with his eldest daughter? His pride and joy? He'd done so much for me, given me life and a home, when I'd taken from him the thing he loved most. He was generous and good and here I was laying in the dirt with his daughter.

Fuck. What was I thinking? This couldn't happen and I was a fucking idiot for thinking it could.

I cleared my throat. "Um, let me help you up," I said, my voice a rough rasp.

Her eyes blinked open and I saw the moment her confusion turned to fury. She shoved away from me, muttering to herself and getting to her feet, dusting off her jeans and legs. When she turned away I adjusted myself and got to my feet.

Her shoulders were tense and she wouldn't face me. "Kat, I—"

"You don't need me, do you?" she asked, her voice cold and unfamiliar.

"To fix the fence?" I asked.

She nodded, still not facing me.

"I guess not," I replied. "But Kat, I—"

"Okay, I'll see you later then," she said and headed to her horse, swinging into the saddle and tugging the reins. Before I could even say anything, she flew across the pasture out of sight.

"You dickhead," I grumbled to myself.

I had fucked up, like I kept doing around her. I busied myself fixing the fence as best I could with splintered wood and basic tools, calling myself all the names under the sun.

I stepped back and surveyed my work. It was good but not good enough to hold forever. I would go into town and get some more wood and rebuild this section. My joy at having a project dimmed slightly at a rustle and movement from the tree line beyond the fence. I glanced up just as Chester next to me whinnied. Not a loud one, just a little warning. I was sure I could see something in the trees and down here it could be anything from a deer or bison to a bear.

"I think we're done here," I murmured and grabbed all my tools before leaving and heading back to the stables with Chester. The ride back didn't thrill me like it normally did, I was still too annoyed at myself for my slip-up with Kat. I wondered if I should find her and apologize. On the way back to the cabin I detoured to the house and knocked on the door.

Leo opened it, a dishtowel in his hand.

"Hey man, is Kat here?"

"In the shower," he replied.

"Ah okay."

"Didn't do anything dumb out there in that pasture when you were all alone, did you? Would hate to have to kill you when I'm just starting to like you." He flashed his teeth at me.

I snorted. "I may have."

Leo looked over his shoulder. "Wanna stay for dinner?"

I gave him a skeptical look. "Are you joking? I'll get shot at that dinner table."

He tossed the dishtowel over his shoulder. "Everyone

likes you, except Daisy but she doesn't count."

"Heard that, asshole!" Daisy shouted as she walked by. "Go and shave your back, you rodeo clown!"

He shrugged one shoulder. "See? She hates everyone, so she doesn't count."

I glanced into the house. "I don't know, man."

Leo reached out and tugged my arm and I stumbled over the threshold. "Look at that, you're inside now. So you might as well stay for dinner." He shut the door and I stared at him like he was crazy before I started laughing.

Leo gestured to follow him and disappeared through the open archway to the left. The air smelled delicious and my stomach rumbled, reminding me that we'd spent all day wrangling cattle and I hadn't eaten.

I glanced around the cottage style kitchen with its soft wood and checkered patterned chair cushions and tablecloth. It was homey and warm and now that I was here, I didn't want to leave.

"Hi Jack," August greeted me.

I waved at her, awkwardly, taking in the wooden sideboards that held ornaments and pictures of Charlie and Sherry. That guilt flared up inside me at seeing her face. I was shocked at the gall I'd had coming into this room, and now, what, I'd sit down to dinner with Sherry's daughters who had lived without her because of me, like we were one big happy family?

"I'll, uh, take a raincheck," I mumbled. August followed my gaze and her features softened. I stumbled from the kitchen with Leo shouting after me but my chest was tight and my heart pounding.

"Jack?" I heard Kat call but I didn't stop. I needed to get out. I shouldn't have come in the first place.

I wasn't welcome here.

CHAPTER SEVENTEEN

Katarina

He pulled away from *me*.

We were moments away from a kiss that I knew would have destroyed me, and he pulled away. The fact that I was willing to kiss him, but he wasn't willing to kiss me hurt. In a way I hadn't expected it to, but I guess it was the right thing. I shouldn't have wanted to kiss him in the first place and the shame I felt at that was still heating my blood even now. It was all I could think about during dinner, which Tilly was strangely absent from.

I glanced around the table. "Anyone seen Tills?"

"She's at a friend's house tonight," Leo mumbled round a mouthful of food.

"And Maddy?"

"Another date," he said, slightly less cheerful this time.

"She's sure having a lot of dates at the moment," Daisy mused, smirking at Leo, who flipped her off.

"Shame Jack couldn't stay for dinner. I like having another guy around the house," Leo said.

"If you're sick of the estrogen then go home, bucko," Daisy grumbled.

"Naw, you like having me here too much," Leo grinned, pulling her into his armpit and rubbing his knuckles across her scalp. I lost myself in their back and forth, pushing any thoughts of Jack from my brain.

I cleared up after dinner and took some wine out onto the porch, settling myself in my usual chair and watching the sky, picking out constellations. When my brain couldn't push Jack away any longer, I grumbled, "Why him?" The words echoed in the night and hung there, annoying me.

Then suddenly I saw a shadow coming down from the hill. I recognized the gait, the height and width of those shoulders. I wasn't going to draw attention to myself, just watched him, as usual, hoping to go unnoticed. I was riled up, volatile and I didn't want to lose it on him again.

I thought he hadn't spotted me. He was so close, and I was nearly home free but then his stride faltered and he looked up, glancing around wildly until he spotted me in the chair.

He pushed out a breath as he approached the side of the porch. He didn't climb up, just watched me through the wooden slats of the railing.

"Katarina," he greeted me.

I scoffed. Just the way he said my name pissed me off.

He sighed. "I wanted to speak to you earlier."

"But you took off."

"I didn't feel comfortable in the house." The words

seemed to just spill from him and it shocked me that he was so open. He bit his lip and looked away quickly before his gaze flitted back. He opened his mouth but then snapped it shut.

"Goodnight Katarina," he said and tapped the porch before walking off.

That's it? He pulled away from kissing me, even said he wanted to speak to me and now he was leaving again?

I shoved myself out of the chair and hopped over the porch like I was a teenager again. My back cracked from the exertion, but I ignored it.

"Wait one second!" I shouted after him, but he sped up, almost jogging towards the cabin.

"Jack!" I shouted, running after him. I climbed the porch and found him trying to jimmy the door open. "You don't get to walk away from me!"

"Just trying to save you from being in my company any more than you have to," he growled and shoved the door open, stalking inside. He tried to shut the door but I blocked it with my foot and pushed it open.

"Kat," he sighed, his head dropping back. I scrutinized him. He seemed tired, exhausted even. I knew today was a lot of work but it seemed to have taken its toll.

"What's with you?" I demanded. I didn't like that I noticed he was weary or how much it bothered me. And I also didn't like how much I'd been getting the brush off when he should have been chasing me.

"Nothing, Kat. Please, just go." He gestured to the door. Teddy came out from the bedroom and sat down at my feet, staring up at me lovingly. I stroked his head a few times before he settled himself by the fireplace.

I fixed my stare on Jack. "Why did you want to talk to me?"

"What do you mean?"

"Before, when you were in the house. You said you wanted to talk to me. What about?"

He shrugged and hunched his shoulders in, looking uncomfortable. "I just wanted to apologize for earlier, I shouldn't have put my hands on you. Shouldn't have tried to…" he trailed off, his eyes dropping to my mouth. The tension grew the longer he stared, and my heart pounded in my ears.

We were alone, in his cabin, just the two of us and he was staring at my mouth. Again.

"Jack," I whispered, and it was enough. He took one step forward, then another, until he was right up against me, pressing me back against the door.

"Why are you here?" he demanded, his voice low.

"I…" had no answer. I didn't know why. Only that I'd felt something I hadn't felt in a long time, if ever, and I didn't want to leave.

He reached behind me, putting us closer together. His intoxicating scent had my eyelids fluttering closed, especially when his cheek brushed against my arm. He twisted the doorknob, opening the door a crack, bumping it into me, the action moving us closer together.

"Door's open, you can leave."

But I didn't. I just stared into those soft blue eyes that held so many sad moments, so much pain. And shockingly, I wanted to ease it.

"Leave, Kat, please," he begged, his brows dipping in. He pressed his forehead to mine, his breath caressing my lips. "Please leave."

I shook my head gently, reaching behind me and closing the door. The sound of the tumbler dropping into place was a scream in the quiet of the cabin. I could only just hear it over the beating of my heart.

"Kiss me," I whispered, fool that I am.

He brushed a lock of hair back, his fingers lingering and stroking the shell of my ear, trailing along my jaw, just like he had earlier. His thumb rested on my lower lip before he plucked it between his thumb and finger. The anticipation had me on edge, ready to detonate with the slightest movement. Our chests expanded together with each labored breath.

"So pretty," he murmured, and I swear to God I whimpered. He pressed against me, our bodies lining up and I felt his hot, hard length, and melted into him. His body held me up and he released my lip. He hesitated, indecision warring with desire. Why was he taking so long?

"Kiss me," I demanded again.

"I haven't done this in a long time, so I'm sorry if I'm not that good at it," he spoke softly, his chest hitching. Vulnerability radiated off him and I reveled in it. Drowned in it and was eager for more.

"Why are you apologizing?"

"Because right now, the way I feel about you, I want this to be the best damn kiss you've ever had."

I swallowed, my throat dry and my body ready to burst into flames at his admission.

"It already is."

I barely said the words before his mouth slammed into mine, hard. Giving and taking every little thing I had to offer. His lips were firm, insistent but gentle, sipping at mine, tasting and sampling. His tongue slid along the seam and I shivered against him, opening wide on a moan and letting him in.

His tongue chased mine, delving and sliding together in a hot wave. A shock zapped right through me, waking up nerve endings that were long dead. I moaned, tangling my hand in his hair and tilting his head so I could get deeper. I was hungry for him and couldn't get enough.

He tasted divine, like sex and sin and promises of pleasure like I'd never known. He licked and sucked on my tongue, rubbing himself between my legs, right where I needed him and my knees gave out. He tapped my thighs and I leapt up, wrapping them around his waist and he turned, stumbling through the cabin as we ate at each other's mouths.

The next thing I knew, my back was hitting his mattress and his weight settled on top of me, heavy and so perfect. I frantically pulled at his shirt, desperate to feel his warm skin on mine. Our lips parted for a moment when his shirt went over his head, then his tongue was trailing a path down my neck, sucking hard and my clit throbbed sharply, desperate for him. I clung to him, writhing against him, my eyes rolling back in my head.

"Fuck me," I begged. I hadn't meant to beg, but how could I not when he was getting me so hot, and yes it had been a while, but my senses were destroyed by this man.

"What?" he asked, his voice thick and heavy, as passion-drunk as I was.

"Fuck me, please, Jack?"

He stiffened, and not in a good way. His demeanor changed completely, and he slowly untangled our limbs, a heavy silence filling the room. I was left cold, aching and vulnerable at the loss of his touch.

It was fine if we were in this together, if we were both giving in. But for some reason him pulling away set a clear boundary. We were not in this together, and my stomach churned.

He pulled his shirt back on but didn't say anything. I didn't move, fear locked me in place. What was happening?

"I think you should go," he said quietly.

"What?" I whispered.

He wouldn't look at me, just kept his back to me. "I think...I think you should leave, Kat. This was a mistake and we both know it."

I swallowed back the tears that sprang to my eyes. I had felt a connection growing between us over time as we'd worked together. We'd shared a few moments with each other where we'd opened up, whether intentionally or drug-related. I'd shared how the ranch was falling apart, how *I* was falling apart and I'd felt like I wasn't alone in this.

I tried to bite back my sob but it slipped out. Mortified, I clambered to the end of the bed, desperate to get out of there before I embarrassed myself even more.

"Kat, wait," he began once I was running out of the room. I heard him curse as he stumbled after me. "Wait, it's not what you think," he said but I didn't care. My sobs weren't staying quiet and I needed to get out of here, I didn't want to be weak in front of him.

I threw open the front door that I'd closed only moments before and ran out towards the house, past the wine I'd left on the porch, and straight inside.

"Yo Kat, we're watching *27 Dresses* if you're up for it? B-b-b-Bennie and the Jets!" Leo shouted from the living room.

"Bennie!" Daisy replied in a high-pitched warble.

I didn't reply, just ran up the stairs and into my room. When I was safely inside, I pulled in deep breaths, trying to calm my pounding heart and stop the shakes in my hands.

"Pull yourself together!" I hissed, patting my cheeks to dry my tears and shake some sense into myself.

But I couldn't.

Jack unleashed something in me.

The tears I'd been holding back were brought to the forefront, refusing to be ignored, and they wouldn't stop. I tried to distract myself but they kept falling. I got into the shower and stood under the spray but my tears still fell, just trickled down with the water. Eventually I gave up trying to stop them and embraced them. I got into bed and cried myself to sleep, cursing the day I'd asked for a sign and Jack Drayton turned up on my porch.

*

The next morning, after ignoring a text from Jack that read *Can we talk?* I dragged my ass out of bed, my eyes puffy and swollen from hours of crying but it was fine, I wasn't planning on seeing Jack on a Sunday, so it didn't matter. I'd just lie to my sisters and say I had a rough night's sleep or was hungover or had allergies, or what-the-fuck-ever.

What ruined everything was looking out the kitchen window while the coffee maker percolated and seeing cows everywhere. Again.

"For fuck's sake!" I shouted, slapping the worktop in anger. How the hell had they gotten out again? Jack must not have fixed the fence or shut the gate properly after I rode off. Either way it was Jack's fault.

A moment later there was a pounding on the front door, and I peeked around the archway of the kitchen and saw the man himself pacing the porch.

"For fuck's sake," I hissed again. Then he saw me.

He pointed behind him. "You seeing this shit?" he demanded, his voice muffled through the glass door.

My eyes rolled towards the heavens, praying for someone to just give me a break. I didn't want to spend the day with him rounding up cattle and fixing fences or gates. I wanted to take my coffee back to bed and cry some more.

I held up my hand, telling him I needed five minutes. I ran back upstairs and washed my face, praying for the puffiness to go down in the next four minutes. I dressed and headed back down but Jack was nowhere to be found.

Assuming he'd gone back to the cabin to change, I pulled on my cowgirl boots and headed towards the stables to saddle our horses. I was amazed when I entered and he was already in there, cooing to Chester. My insides squeezed sharply at the soft words he was speaking to the horse but I ignored them. From now on, any bodily reactions I had around Jack couldn't be trusted.

"Hey, I've just finished Chester, you want me to—"

I shook my head. "Nope," I replied, popping the *p*. I began saddling Sunshine and I could feel Jack watching me. I could practically feel him vibrating with the need to talk to me, but he showed some sense and didn't.

We rode back down towards the house and worked together to herd the cattle, Jack continually anticipating my moves and needs which annoyed me. How were we so in sync? I even tried a few guff moves to throw him off but he knew what I was doing. Eventually we got them back down to the south pasture and yet again the gate was still closed.

Jack rode on and opened it. Once the cattle were all inside safely, I rode off to do the perimeter check again and of course, found the corner fence trampled.

"What the hell?" I murmured.

"I fixed that, admittedly not the most amazing work but it was sturdy, I swear. I tried rocking it and it wasn't giving," Jack assured me.

Sympathy tried to unfurl inside me at the worried

expression pinching his face, like I was gonna lay into him over it, but I tamped it down.

I jumped off Sunshine and inspected the area, including the dirt and hoof prints. Jack continued talking while I inspected the mud. Wait a minute, was that...

"Son of a bitch!" I shouted, silencing Jack. I spun around, glancing towards the tree line. "Where are you, you bastard?" I called, eyes peeled as I looked for any movement.

"Uh, what's happening?" Jack asked, looking at me like I was crazy.

"You see this?" I demanded, pointing furiously at the hoof prints in the mud.

"Um, no?"

"This is a cow hoof, see, it's almost teardrop in shape."

He just continued to look at me like I was crazy.

"This here, that's not a cow hoof."

"It's not? But they look the same?" Jack asked, tilting his head and squinting at the mud.

"Similar but it's more angled. It's the hoof print of a bison," I said, then spun towards the tree line. "A pesky bison who likes to cause trouble. A bison called Bert!" I shouted. At that moment, like he had been summoned, Bert the Bison emerged from the tree line, munching on some grass like he didn't give a shit about all the destruction he'd caused. Because he didn't. He craved chaos, the big shit.

I stomped over to him, ready to give him a piece of my mind, when strong arms banded around my waist.

"What the hell are you doing? Are you crazy?" Jack shouted, pulling me away from Bert whose smug gaze followed me.

"What are *you* doing?" I shouted back. "Put me

down!"

"No, you're going after a wild bison, what's wrong with you?"

"Bert's not wild, he's an asshole!"

"Really, the random bison is an asshole?" Jack looked at me doubtfully.

"Yes, he is! He does stuff like this all the time, he's a menace!"

Jack looked over to where Bert was munching on some grass, kicking his hooves on the ground like a naughty child. "I'm so confused right now."

"Years ago, Bert appeared. He got separated from his herd or they kicked him out or whatever, and ever since he hangs around the town, causing drama and mischief to entertain himself, because he's bored," I huffed. "And an asshole!"

"Bert the Bison is an asshole," Jack replied, and I could see him smothering a grin which only made me madder.

"Don't laugh at me!"

"I'm not, I'm just…it's interesting is all."

Bert had crept a little closer and was now within throttling distance. Like Jack knew what I was going to do, he moved and placed himself between me and Bert.

He bent down and put both hands on my shoulders, peering into my face. "We'll fix the fence and make it Bert proof, how about that?"

Ugh, why was Jack being so helpful and perfect. Why couldn't he be a dick like he was last night? The memory had me clamming up and shrugging him off me. "Fine," I grunted and turned away, kicking at the grass petulantly, just like Bert.

"Just let me go back to the cabin. I'll get some more wood to reinforce it and make it Bert-proof."

Jack rode off and I sat down in the grass, picking at it and wondering how my life came to be that I was a thirty something orphan, with a bankrupt ranch, chasing off a tricksy bison, rejected by the last person I would ever want to hook up with, and then stuck having to rely on that person.

"Screw you, universe!"

I glared at Bert who kept trying to schmooze his way over. "Don't be coming over here to apologize," I grumbled at him. He hung his head and I stuck my tongue out at him. He obviously didn't return the gesture but I could tell he wanted to.

Sometime later, Jack reappeared and set to work fixing the fence. Under the sun and Bert's watchful gaze, he stripped off his damp shirt and I was treated to all those glorious muscles flexing and doing manly things.

"You don't need me, do you?" I croaked around my dry throat.

"Uh, yeah?" Jack said and pointed to Bert. "Don't leave me with this menace, who knows what he'll do."

I snorted. Jack smirked and the impact it had on my insides had me frowning and turning away. Eventually he was finished and with a terse warning to Bert, we were on our way back.

We untacked the horses and headed back to the house, me ten paces in front of Jack. I was so close to the porch, so close to being away from him when he called after me.

"Can we talk?"

"Nope," I shouted back.

"Kat, please? Let me explain?" he sighed.

I whirled on him, storming back and getting in his face. "You said you'd do whatever I asked?"

He nodded, his eyes flitting over my expression.

"Then leave me alone and keep this professional,

please?" I arched a brow when he opened his mouth to argue.

Eventually his lips pulled into a mulish line and he nodded just once.

"Great," I replied with a bright smile and headed on into the house.

That night, like an addict needing a fix, I sat in my father's study in the dark and watched him.

CHAPTER EIGHTEEN

Jack

Five years ago - day 3,290 in prison…

Charlie stared at me across the cool metal table, his eyes running over my face and although he kept his expression neutral, I saw the tic just below his eye.

"You need to make some more friends," he grunted, eyes flicking away from the horror show that was my face.

"The men who did this to me were my friends," I joked weakly, cracking a smile and hissing as my swollen lip split and I tasted blood.

"Who did you piss off?"

"No one. I had the gall to get up in the morning and this is what happened."

Charlie shook his head, his lips pinched tight in anger. "Jack, you gotta stop—"

"I don't know what you're about to say but I need to remind you where we are. This is what happens in here, we don't sit around braiding each other's hair and writing in fucking dream journals, Charlie."

"Watch your tone, son. I know exactly where we are." There was a warning in Charlie's voice. I knew the words he choked back, that he knew exactly where we were and *why*. I ducked my head, looking down at the hands twisting in my lap. My scabbed knuckles. I was so busy dodging the shiv that I didn't dodge the knuckle dusters the guys who jumped me had. I fought my way out, only just though, and not without taking a serious beating. My eyes were black and blue, and I was pretty sure I had a couple of cracked ribs. I'd been pissing blood for a couple of days thanks to a few hard jabs to the kidneys, but I'd been there before and I'd be there again.

It was just that Charlie had never visited when I was recovering before.

"I get it. I'm sorry, I know you can't help it. It just…kills me to see you like this," Charlie said, his voice cracking and a lump formed in my throat.

Some months it was really hard to see Charlie. Some months we were both emotional and some months we were jovial. Some months were a swing and a miss but he'd never missed a visit, not once. He'd shown up for me more than anyone in this life and I owed him everything I had just for that.

"I know and…thanks, I appreciate your concern," I replied, my voice rough.

Charlie sniffed and clapped his hands together. "So, I've been thinking, we need to start planning what you're gonna do when you get out of here."

My stomach dropped. Occasionally he tried to bring up this conversation and I managed to swerve it. I guess it couldn't be avoided forever.

"I've got five years left, give or take a few weeks, bit early to be thinking about that," I scoffed.

Charlie pshed. "It's never too early. I was thinking, how about you come by the ranch when you're out. We can talk about it closer to the time, but I'd love to have you there."

I didn't know what to say. I just stared at the man in front of me who I'd broken in so many ways and yet he continued to help me. To show up for me.

"You can't do that," I replied.

He shrugged. "Sure I can, it's my ranch, I do what I want. Have you thought about a career?"

"Not really."

He reached across the table and placed a hand on my arm. "I know it's hard. You've been here a long time and there's still time to go. But I want you out of here and in one piece ready to start your life. You need to focus on what you want when you can finally take life by the balls and get it."

"No touching!" A guard shouted and Charlie gave my arm a quick squeeze and withdrew.

I rubbed a hand along my jaw and then flinched when I put pressure on a bruise. "I like woodwork, I've been reading about it."

Charlie's eyes lit up. "Yeah? Woodwork is good, carpentry is a solid career. I would need some help like that at the ranch, you could start there and get some experience before you take on some bigger jobs."

"I can't stay at the ranch, Charlie," I said. The old fool was getting far too ahead of himself.

"Why not?"

I leveled him with a look. "You know why."

"Well it ain't called Redemption Ranch for nothing,"

he winked. "Just say you'll think about it?"

I nodded. "Sure, I'll think about it." I could do that at least.

He smiled wide and I found myself smiling in return. "I can't wait to bring you home from this place."

My chest ached at his words, at the simplicity in them, like we didn't have a million miles of shit and baggage between us. "I'm not a stray puppy at the pound that you can adopt and bring home."

He smiled again. "I know you're not. You're family."

*

Present day…

I woke up from my dream, calling out Charlie's name, my heart aching and missing him like hell and it hit me all over again that he was gone.

Grief was a funny thing. You think you're okay and getting by just fine. Then something comes along and knocks you on your ass. That was me today.

I didn't get out of bed. I lay there, lost in my thoughts and memories, thinking about all the ways my life was what it was because of him. I was still around because of him. I'd had dark thoughts while in prison, considered doing some things to end the suffering.

But I didn't.

I kept going because of that pipe dream that I would one day be out of that place and at the ranch, working alongside Charlie. That became my dream. But that died the moment I found out he had too.

I tried to be excited about life but hadn't been that successful until recently. I'd started carpentry, I'd grown excited about my future. I'd worked at the ranch, side by side with not Charlie, but Katarina.

It had been weeks since she lay beneath me, begging me to fuck her.

I'd done what she'd asked, I'd stayed away from her. I'd kept it professional and it was killing me. I didn't know how much longer I could go without experiencing the perfect feeling of her long legs wrapped around my waist. The intoxicating sensation of her skin against mine, her hands in my hair and the drugging feel of her lips on mine.

She had me under a spell and yet, when she'd uttered those words while writhing under me, I'd freaked out. I'd gotten scared. And I'd ruined everything. I was a thirty plus virgin and I panicked because although I knew the mechanics of fucking, I didn't know how to *fuck her*, the way she wanted, the way she needed. What if I disappointed her?

And I knew I shouldn't have been doing that anyway. I tried to put up defenses against her but the second she chased me into my cabin, I knew she wanted it as much as I did. She was the only one I was concerned about. I would never do something she didn't want, so the fact that she chased me, begged me, was a green light. No matter how many ways of fucked up it was that I wanted her.

So I'd done what she asked, I'd kept it professional. No matter how much I wanted to touch her, I kept my hands to my goddamn self and it was killing me. It was all of my own doing but I couldn't handle it much longer.

Riding with her all day, working on the ranch, seeing her around town, it was too much. Sometimes I thought she was watching me but I never caught her. She had made it abundantly clear that she didn't want anything from me so I must have been imagining the warmth of her stare as it lingered, tracking me from head to toe.

Made me hard from just my imagination. Made me want to fuck her just like she asked, like she *begged*.

By the time I got out of bed, the sun was setting and Teddy was whining and nudging my arm. I fed him, showered and pulled on my white Henley, black jeans and wrecked boots, ready to head to work and hopefully shake myself out of my funk.

I walked to The Lonely Bison. The fresh air filled my lungs and the tightness in my chest started to lift. The sun set as I headed into town and when I pushed through the saloon doors of the bar, I was beginning to feel normal again.

"Here he is!" Max shouted, flinging me a big grin. I waved and tried out my smile for the first time that day and was surprised to find it worked.

The bar was full to bursting with folks looking for a good time. The overwhelming scent of perfume, cologne and alcohol was oddly comforting, and I ducked behind the bar and got to work.

Halfway through my shift, Max sidled up next to me, groaning and shaking his head, gesturing to the woman walking away from me. "What's the matter with you, dude? That woman was practically begging for a ride on the Jack train."

I shrugged. I knew I should be looking to have a little fun and experience some feminine company but honestly, the thought of anyone other than Kat gave me the ick.

"Still hung up on the oldest Cartwright sister, huh?" he asked, grinning at me again and I kinda wanted to slap it off his face. But he was my only friend so I couldn't.

"Speaking of Cartwright sisters," I said and nodded towards the door where Tilly, the youngest, was peeking in.

Max cursed and when Tilly spotted him, her eyes

practically turned into hearts. "What is her deal?"

"She's infatuated, that's all. You never had a crush when you were fifteen?"

Max flipped me off and went over to Tilly, sharing some tense words before he closed the door on her. He came back to the bar, shaking his head.

I flung him the same grin he gave me, and he glared when he spotted it. "Not a word," he warned and I laughed, feeling my chest ease again.

I dodged a few more women through the night, dug my hands in my pants pocket and managed to find two phone numbers which had been snuck in there and promptly put them in the trash.

The band had pulled Max up on stage with them to sing a few songs and although he pretended he didn't want to, Max sang with a gusto that suggested he might be a fan of the limelight.

I was tidying up when I spotted that telltale light blonde hair hiding in the corner. I made my way over to Tilly. "You shouldn't be here."

She glared up at me but her eyes were glassy. "You're here," she replied, not making sense, then she hiccupped.

"Shit," I murmured on seeing how wasted she was. Max would be furious she was here and drunk. If anyone spotted her and thought that Max had given her alcohol he could get in a lot of trouble. "Come with me," I grunted and hauled her by the arm to Max's office. I grabbed some water on the way and pushed her onto the couch, shoving the glass at her.

"Drink this." I grabbed my phone from my pocket and opened my chat with Kat that had plenty of messages she hadn't responded to. She'd left me on read, as I discovered was the lingo. I messaged her that Tilly was here and needed to go home.

"Your sister is coming to get you," I said when I got Kat's reply. "I need to get back out there. Stay here, drink your water, and don't touch anything."

"He's the only one," Tilly said sadly, turning to me with her huge green eyes magnified by her tears.

"Max?" I asked. "What did he do?" Anger snaked down my spine at the thought of Max doing something to hurt Tilly. He'd been great to me, but I didn't really know him and there was a reason Tilly was hanging around so much.

"He was the only one who didn't treat me like some dumb, grieving kid. He spoke to me like I was an adult, like he understood."

"That's all that happened, you guys just talked?"

Tilly nodded. "Talked, fell in love. At least I did…" She broke off, sobbing into her water. I was relieved but also felt sad for Tilly. She was the youngest sister and had a lot to deal with in her short life.

"Just…stay here. I'll be back," I said. I headed to the bar and served a few patrons but Max was living it up on stage and hadn't noticed I was missing, so I snuck back into the office to Tilly.

She saw me and began sobbing again and my heart broke for her. I sat down on the couch and put an arm around her awkwardly trying to console her. She flung herself at me and wrapped her arms around my neck.

"Shh, it's okay," I said, feeling stupid. I didn't know what to say to make her feel better and then I remembered something. "You were always Charlie's little girl. The way he talked about you, he was so proud of you."

Tilly's sobs were muffled in my chest, but I was sure she was quieting down.

"He told me about how one time when you were nine,

you got out to the horses and managed to mount one and rode it bareback like a little rebel. He was torn between whooping your ass and being so dang proud of you. He laughed so much when he told me, and I always wanted to know how you managed to get yourself up on that horse?"

She snuffled quietly and looked up at me, eyes streaming, cheeks red and splotchy, nose leaking. "I climbed one of the stalls."

I laughed. "You're a little rebel, fearless, just like Charlie said you were."

"He…he said that?"

I nodded and her face seemed to light up a little and she wiped her tears, her chest hitching as her sobs subsided. "What else did he say?"

"He said you made it down to the south pasture before anyone could get after you. Said you were out like a shot, so fast and so confident on that horse. He was amazed at how well you rode, especially bareback."

"I'm not afraid of being thrown," she said, and her chin jutted out stubbornly.

"I'm not surprised. Maybe we could ride together one day? Give me some pointers as I'm kinda new at it."

"I know, I've seen you ride," she replied.

I burst out laughing at the sass from this fifteen-year-old. Damn she would have a mouth on her when she was older, and I couldn't wait to see her go toe-to-toe with Daisy's snark.

There was a knock at the door and Kat's blonde head peeked around the frame.

"Hey," she whispered, her eyes locking with mine and my damn heart started pounding. When she spotted Tilly, she frowned, concern pinching her brow. "What have you gotten yourself into now?"

"It's okay, Kat," I said gently. "She's okay, Max didn't see her. No one knows she's here and she's okay." There was so much on Kat's shoulders at the moment and if I could help in any way then I would, even if it was just hiding her drunk sister from a bar owner.

Kat's stare didn't linger on me, if anything she tried to avoid me. "Come on, kid. Let's get you home and sober you up."

"I am sober," Tilly grumbled but pushed to her feet.

As they were leaving, Tilly turned back to me. "I'd love to ride together some time."

Kat's eyes swung to me and burned me with their intensity. I rocked forward on the balls of my feet. "It's a date," I replied.

Kat frowned before they left and I headed back out to the bar, sighing deeply at the crisis averted. The night wore on but eventually all the patrons headed out leaving me and Max to tidy up.

"What did you say to Tilly?" I asked.

Max shrugged. "Nothing really. Everyone's been treating her with kid gloves and I hated it when people did that to me when I was younger. So I just told her how shit was."

"I think you really struck a chord with her, she's got a little crush on you," I teased.

Max blanched. "That's the last thing I need, some kid mooning over me, thinking I'm her hero."

"Must be nice being idolized. Why's that so bad?"

Max sighed. "Because I'm no one's hero."

That night as I lay in bed, trying to sleep, my phone pinged. I squinted as the bright screen pricked my eyes and saw a message.

Kat: Thanks for looking out for Tilly.

I read the message over a dozen times before I put my

phone down and fell asleep with a smile on my face.

CHAPTER NINETEEN

Katarina

I couldn't fault him.

He'd done exactly what I asked so why was I so pissed at him? It was because he kept doing things that were annoying, like showing up for me, looking after my sister, putting us first, and doing things with planks of wood in almost no clothing, painted in sweat.

I should be focusing on how to save the ranch but instead, my hormones were acting like I was fifteen again and going boy crazy.

"Yoohoo!" Daisy sang, waving her hand in front of my face. I blinked, warm soap suds running down my arm where I'd drifted off while doing the dishes. "Where did you go?"

"Oh, sorry," I said, handing her a plate.

"Somewhere nice I bet, based on the flush of your skin," she teased.

I snorted. "No, my hands are in hot water, that's why I'm flushed."

"If you say so."

She dried off the plate and ducked down, pulling a cabinet door open and it practically fell off its hinges. "This place is falling apart. If it's not this, it's the bathroom door, or the wonky table or the drawer that sticks on the sideboard," Daisy grumbled.

"Nothing stopping you from fixing any of it," Leo said as he walked into the kitchen.

"Do you just live here now?" Daisy asked, arching a brow at him as he dropped a plate in the sink and crammed the last of his toast into his mouth.

"Yesff," he replied around his mouthful. He chewed and swallowed before adding, "You know, there is someone who could come and fix all of this."

My stomach tightened at his insinuation. *Not Jack, not Jack, not Jack.*

"Do you mean Jack?" Daisy practically snarled.

"Yep."

Daisy grunted but didn't disagree like I expected her to.

"We're done here, you kids go and play," I teased, flicking water at them both, wanting them out of my kitchen so they wouldn't notice how weird I acted when anyone mentioned Jack.

"Come on Daze, let's go watch—"

"If you say The Devil Wears Prada…"

"The Devil Wears Prada!" Leo shouted, slinging an arm around her neck.

"So weird that that's your favorite movie."

"You're weird," Leo shot back and eventually they left the kitchen. I finished the dishes, thinking about how Jack was with Tilly last night. He'd treated her with care and concern and spent time listening to her and cheering her up. He kept doing nice things and it was making it harder to stay mad at him.

I made my way to Daddy's study, determined to go through the rest of the paperwork and get a solid grasp on the finances. I'd procrastinated long enough.

So far, things weren't looking great. We were in trouble, big time, with a couple of different creditors. And another ranch owner who had done a few deals to help us out.

I went through the papers until my eyes were stinging and I'd uncovered all the financial hardship. There were final notice letters and overdue payment letters, and the bank account wasn't exactly flush with cash to pay any of them. I needed to come up with money and fast. But how? I was drawing a blank and didn't understand why my brain couldn't deal with this.

I leaned back in the chair and pushed my palms into my eyes, rubbing away the tiredness. I stood up, stretching my legs and then decided to call it a night, flicking off the lamp on the desk. As I turned, I looked out the window and immediately fixated on the cabin.

Jack was in there, post-shower judging by the towel hanging around his waist.

"Stop watching him," I scolded myself. It was wrong and shameful but I couldn't help it. I leaned against the wall and watched as he puttered around. He ate an apple while leaning against the small worktop of the kitchenette, taking huge bites out of it. I remembered the feel of his lips and teeth clamping down on my neck, my knees shook and I almost moaned.

Like he knew what I was thinking, his eyes snapped up and I froze when they collided with mine in the dark. I knew he couldn't see me but I stood stock-still as he tilted his head from side-to-side. Then he disappeared. I released the breath I was holding but he reappeared, this time at the window, staring straight at me.

He ran his hand down his chest, slowly.

No way could he know I was here. This was crazy.

My breathing grew labored, like I'd just come back from a run. He trailed his hand lower until he gripped himself through the towel.

I gasped as he stroked himself, my cheeks heating and the pulse between my legs throbbed sharply. Oh my God, was he really doing that with me watching? He had to know.

He continued stroking over the impressive length that I wanted in my hands, my mouth, my pussy. My mouth watered as his head tipped back and I swear I heard his moan from here. I spun away from the window. I couldn't do this, couldn't violate his privacy any more like I had been. Even if I thought he was doing this for me.

A moment later, my phone pinged in my pocket. I pulled it out, turning down the brightness in case he could see me. I scrolled down the top bar and saw I had a message from him.

Jack: Enjoying the show?

My heart stuttered. He *did* know I was watching. But how? How did he know? It was pitch black in here. I sank back in the shadows, my heart pounding, pulse throbbing. And my phone pinged again.

Jack: Unless I'm crazy…

Jack: Yeah I'm crazy. No way are you watching me, I guess I can keep going…

"Oh my God," I groaned, clutching my phone to my

chest. Did I dare peek? I slowly glanced around the window frame and saw him standing in the same spot, phone out, a massive grin on his face. I was simultaneously disappointed and pleased he wasn't jerking off.

My phone pinged again, lighting up my face and I cursed and ducked back.

Jack: Gotcha.

Jack: Night, Kat. Sweet dreams x

I sank to the ground, a quivering mess of need. How did he get me so riled up like that? I wondered if he would have continued if I didn't duck away. If he would have climaxed right there in front of me. I suddenly wanted to see that more than anything: his head thrown back in ecstasy, mouth open as he grunted his pleasure.

I shook my head, pulling myself off the floor and refusing to glance out the window again and headed up to bed.

The next morning, Jack was on the porch, sipping the coffee that Tilly had brought him, and he smiled at me when I appeared. It was a pleasant smile but a knowing one and my cheeks flushed.

"Sleep well?" he asked, as we headed towards the stables. The insinuation in his tone had shivers racing up and down my spine, goosebumps spread across my bare arms. I didn't answer him, didn't know what to say. I felt guilty but also ridiculously turned on and frustrated. I was still mad that he rejected me and it all felt like we were playing with fire.

I managed to avoid him all day, he was out fixing fences and I was with the horses. When I came out from the stables to get some lunch, there were two men on the porch. One was dressed in a sharp suit, the other in black jeans and a t-shirt, arms folded across his massive chest. I headed towards them, fear sending my adrenaline skyrocketing when Daisy came out from the house instead.

"Shit," I hissed and jogged towards the porch, trying to get there quicker. "It's okay Daisy, I got it, you can go," I said, terrified she would learn the truth.

Her gaze flicked towards me and she frowned. "Do we owe these people money?"

I waved her off. "It's just a misunderstanding. Daisy please, I'll handle it, go inside," I tried to smile but my panic twisted it into a grimace. She reluctantly disappeared and I turned towards the men. "Can I help you?"

The one in the suit turned towards me, a smug smile dripping from his lips. I wanted to slap it off his face. His muscle man breathed heavily behind him, trying to appear threatening.

"Are you Katarina?" Suit asked.

"Yes, and you are?"

"Martin Mirander from Mirander Associates." He held out his hand but I ignored it as my stomach plummeted. This was one of the companies we owed money to.

"How can I help you?" I asked through gritted teeth.

"We've been trying to contact you regarding the debt you owe us," Martin spoke smoothly.

"I don't owe you anything," I said, trying to play dumb.

"Well, not you specifically. The ranch, which has now passed to you, ergo, you."

"And?" Playing dumb was only going to get me so far and my hands began to shake from fear.

"We've come to collect," Martin said, and Muscles cracked his knuckles. My eyes must have widened because Martin hastened to add: "Assets, to clear the debt. We'll take what we're owed from the property, it's all legal."

My brain went into overdrive, so many thoughts racing that I couldn't put together a plan of action. I was completely helpless in this situation.

"That's not a wise decision." Jack's voice was firm, barely restrained anger simmering in his tone. I felt his heat as he came up behind me and everything in me screamed to lean back into his touch, let him carry this burden for me.

"We've written to the ranch a number of times to advise—"

"And you'll know that the owner of the ranch has just recently passed away. Surely it would be good of you to allow the family time to grieve before riding in here for your pound of flesh?" Jack put his hand on my shoulder and squeezed gently, comforting me and I nearly sobbed with relief.

Martin pushed his glasses back up his nose. "Yes, I was terribly sorry to hear about Mr. Cartwright, he was a great customer. I don't wish to be insensitive but—"

"Which is why you'll leave today, empty-handed, and give us some time to get the money together. I think that's reasonable, don't you?" Jack offered, his voice leaving no room for argument. He was beside me now, putting on a front like we were a team. I couldn't look at him, I was so ashamed of how I'd neglected things and now needed him to come rescue me.

"Well, we've been patient and given plenty of opportunity—" Martin spluttered.

"If you step one foot inside that house, I will destroy you." Jack's low voice held a warning note and even I was scared. "I'm asking you *nicely*, to come back in two weeks, then we'll have this settled."

Martin looked to Muscles who shrugged, and Martin

sighed. "Two weeks, we'll be back."

I nodded, it was all I could do, and they left. Once they were gone, I pushed out the breath I was holding and started trembling.

"Hey, it's okay," Jack soothed, his big hand stroking up and down my back.

"Thank you," I whispered. My hands were shaking as I brushed away the tears that threatened to fall.

"Goddammit Kat, you're killing me here," he growled and tugged me into his chest.

I buried my face in his shirt, feeling his taut muscles press against my skin, his wood and pine scent soothing me.

"Kat?" Daisy called gently. I pushed away from Jack, ignoring the hurt look on his face, and turned to see her in the doorway, arms hugged around her tightly, glancing between us. "What's going on?"

I tried to put on a bright smile. "Nothing. Everything's fine, Daze."

She actually stomped her foot. "Don't lie to me, what's going on? Is the ranch in trouble?"

"Daisy, please," I begged her.

"You don't need to hide stuff from us, we can help!" Daisy said.

"I appreciate that but it's fine, I can handle it," I replied and smiled again. Her eyes flitted to Jack and she stared at him for the longest time before she disappeared back into the house.

I wasn't aware of it, but Jack had been stroking my back the entire time. Like he realized, he stopped and dropped his forehead to my shoulder. "Kat, please let someone help?"

I leaned my head back against him, reveling in his touch, forgetting that I shouldn't like it this much, that it shouldn't feel this right.

"I have to do this myself. I can fix it, I can. Thank you for being here and buying me an extra two weeks to figure out what to do."

"*Us* an extra two weeks," he replied, lifting his head and spinning me to face him, his hands on my hips, squeezing tightly. "We're in this together, I don't care what you say. You forget, sweetheart, you gave me that cabin, which means I own property here. This impacts me as well. And I'm not letting anyone fuck with my home now that I've found it. Or your home either."

He was right. If people kept showing up all the time then he was involved, whether I liked it or not. And honestly, it felt great to have support and someone stand up for me and the ranch.

I nodded. "Anyway, get back to work. Dinner's at six, don't be late."

"Dinner?"

"Yes, it's my way of saying thank you."

"I don't want to make Daisy uncomfortable," he hedged, looking towards the house.

I shrugged. "She won't be. I think she's warming up to you."

He grinned at me, and I swear my knees knocked together. I wanted to lick my tongue across that smile, tangle my fingers in his hair, drag my teeth down his neck, beg him to fuck me and have him give in.

As we continued to look at each other, his smile slipped and his eyes darkened with a heat that left my body tight with anticipation.

I cleared my throat, breaking the spell and headed off towards the stables again. I didn't see him for the rest of the afternoon. I went home and showered before dinner, feeling gross from mucking out the stables and baling hay.

When I came down there was chatter in the kitchen and I paused for a moment on the stairs, enjoying the full house and pleasant, happy voices.

Everything was okay.

I entered the kitchen and glanced around, seeing a full dinner table and Jack sitting there, in his nicest lumberjack shirt, it was like something clicked into place. This was family, this was *home*.

He was talking to August but when I came in, he glanced over and smiled at me, raising an eyebrow as if asking, *Are you okay? Is this okay?* I nodded back to him, everything was fine. Daisy didn't even complain, just glared at him a few times.

"Where's Leo?" I asked, glancing around the table, noticing he was missing for the first time in days.

"He's got a date," Daisy answered. My eyes swerved to Maddy who poked at the food on her plate.

"Jack, after dinner would you be able to look at my closet doors? They're sticking and I don't know why. I heard you're good with wood?" August asked innocently.

Daisy snorted at the innuendo, and I glared at her.

Jack smiled. "Of course, I'd be happy to."

"Also, my bedroom door handle is kinda hanging off, could you help with that?" Tilly asked.

"Sure thing," he nodded, and I could see him glowing from their requests, like he wanted to be needed. It made me ache a little for how much of his life he'd spent alone. I didn't pipe up that the girls knew exactly how to fix all of those things. They just wanted him to feel included.

"Anything out of use that you'd like him to take a look at?" Maddy asked, pulling herself out of her reverie enough to raise a brow at me. I flicked a green bean at her and she snickered. I looked over at where Tilly was showing Jack something on TikTok and found him staring at me, and not at her screen. My cheeks flushed and I ducked my head.

The rest of dinner went off without a hitch and then Jack was upstairs fixing August's closet and Tilly's door. Then he was saying goodnight and thanking us for letting him stay, shooting me a lingering look that had my knees weakening. He left the house and took all the air with him when he went. I didn't know what to do with myself. The girls went off to watch TV and I tried to lose myself in whatever crap they were watching but my thoughts distracted me.

I went into the office, ready to come up with some ideas on how to save the ranch. I bent down to flick the lamp on but before I did, I stopped. Jack was in the window, staring out. I watched him, interested to see what he would do.

He took out his phone and brought it to his ear and a moment later mine started buzzing. I pulled it out.

"Yes?" I answered, breathlessly.

"Kat," he said, his voice echoing in my ear as I stared at him. His breathing was heavy and deep. I could even see his chest expanding with each inhalation. Tension pulled taut between us, the air electric, and I practically vibrated with need.

"I need you," he said. The wanting in his voice was too much. I ended the call and ran from the room and out of the house. He was in the cabin doorway waiting for me. I threw myself into his arms and he caught me, pressing me against the door and slanting his mouth over mine, groaning as our tongues touched.

The electricity I'd felt earlier was nothing to the heat between us now. I was pulling at him, trying to get closer to him as our tongues frantically worked together.

He pulled away, trailing his lips down my neck, tasting my skin and sucking my neck again, tearing a moan from me. He dragged me into the cabin and shut the door, his palms cupping my breasts and squeezing them as he licked the dip at the base of my throat before trailing his lips along my collarbone.

My hands tangled in his hair, pulling at the strands. "Please, Jack. Don't make me ask you again."

CHAPTER TWENTY

Jack

Don't make me ask you again…

She wanted this, needed it just like I did. All day I'd been dying to touch her, needing her with an intensity that terrified me.

When I'd spotted those men on the porch, the need to protect Kat roared to life with a ferocity that I'd never known. It hadn't left me. The need to mark her, to make her mine. A need I had no right to be feeling.

I ground myself into her, desperate for relief only she could give me. "I told you, anything. I'd do anything you ask, sweetheart."

I pulled back and stared into her eyes, hazy with lust and need, her lips swollen and puffy and my cock jerked, desperate to get to her.

"Then, *please*, Jack…"

I lifted her off her feet, her long legs wrapping around my waist and squeezing tight as I stumbled through the cabin to the bedroom. I dropped her down onto the bed and pulled my shirt over my head, desperate to feel her skin to skin. I never realized how much I'd needed touch before, having gone without it for so long. But I wondered if it was only *her* touch that I craved all this time.

She shuffled to the edge of the bed on her knees and placed wet kisses over my stomach and chest, laving her tongue over it like she was branding me. She cupped my ass and pulled me to her mouth, nipping gently and my hands wove their way through her hair, holding her closer.

One hand left my ass and came around to grip me through the denim and my breath stuttered out as she stroked.

"Hang on a minute, sweetheart, I need to talk to you," I said, groaning as I pulled her mouth off me.

"Are you fucking kidding me right now?" she shouted, and I was startled at her anger. "You're gonna push me away again?"

I gripped her hands and sat down beside her, pulling her onto my lap. "No, I'm gonna tell you why I did last time."

She folded her arms over her chest and pushed her breasts up, momentarily distracting me. "I'm waiting," she sassed when I didn't speak.

I opened my mouth but words wouldn't come out. I huffed and laid back, placing my hands over my eyes and she shifted so she was straddling me. "I've been in prison."

"I'm aware," she said. "And?"

"So, I've not..." I trailed off, pulling my hands away

from my eyes and swirling them over each other in some random gesture that I imagined represented sex, which it didn't. At all.

"It's been a while, I get it. It's okay if it's quick the first time, we can go again," she said, bending down and placing a kiss to my chest, licking her way to my nipple and tugging it between her teeth. My eyes rolled back in my head and my hips shot off the bed, searching for her, loving all these new sensations.

"No, I mean I haven't…"

She stilled, her eyes sliding to mine and she placed her hands on my torso, resting her chin on them. The movement had her falling into a deeper squat and the added pressure to my dick had me taking deep breaths and counting back from ten.

She regarded me quizzically. "You mean you hadn't before you went to prison?"

"No." I said it through gritted teeth as she shifted, rubbing herself over me.

"Oh…" Her eyes widened. "Ohhh…so this will be your first time?"

"Yes. Which is why I stopped the other night. You wanted it a certain way from me, and I wasn't sure I could give you what you needed."

She quirked a brow. "So you decided to not give me *anything*? Rather than explore together?"

My hands clapped over my eyes again. "I'm an idiot." The idea of exploring together was so intriguing and arousing that I realized I was an idiot for not doing it sooner.

Her deep chuckle wafted over me. "I'm not arguing with that." She leaned forward and nipped my chin, kissed her way along my jaw before stopping by my ear. "I'll be gentle," she purred.

I groaned. "Good God, I hope not."

"We'll take it slow. First, you can take my top off," she said, sitting back and pulling me up with her. I gripped the hem of her shirt and tugged it off. Her hair settled around her in blonde waves that just begged to be fisted. I stared at her chest, her red satin bra covering the sexiest tits I'd ever wanted to see.

"Take it off," she said, her voice deepening. I reached around the back, found the strap and fumbled slightly, cursing myself for how clumsy this was, before I whipped off the demon bra. Her breasts bounced free in front of my face and I couldn't stop myself from leaning forward for a taste. I palmed one and sucked the nipple of the other, pulling the bud into my mouth and swirling my tongue around it before tugging gently.

Her fingers dived into my hair again, pulling at the strands as she panted through her pleasure. "Yes, Jack, just like that," she breathed, and it spurred me on. I rolled her other nipple between my thumb and forefinger, plucking and stroking until she was arching into my mouth and rubbing herself against my lap.

"Take my shorts off," she begged.

I unsnapped them and slid them down her legs and she balanced herself as they came off. Then she was back in my lap in just her panties. I spied a wet patch on the red material that matched her bra. My gaze locked onto it and I nearly came in my pants like a teenager just from seeing how aroused she was.

"Is that for me?" I asked, I don't know where the words came from, only that I needed to know. My inexperience demanded to know if I'd gotten her this worked up.

"Yes," she moaned. "Please touch me."

The other night I'd toyed with her, touching myself

while she watched and now, I wanted to watch.

"Show me how you play with yourself," I murmured against her skin.

She didn't hesitate and God that only riled me up more. Her fingers dipped inside her panties and she began stroking herself. I immediately realized my mistake in not removing them because I couldn't see what she was doing, but I could hear it, hear her wetness as she pushed two fingers inside herself and pulled them out of her underwear and ran them along my bottom lip.

My tongue swiped out and eagerly licked up her taste, musky and feminine. She pulled her panties off and then she was naked in front of me. I'd never had a naked woman standing in front of me and I took my time looking my fill of her magnificent body.

I loved the dip of her smooth navel, the wide swell of her hips patterned with stretch marks and her strong legs that had been honed from riding and hard work. Her pussy, wet and ready for me.

She grabbed my hand and placed it over her so I was cupping her heat. She covered her hand with mine and rubbed herself back and forth, her breath hitching each time she hit the right spot. I stared, mesmerized by my hand on her, our hands working her together. Eventually I explored and pressed a finger inside her.

"Holy shit," I stuttered as her heat clenched down around me, trapping me inside. I squeezed another one inside her and she bucked and rode me wantonly. I buried my face in her chest loving the closeness and the feeling of her skin on mine.

Before I knew what was happening, she was gasping and shaking. I pulled back to watch her, her eyes squeezed shut and her mouth open, little gasps slipping from her until she collapsed against me.

"Fuck, you're so sexy," I groaned as her wetness flooded my hand and I couldn't wait for what came next. "I don't know how long I'll last, but like you said, we can go again."

"That's the spirit." She smiled at me lazily and it was a smile that branded itself on my soul. I wanted to see it for the rest of my days.

I lifted her up wrapping her legs around me as I leaned forward, rummaging in the bedside cabinet I'd made for the condoms I purchased a few weeks ago, knowing this moment was inevitable.

She took the packet from me, ripping it open. "Take your pants off."

I maneuvered under her, sliding my pants and boxers off and laid back. My nervousness reared its head again, doubts creeping into my mind. *Would I be enough for her? Would I ruin the moment with my inexperience?* All of that disappeared as her eyes widened when my dick was freed and all I could think was that I needed her, *now.*

"If you keep staring at it like that, I'm going to embarrass myself. Please, Kat," I begged. She snapped out of her daze and leaned forward, wrapping her fingers around my length and I rose up on my elbows as she stroked me, squeezing until a drop formed at the slit tip and she dipped down, her tongue sliding over me and catching it.

My breath caught in my throat at the wet slide of her tongue and I cursed. "Please sweetheart, no more, I can't, the thought of me in your mouth…" I trailed off, unable to form words when she looked at me like that. She took pity on me and rolled the condom down over my length.

I flipped us, pressing her under me, loving the feel of her. Her legs spread slowly and I was cradled by her. I cupped her jaw, rising up on one hand, trailing my thumb over her bottom lip. I reached between us, slightly shaking because this was the moment I had been thinking about for too long.

She helped me, guiding me to where I needed to be and then I pushed slowly. I was an inch inside her when she clenched tightly and stars burst behind my eyelids at the feeling. I thrust again and slipped in further and continued until our hips bumped together. She wound her legs around me and rocked, moaning softly and my arms rested on either side of her face, stroking her hair back so I could see every single emotion that skated across her features.

I thrust again, the tight sensation unlike anything I'd ever felt. Her eyes flew open to meet mine. When I did it again, we both cursed. I dropped my head and kissed her lips and then, like something snapped in me, I fucked her. I thrust and she lifted her hips to meet me, just as desperate. Her hands raked down my back and she cried out with each thrust which drove me insane. It took everything in me to keep it together when I saw how much she was enjoying this, how good I was making it for her.

"Yes Jack, so good, you're so good," she moaned, and I felt that telltale heat forming low in my gut. I was barrelling towards the edge, sooner than I'd hoped but I needed her to fall with me. I reached between us and fumbled before finding her clit and working my fingers against it.

"Come for me, sweetheart, I need to see it again," I murmured against her lips, bending my head down to suck her nipple into my mouth. I was so close and when she gripped my ass cheek and dug her nails in, holding me against her as she clamped down around me, I couldn't hold back any longer.

"Fuck!" I shouted as I climaxed, spilling into the condom as we lay together shuddering. I dipped my head, resting against her chest as I got my breath back. Her hands continued working their magic in my hair, stroking it, tugging it as she moaned before she released it.

After a few minutes she chuckled.

I lifted my head, looking at her flushed cheeks, blissed-out expression and bright eyes. She had never looked more beautiful. "What?" I asked, kissing her chest, her neck.

"Well, you made me come twice, not bad for your first time. Something tells me you'll be a quick study." She patted me on the back.

"I just need the right teacher," I replied, trying not to let my ego inflate over making her orgasm two times.

"There's a lot to show you," she teased. "We'll probably need hours and hours of study."

"I can't think of a better way to pass the time."

CHAPTER TWENTY-ONE

Katarina

I woke up warm, satisfied and kinda horny again.

I tried to roll over in bed but the massive arm draped over me, locked across my chest with one big palm cupping my breast, held me in place. Now I knew why I was already turned on again: his scent, his heat, his perfectly calloused hand rubbing deliciously. I stretched, pushing my ass back into his groin and plunging my chest deeper into his palm. We both moaned, his sounded sleepy, like he wasn't properly awake. I ground against him once, twice until he started pushing back.

"What a way to wake up. Is this why people never get out of bed?" His voice rumbled in my ear, raspy from sleep and making me shiver. His grip on my breast tightened and his thumb started stroking over my hard, begging nipple.

My eyes squeezed shut and I bit my lip to keep from moaning too loudly and inflating his ego any more. But then his other hand snaked over my hip and under the seam of my panties, immediately finding my swollen clit and pressing down on it.

I squeaked and his chuckle vibrated through my chest.

"Not fair," I groaned.

"You think you play fair, sweetheart? Pushing that perfect peachy ass back into my dick and making it as hard as you can?"

His finger continued its magic until it was joined by another and he pinched the two together. "Oh fuck," I shouted, accidentally letting it slip out. He maneuvered quickly, shifting his weight and turning me towards him so we were face to face. He quickened his pace and then dipped down and slid two fingers inside me, pumping them, the wet sound making my cheeks flush.

We didn't speak, our breaths making plenty of noise and saying everything as he continued pumping and dragging his fingers wetly through my flesh. Coaxing me, stretching me with a third one, and finally shattering me. I practically screamed as my body clenched down on him over and over again.

"I love watching you come," he murmured, placing a kiss to the side of my mouth. I didn't say anything, hadn't even opened my eyes yet.

When I finally caught my breath, him still pumping inside me, I opened my eyes and immediately found him staring into them. His blue had deepened to the dark navy of the deep sea, so many thoughts and emotions swam behind them.

"Hi," he whispered.

For some reason, emotion swamped me and my throat closed. "Hi," I replied, my voice shaky.

His brow furrowed. "Hey, what's wrong? Was that too much? I'm sorry I didn't mean to—"

I flung my arms around him, cutting him off. I don't know where the emotion came from. I'd bottled so much up recently that maybe the physical release had started a chain reaction to an emotional one too.

"I'm okay," I said, my voice muffled against his neck. His hand stroked my back, holding me tightly to him.

"It's okay, you can talk to me if something's not okay?"

"No, I'm fine, honestly. I think the intensity just took me by surprise."

"Oh yeah?" I heard the smile in his voice and rolling my eyes, I pushed him off me. He pressed a kiss to my lips, I panicked about my morning breath but he didn't seem to mind.

He didn't seem to mind anything with me.

I kissed him back, my tongue tentatively searching for his, needing the connection, needing him. When his slid against mine, my body sighed. I pressed against him and felt his hardness on my bare stomach, a little damp where he'd clearly enjoyed what he was doing to me.

I pulled away when I realized I could see his features which meant it was daylight.

"Shit!" I threw back the covers and searched for my clothes.

"What?" he asked, sitting up, his tanned skin on display and making my mouth water for a taste. Did he have any idea how sexy he was? How were more women not throwing themselves at him? How was he still a virgin?

Not anymore…

"I need to get back, before the girls are up and wonder where I've been."

There was a pause before he said, "Are you bothered if they know where you've been?"

It was a loaded question and one I wasn't prepared to answer right now. I didn't know how I felt about what was happening other than it felt good, but did it feel *right*? Given our history, everything should be screaming at me to stay away from him and yet I couldn't, or my traitorous body couldn't.

"No, I just…" I trailed off, not really knowing how to answer. I turned to him, seeing him sitting in bed, his dark hair unruly, his gaze penetrating me with an intensity I both loved and wanted to shy away from.

After a moment he waved his hand. "I get it, it's fine. You go on and I'll see you soon."

I wanted to say we should talk about it but I couldn't put words together so I didn't argue, just gave him an awkward wave and hurried out of the cabin. I finger-combed my hair and slapped my cheeks, taking some deep breaths just in case I bumped into one of the girls up early.

I crept in through the front door and hearing complete silence, I carefully slipped my boots off. I paused, and still hearing nothing I released the breath I'd been holding and headed for the stairs.

"Good morning, Katarina," Leo said.

I yelped and turned on the bottom step to find him leaning against the kitchen archway, a cup of coffee in his hand and a smirk on his face.

"Nice morning?" he asked, waggling his brows and taking a sip of coffee.

"Yes, you?" I replied casually.

"So far."

"Great," I said and then turned.

"I just saw the most interesting thing," he began, a teasing note in his voice. I slowly turned, glaring at the little shit. "I saw someone leaving Jack's cabin this morning who looked a lot like you. That's interesting, don't you think?"

I smiled at him, full of teeth. "I don't think that's interesting at all. Some people might wonder what you're doing here so early in the morning in a house you don't live in. Maybe some people should revoke your house guest privileges?"

He laughed. "My lips are sealed, Kat."

I nodded. "I'm glad."

Then his expression turned serious. "Just, be careful. I'm happy for you but you're like my big sister, I don't want you to get hurt."

I scoffed. "I won't get hurt, it was just a bit of fun."

He cocked his head. "For both of you?"

I faltered. *I* knew it was just a bit of fun but did Jack?

Of course he did. He was out of prison and finally free, the world was his oyster. He wasn't attached to me.

"Don't get hurt, but also remember, he doesn't have anyone."

My stomach lurched at Leo's words, hating that he was right. Jack didn't have anyone and what if he did attach himself to me? Did I really want to think about the consequences of that?

"Don't let the door hit your ass on the way out!" I called over my shoulder as I headed upstairs for a shower.

Once I was clean and dressed in my denim overalls, hair held back in a ponytail and a red bandanna tied around my head to keep the stray strands from my eyes, I was ready for the day. Not that I hadn't had the best sleep ever and woken up the best way possible, but now Leo's words had thoughts pinballing around my mind about what had happened with Jack and what the impact of that was.

What if my sisters found out, would they care? Would they be mad or disappointed? How did *I* feel about it? Yeah, it had been amazing, the man was magic with his hands despite his lack of experience. And the thought of helping him build that experience had me fighting off a shiver. But it couldn't turn into anything serious. It was casual. Jack would think it was casual too. We were just two random people who casually had mind-blowing, amazing, toe-curling sex.

When I met Jack on the porch thirty minutes later, my cheeks flushed of their own accord. My eyes trekked over him slowly, taking in the navy muscle tee that hugged his biceps, biceps I'd bitten last night to fight off a scream as he pounded inside me. The material was pulled taut against his chest, a chest I'd licked and nipped. His thick denim clad thighs that I knew held so much power and don't get me started on his round, luscious ass. Even his feet were nice, and I hated feet.

Casual.

Clearing my throat, I asked, "Ready?"

He smirked at me, like he knew my mind had plummeted straight into the gutter. He did his own lazy perusal and it was downright lascivious. "Ready."

"Great," I said, smiling tightly, and set off at a gentle jog towards the stables. He kept pace with me, putting us closer together and I veered off, creating some space between us but he didn't say anything.

When we reached the stables, I spotted Tate Wilder, Reverence's farrier and veterinarian already looking at the horses.

"Hey Tate," I called, waving at him. He came by to run health checks on all the animals and change the horseshoes too when needed. He lifted his head, his black hair falling over his forehead and pushed his glasses up his aquiline nose. He had the most gorgeous high cheekbones, and jawline that I'd ever seen. He'd filled out a lot since high school. Tate used to be the quiet, shy boy in the corner who most people ignored. He lived next door to my best friend Gertie, so I used to see him a lot. He was very studious, sometimes his seriousness was off-putting but I liked him. And he was passionate about animals which was always a plus.

"Good morning, Katarina," he replied. His stiffness meant he always full-named me even though we'd known each other for twenty years.

Jack stepped forward and held out a hand. "I'm Jack, nice to meet you, Tate."

Tate eyed the hand that had been stretched out before replying. "Yes, I know who you are. Nice to meet you too, I guess." Of course Tate knew who Jack was, the whole freaking town did.

Then Jack did something bizarre. He rested his hand on my lower back and stroked his thumb over my spine. My breath hitched at his touch but I pulled away. I didn't want anyone, including Jack, to think there was something more going on here. I felt his eyes on me but I ignored them.

"What are we thinking then, Tate? Who needs what?"

Tate's signature frown appeared. "Marshmallow looks good, I know August takes great care of him. But I think Pickles has an infection in her hoof so I need to look into that."

Tate rattled off a few more things and then I sat and watched him as he took out his instruments and laid them out ready, counting each time he did it before carrying on with what he was doing, which was a little odd. I watched him get to work, the movements aggressive and forceful and I flinched a few times as he dug out the mud and grass from the horses' hooves even though I knew it didn't hurt the horses.

"How do you know there's an infection?" Jack asked. He'd been watching Tate closely, like he was trying to learn as much as possible from him.

Tate frowned again before pointing to the side of the hoof. "See this swelling here?" Jack nodded. Then Tate lowered the hoof to the ground and walked Pickles in a circle. "See her reluctance to put her full weight on it? That tells me there's an infection here."

"Ah yeah I see it," Jack replied, nodding. Then he asked more questions about the horseshoes. It was cute how he wanted to learn it all. I shook my head, turning away from his eager questions and went over to stroke Chester. The gentle giant nudged my hand and I reached into the treat bag and dug out a couple of sugar cubes to give him.

There wasn't a huge amount to do today so we spent the morning with Tate and weirdly, I felt bad pulling Jack away when he was learning so much. So I left them to it and went off to investigate one of the pastures but soon Jack found me.

"You need me to do anything today?" he asked, tucking his hands into his pockets, his forearms flexing as he did.

"Nope, I can handle everything. You can go back and enjoy learning from Tate," I replied.

He reached for me. "You sure?"

"Yep!" I spun away and kept going. I knew I was being off with him but I couldn't help it, I had a lot of feelings I needed to sort through and I needed space to do it. I had too many things on my mind, trying to save the ranch, mainly coming up with a way to fend off Martin in two weeks when I inevitably didn't have any money.

Throughout the day, I grew progressively moodier. I didn't know what to do or where to start. I didn't see Jack again and after dinner, I shut myself in my father's office in an attempt to come up with ideas.

I felt so incompetent at all this, and it brought up all the old feelings of doubt over my abilities, stemming from back when I was at college. I was a failure all over again, only right now it really mattered. Except I wasn't learning, there was no safety net. The training wheels were off and I was flailing to try and keep myself upright, to no avail.

The only thing I could think of was taking out one big loan to try and cover all the little loans and then at least I would owe the bank and not a bunch of random strangers who could turn up at any moment. I decided the next day to try that and was buoyed by finally taking some kind of action.

When I saw Jack the following morning, looking gorgeous in a light blue Henley that matched his eyes and a baseball cap, I had the annoying urge to run into his arms but I didn't. I needed to put some distance between us.

"You'll be working with August and Maddy today," I said when he smiled and said good morning.

His expression faltered. "Sure. Everything okay?"

I nodded sharply. "Yeah, I just have some errands to run."

He looked me over from head to toe. I'd worn my nicest dress and heels and put my hair into a bun, hoping to impress the bank with my appearance at least.

"If you need me, you only have to ask," he said softly.

He always wanted to help, was eager to help, but this was my burden and I needed to fix it to prove that Daddy was right to put the ranch in my hands. That I could cope on my own, that I hadn't wasted thirty years of my life and was still unable to stand on my own two feet and manage the ranch.

I didn't say anything and when August appeared at our side, I left. I could feel Jack's stare on me as I got in the truck but I tried to put him out of my mind as I drove into town.

The bank was in an old church that had been remodeled. Its high ceilings and bare white walls created an echo so everyone spoke in hushed tones. I sat down with my advisor who practically laughed me out of the building. I was not a viable candidate for a loan. I had nothing to offer up as collateral except the ranch which was not an acceptable asset being that it was so in arrears.

I sat in my truck afterwards, trying not to have a panic attack and give in to my spiraling thoughts. The ranch needed me, the girls needed me. I needed to fix this and I needed some time to refocus my thoughts and come up with another solution.

I went home and shut myself in Daddy's office and started going through everything from the beginning, praying I would find an answer somewhere.

CHAPTER TWENTY-TWO

Jack

She was pulling away from me.

I could feel it and it didn't feel good. Ever since our night together I had been craving her company more and more. I wanted to watch how her smart brain worked through challenges, how she came alive with the hard work she put in at the ranch. Even how she was around her sisters and the bond they shared.

And yet she felt further away than ever. Any time I tried to get close to her she pushed me away, brushed me off and dammit she was hurting my feelings. I felt like a lovesick puppy trailing after her but she wanted nothing to do with me.

I'd thought there was something between us but I guess I was wrong. She wanted it strictly business. But

233

sometimes when she looked at me, I could feel *something*. Like I hadn't made it all up in my head. I played our night together over and over in my mind, wondering what I did wrong, but I couldn't figure it out. Maybe I was too attached, maybe she wanted no strings and here I was trying to tie her to me.

There was a knock at the cabin door and my heart pounded in my chest, hoping it was her. I swung the door open and was immediately disappointed.

"Happy to see you too, bud." Leo frowned at me. "Come on, we're going for a drink." He jerked his head towards his truck and then walked off.

"I don't drink," I called after him.

"No shit," he shouted back. "Bars sell root beer too, ya know."

I kinda wanted to stay in tonight and sulk, like a grown ass man, but getting out of the cabin and socializing might be kinda nice. Just the sheer fact that someone in this town wanted to spend time with me was a great feeling and hell, I needed friends.

I grabbed my phone and followed him, running to catch up. "You know I can't drive us home if you get shitfaced?" I said, tugging open the door to Leo's truck.

Leo sighed like he was running out of patience. "Yeah, I know. That's why I'm having a root beer too." He put the truck in gear and reversed out, rolling the windows down and the cool summer breeze drifted in, bringing the smell of the ranch, the sweet soft scent from wildflowers, and birds singing their final song of the day.

We rode in silence and I closed my eyes, tilting my head back against the headrest, enjoying the drive. God, I'd loved driving. I missed it so much and this way I still got to experience it, just not to the fullest.

Leo pulled up at The Lonely Bison and we got out,

heading inside. "I take it you're okay coming here on your night off?" Leo called over his shoulder.

"Yeah, I like it here." It was true, there was such a great feel to it, small town comfort.

Leo went to order the drinks and I grabbed a high-top in the corner, away from the band. I looked around, conscious of being here for the first time as a customer. I took in the people dancing to the band's bluegrass music, heard the excited chatter coming from other tables and laughter from where friends egged each other on at the mechanical bull.

Leo slid the bottle of root beer across the table to me and sat down on his chair. We clinked the necks together and I took a deep swig, the bubbles fizzing my nose.

"Look at us, two young, hot single men out for the night and sitting here all alone with root beers," Leo joked, and I chuckled.

"So what's your deal?" I asked. I liked Leo but I didn't know a lot about him.

He shrugged. "What do you wanna know?"

"Firstly, why you've dragged me out for a drink?"

Leo's bottle stalled halfway to his mouth. "I felt bad for you."

I winced. "Thanks."

Leo grinned. "Nah man, I don't mean like that. I could tell that you were enjoying the free life and then, all of a sudden, the last week or so you've been down. And I thought it might have something to do with our Katarina sneaking out of your cabin the other morning."

Busted. I rubbed the back of my neck. "I just can't figure out what she wants."

Leo snorted. "Can any man figure out what a woman wants? Take Maddy for instance, she keeps going on all these dates but...you know what," he held up his hands, stopping the rant before he truly got started, "this is about you, not me."

"No, no, share with the class."

Leo paused, picking at the label on his bottle. "Well, she's always known she never wanted to settle down and have a husband and kids. I don't know why, she's never really elaborated on that. But all of a sudden she's going on all the dates like she's trying to find Mr. Right and I don't really get why."

I eyed him up, the way he was pouting. "And you don't like that someone else is playing with your favorite toy?"

"Don't talk about her like that." His tone held a hard warning.

"Calm down Buckle Boy, it's an expression. Why are you bothered? Aren't you just friends?"

He shrugged. "Well yeah, best friends, have been for over twenty years."

"So what's your issue?"

He fixed me with a glare. "Starting to regret feeling sorry for you and bringing you out here for some fresh air."

"I ask the hard questions," I joked.

"Then let me ask you one." He took a swig from his bottle. "What's happening with Kat?"

I pushed out a big breath and started picking the label of my bottle. "Fuck knows." Leo laughed, a hearty deep laugh and I started laughing too. "She's pushing me away and I don't know why."

"You really don't know why?" His laughter subsided. "I don't think it would go down well with people in town, given your history."

"I know that. Of course I know that. I just thought...hell I don't know what I thought. It felt

236

different, like things were changing between us and maybe she didn't hate me anymore. Surely she couldn't hate me if we slept together?"

Leo shrugged. "I dunno, hate sex is some of the best kind."

"I guess I'll never know."

"Just, maybe give her time. It's a lot to process and she's had her fair share of shit lately. If it makes a difference, you're the first guy I've seen her with in a real long time, which has to mean something. I'll be back, gotta take a leak."

Leo went off to the restrooms and I played his words over. Kat had come to me, she had wanted me and if she hadn't been with anyone for a while then Leo was right, surely it had to mean something? I felt strangely uplifted by his words, like I had some hope now.

When Leo came back, we played pool and chatted some more. He told me about his career and how Charlie helped him get started in rodeo.

"There's a big competition coming up," Leo said.

"And?" I asked when he didn't elaborate.

"I dunno, man." He ran a hand over his jaw. "It means leaving for a while and I don't know if I could."

I smiled. "Leave Maddy you mean?"

Leo just nodded.

"I can't speak for whatever is going on between you, because clearly there's something," I added when he opened his mouth to deny it. "But you need to think about your future too. She'll be here when you get back."

He just nodded again and then changed the subject.

When he dropped me off at the cabin later, I thanked him for taking me out. "Felt good to talk to someone."

"Same," Leo said. "Does this make us besties now?" I flipped him off and he laughed. "See ya later, bestie," he added and drove off.

Teddy was thrilled to see me. I took him outside and played fetch in the dark, the lights from the cabin illuminating the ground enough so that I could just about see. I'd been neglecting him recently in my pity party so I spent extra time playing with him. When he brought me back a massive stick, I told him I wasn't throwing that and he took himself inside, sulking.

Grabbing a glass of water from the faucet, I contemplated going to bed but my eyes flicked out the window towards the study. I could see Kat inside working away, doing whatever she was doing. God, I wish she'd just let me in to help her but she was stubborn as an ox.

I took a shower and came back out, topping up Teddy's food before bed, knowing he loved a midnight snack. When I stood up and looked out into the night, the office window was dark. I turned away but stopped in my tracks when I felt the telltale prickle on the back of my neck.

Goosebumps raced up my arms as I slowly turned back. I'd been dying to feel those eyes on me all week and now finally they were. I couldn't see any movement, nothing but a dark window but I knew she was there.

I grabbed the phone I'd left on the kitchen counter and pulled up her number and hit call. I couldn't hear anything but I saw the light flash in the window of the office. I could see it flashing before it moved and a moment later her voice came down the line.

"Yes?"

I smiled. "You're watching me sweetheart."

"What makes you so sure?" She didn't deny it.

"Are you gonna pretend you don't watch me in the dark?"

She didn't speak, but I knew she was still there. "Why

do you watch me Katarina? What are you looking at? And yes I know you do, other than the fact that I can see the light from your phone? I can feel your stare on me, your eyes sliding over my skin eagerly. It gets me so hot, knowing you're sitting in the dark watching me, *wanting* me."

Her breath hitched and I could hear as she slowly exhaled. My dick hardened, I'd heard that sound before, when she was laying underneath me as I pounded into her.

"You gonna come down here, sweetheart or just keep looking?"

She sighed, the noise speaking volumes. Reluctantly she replied. "We both know the answer to that."

There was silence as she ended the call and triumph glided through my veins. I stood by the door to the cabin waiting. She made me wait. Made me worry. And finally she walked in, pausing in the doorway and giving me a meaningful look.

"You can stop playing hard to get," I said, running my eyes over her. She was in satin pajamas, little cartoon frogs on them and the slogan, *It's hard work finding a prince.* I smirked at them, so at odds with Kat's stubborn, controlled demeanor.

"I *am* hard to get," she replied, closing the door and strutting over to me.

"No, sweetheart. You're hard to *keep.*"

She stopped when we were chest to chest. I glanced down at the hard glint in her sky-blue eyes. She wasn't willing to give in to me yet, she wanted me to fight for it. To earn it.

I dipped down, our mouths a breath apart and I watched her eyes flutter closed, her chest lift slightly in anticipation.

"You've been avoiding me," I whispered, and her eyes flew open. She opened her mouth to argue but I didn't let her, I covered her lips with mine.

We fought for dominance. She was mad, so was I. I'm not sure what she was mad at and in that moment I didn't care. I just wanted her. Wanted what was *mine*.

Her arms looped around my neck and she went up on tiptoes, pushing back against my mouth and trying to take charge. I cradled the back of her head, fingers twining with her hair so I could change the angle, finding a perfect fit. I pulled back, dropping a few chaste kisses against her mouth that she tried to deepen.

"Don't stop," she whined, and I loved hearing that tone, seeing how I affected her. She tried to put her walls up but I would decimate them. I liked that I could put cracks in her foundation and have her crumbling; because that's how she made me feel too.

"Tell me you want me," I demanded. I didn't know when I'd become so needy and insecure with her but I wanted reassurance. She was the first woman I'd ever truly cared about and the idea that she might not feel the same ruined me.

She met my stare, her eyes clouded with lust, her lips red as rubies and so inviting. "I want you."

It was enough, almost. "Tell me you need me."

Her eyes heated, I think she liked the way I spoke to her.

"I need you," she whined. I loved that whiney, pouty voice she put on.

I walked backwards into the bedroom, pulling her with me and Teddy let out a sharp bark at seeing Kat. She stroked him for a moment before settling him in the living room and closing the bedroom door.

When she faced me again, she was almost shy. Like the

intensity from before had faded and now she didn't know what to do. I stalked towards her, cupped her cheeks, brushing her silky hair back from her face, and kissed her again. She melted into me, just as I hoped she would. I kissed down her jaw and neck, gently nipped the sensitive spot between her neck and shoulder and she melted further.

Her hands slipped under the hem of my shirt and up my back, stroking the muscles and I shivered when her nails raked over my skin.

God, I loved her touch.

I cupped her tits through the flimsy satin pajamas, feeling her nipples pebble instantly and my thumbs played with them, driving her need higher.

"All I've thought about all week is what you would look like riding me," I said against her ear and she trembled, her nails digging into my skin harder. I lifted her off her feet, wrapping my arms around her waist, my lips glued to her neck as I laid her down on the bed. She rubbed herself against me, writhed under me.

I pulled her top off and couldn't stop staring. She was the most stunning woman I'd seen and I'd never get over the sight of her laying there, naked and needy. I pulled her shorts and panties off and then spread her legs wide, baring her to me. The thin trail of dark blonde hair that led me straight to her wet center. She was ready and eager and I was dying for a taste.

Dipping my head, I kissed a trail up her thigh, kneading the flesh before pulling my hands up and cupping her ass. I hovered over her pussy and glanced up at her, her eyes were wide as she watched me, pulling herself into a seated position.

I slid my tongue through her lips, slowly and tapped that little bundle of nerves with my tongue once, then again, harder and her eyelids fluttered shut. I smiled, clearly on the right track and fit my lips around her clit and sucked hard. Her back bowed with her cry, her fingers snagging in my hair as she arched and ground herself against my face desperately.

She took what she wanted, not worrying at all if she was being too aggressive with her moves. I reveled in it, wanted her to let go. This stubborn woman who needed a release. Her head came forward as she made eye contact with me, her fist still tangled in my hair as she rode my face. She flooded my mouth, like just watching me eat her out was all it took to get her off. I slipped two fingers into her, the pressure of the position made it a tight squeeze and it was enough to tip her over the edge.

She cried out, stilling as she clamped down around my fingers and I felt her pulsing against my tongue. In the midst of her orgasm I flipped us, none too gracefully but it got the job done. She was sitting on my face and I had more movement in my hand so I thrust my fingers, tickling that rough spot inside her that made her whimper and ride my face harder.

For a moment I couldn't breathe and it would honestly be a great way to go. Then her orgasm settled down and she quivered on top of me.

"Oh my God," she sighed, tangling a hand in her hair and giving me a lazy, hot as fuck, post orgasm smile. I lay there catching my breath and trying not to come at the same time. I really wasn't sure how long I was going to last once I got inside her.

"That was…" she trailed off, shaking her head. Her eyes found mine and she stared at me for a moment before something switched in her and she started tugging at my shirt and sweatpants.

When I was naked, she wrapped her hand around my

dick and pumped once, twice and it was my turn to say, "Oh my God." She grasped me tight and twisted her grip as she worked up to the head, then with a naughty smile, she dipped down and licked me from base to tip.

I couldn't speak, just watched as she worked me in her mouth, her tongue flat against the thick vein that ran the length of me. She played with my balls and squeezed them, robbing my lungs of air. And just when I thought I couldn't take anymore, she pulled her mouth off me with a wet *pop*.

"Inside me, now," she demanded.

I scrambled to get to my bedside drawer for a condom but she stopped me.

"I'm good, I'm on the pill and you're the first person I've slept with in a long time. I trust you," she said.

"Well you're the only person I've ever slept with so you know I'm good," I replied.

Sexy I know.

She rose up on her knees and shuffled forward, placing her hot flesh above me, rubbing herself over me, leaning forward and crashing our lips together. As she plunged her tongue into my mouth, she sank down on my dick and I didn't just see stars, I saw the whole damn universe.

She was so hot, so wet and the feeling of her tight around me was unlike anything I could have imagined. All the sensations. I could feel every movement. She lifted up and slammed herself down again and I groaned, my head falling back and I gripped her hips, grinding her against me.

I couldn't tear my eyes away from her as she rode me, her head fell back, her hair tickling my thighs and her breasts bouncing as she worked herself over me. I was wrong before, this was the sight that would stay with me until I died, watching this glorious woman lose herself in my body, in what I could give her. I needed her mouth.

Pushing myself up, I wrapped my arms around her, bringing our chests together. Her nipples rubbing against me as I cupped the back of her neck, our mouths colliding. Each time she brought her hips down, I lifted mine up, both of us working in tandem to get to that magical place.

I was so close but I needed her there with me. I worked a hand between us, finding the place where our bodies joined and moving up until I brushed over her clit, then I rubbed and rubbed, feeling her tighten on me. She gasped, her little breaths coming faster and shorter and I knew she was close.

I bit the side of her neck again as my release barreled into me, shooting inside her and my toes curled, cracking from the intensity of my orgasm. She cursed, loudly and then she was flying over the edge too. I lay back, pulling her with me and she collapsed on my chest, both of us panting and sticky from sweat.

"Holy shit," she sighed a moment later.

I laughed. "Holy shit indeed."

We lay there for a while in silence, just reveling in what we'd experienced, before I moved her onto her side and pulled out of her. I went to the bathroom to get a cloth to clean us both. When I came back she was up and putting her pajamas back on and my stomach dropped.

"You're leaving?" I tried to keep the *needy* out of my tone.

She faced me, her cheeks still flushed and her hair looking like she had been rolling in hay, I loved it. "Did you want me to stay?" she asked warily.

I didn't hesitate. "Yes."

She shrugged. "Then I'll stay." She started to get back

into bed but I stopped her.

"This is a naked bedroom, no pajamas allowed."

She arched a brow at me and then shrugged out of her shorts and top. "That's fine, if you think you can keep your hands to yourself."

I prowled across the bed and pulled her into me. "Sweetheart, I have zero intention of keeping my hands to myself."

The woman honest to God giggled and I decided it was a sound I would move heaven and earth to hear again.

CHAPTER TWENTY-THREE

Katarina

"This isn't very professional," I complained.
Jack had me pinned against the empty end stall in the stables, his mouth on my neck. My eyelids fluttered shut as he sucked on the pulse beneath my skin. God I loved it when he did that, my body turned to putty in his hands. For someone with hardly any experience he sure knew what he was doing.

"Feel free to make a complaint to HR," he rumbled, before diving back down to my throat again. My hands began their own dalliance under his damp shirt. He'd been baling hay before I distracted him. I'd been innocently leaning against the wall, silently watching him.

His back muscles flexed in a way that had heat churning in my gut and I *may* have sighed out loud, which drew his attention and well, here we were…

I raked my nails over him, I loved how solid he was. A wall of muscles covered in thick, tan skin that tasted like salt and sex. He huffed out a breath against my neck as I squeezed.

"If you keep doing that, I'm going to have to find something to restrain you with," he groaned.

I giggled. "You wouldn't dare," I teased, an undercurrent of *do it* in my tone and I was so glad he caught it.

"Right, where's that rope I saw earlier?" He glanced around and shackled my wrists.

"No!" I squealed, trying to pull them away and failing miserably. He gave me a look that said I was in for a ravishing and my excitement grew. He tickled me, I shrieked and giggled and we ended up on the floor of the newly cleaned stall, rolling in the hay.

"Kat? You in here?" Daisy's voice rang out and my stomach dropped in fear.

"Shit," I whispered and shoved Jack off me, leaping to my feet and frantically righting my clothing and wiping my mouth. I glanced down at Jack who was looking at me with a strange expression on his face. Emotion swam behind his eyes, a sadness floating in their depths that made me uncomfortable.

He got to his feet, just as Daisy appeared around the stall door. She frowned when she saw me and Jack clearly looking awkward, her mouth tightened in disapproval and that sinking feeling hit my belly once more. Although she'd let him into the house, she was still wary of him, and I knew she wouldn't appreciate it if she caught us in a compromising position.

"Everything okay?" she asked, her piercing eyes flitting between us.

"Sure," I said, a little breathlessly from all my efforts to act casual. I glanced at Jack who was still looking at me with that expression. A muscle ticked in his jaw before he turned away and grabbed the broom.

"Sure," he said over his shoulder, the word clipped, and I cringed at the tension that now radiated from his shoulders. Guilt clawed at me, and I hated that I rebuffed him in front of someone but I didn't know how I felt about him, about us. And I certainly didn't know how to have that conversation with my sisters. I needed him to understand that this was complicated and I needed time to come to terms with it and figure out how to handle it.

"What's up?" I asked, brightly.

Daisy continued staring between us. "Those men from the other day are back, just thought you should know."

"Okay, I'll be right down," I said. This time at least I was prepared for them. I had a plan. It would be enough to pay them off and make them go away so I had some breathing room to plan what to do with all the other people we owed money to.

Daisy nodded and left the stables. There was an uncomfortable tension between me and Jack, the stall suddenly felt too small. I watched him continue sweeping, not facing me and I wanted to put my arms around him, tell him I was sorry for my panic, but I couldn't move or form the words.

I turned to leave when he asked, "Want me to come with you?"

I shook my head. "Nah, I got this." I tucked my hands into my pockets.

"I don't doubt it," he replied and his faith in me gave me the boost I needed to go and deal with these two assholes.

They were on the porch, waiting patiently for me while Daisy glared at them and blocked their entrance to the house. Martin was there in his stupid suit with a smug smile and Muscles in tow.

"Ah, Ms. Cartwright, we meet again," Martin said, like we just bumped into each other.

"That's what happens when you keep coming to my property," I replied, sharply.

Martin's mouth pulled into a thin line of displeasure. "Well, by all means let's make this quick. My money?"

"I'll have it for you tomorrow," I started. Martin opened his mouth to argue but I held up my hand. "There's a cattle market today, I've got a couple of breeding heifers to sell along with some other cattle which should fetch a nice price. I'll give you an extra five percent for your patience," I finished. It made me sad to sell the cows but I had no choice. At least I only needed to sell some of them.

"Twenty percent," Martin retorted.

"Eight percent," I countered. "And I let you walk off my porch with no injuries." I gave them both my meanest grin and Daisy cracked her knuckles.

Martin glanced at Muscles who nodded reluctantly. "See you tomorrow then. But if any money is missing, nothing, including your boyfriend, will keep me from coming into that house and taking what I'm owed." Martin nodded behind me and I turned and saw Jack was standing about twenty feet away, arms folded across his chest, watching us.

"Wouldn't Mommy be so proud," Martin drawled.

Nausea swam in my gut at his spiteful words. Daisy growled and lunged for Martin but I was quick. I managed to wrap my arms around her waist and drag her back before she did any damage. He chuckled and doffed his imaginary hat at us, waving goodbye.

"You shoulda let me teach him some manners," Daisy grumbled.

"Oh, pipe down," I snapped, unhanding her. I glanced back to see Jack was walking off to the stables, satisfied we were okay. I was glad he hadn't come down here and made a scene, but I also wanted him to wrap me in his arms and carry me away.

"I don't know what's happening there, but it needs to stop," Daisy warned, her voice low. I turned back to find she'd been watching me and the look of longing that was probably on my face.

"Nothing's happening," I replied, my voice wavering and even I wasn't convinced.

"It seems like we've got enough problems without that happening. How much money do we owe?"

I bristled, hating the insinuation that I couldn't fix this for us. "None of your business, Daze."

"It is when it affects where I'm living. How many other slimeballs are gonna come out of the woodwork?"

I held up my hand, silencing her. "I'm handling it." She had a look in her eye like she was planning something and it made me nervous. "Daisy, I've got it under control," I added, firmly.

That night I lay in bed tossing and turning, thinking about Jack and the look Daisy gave us and the way I felt. I wanted to sort through my feelings, but they were so unclear that I didn't know where to start.

I sighed and threw the comforter off me, feeling smothered. I grabbed my phone and opened my chat with Jack. The last thing he sent me was a kissy face emoji and that brought a smile to my face. Then I saw he was online too.

I tapped out a message.

Kat: Can't sleep either?

Jack: Nope, too busy thinking about how I didn't get to taste you earlier.

I smiled so hard and squirmed in my bed.

Kat: Don't say things like that when we're not in the same bed.

Jack: I didn't say anything.

I sent him the eyeroll emoji.

Kat: Fine, don't type that.

A moment later it said he was recording a message. I received the ten second clip and pressed play. It played through once but I didn't hear anything. I turned my volume up and then pressed play again, pulling the device to my ear. His heavy breathing filled the room and I scrambled to turn the volume down right as he moaned my name.

"Oh shit," I groaned, more turned on than ever at what he was doing. I'd slept with a few men over time and none of them ever moaned. Some of them tried, and failed miserably, at dirty talk. But no one had ever made the sounds that Jack did. The heavy breathing, the tortured, pleasurable moans, they did something to me. Something dark and needy.

Kat: Are you doing something you shouldn't be?

Jack: You wanna come down here and find out?

I leapt off the bed and padded over to my door, pulling it open a crack and listening in the dark for any noises. When I heard nothing, I stepped out, tiptoeing down the stairs and snuck out the front door. I ran across the damp grass in my bare feet, the blades tickling and leaving wet kisses on my skin.

He wasn't waiting for me like I expected. I pushed the door and it creaked open. I slipped inside and closed it, leaving damp footprints on the wooden floor, I skipped to his bedroom and knocked.

"Come in," he called, his voice thick and I smiled to myself at the delights that awaited me on the other side.

I crept inside and closed the door behind me. The room was pitch black, I couldn't see in front of me, not even the faint outline of furniture.

Then he was pressed against me, shoving me back into the door and attacking my mouth. There was an urgency to his kisses, an anxiousness that I returned. I didn't know where it came from, only that I needed him now. I hadn't ever needed someone, let alone a man, like this before.

My shorts were down and my leg thrown over his shoulder and before I could even beg, his tongue was sliding over me, pressing down and I slumped back against the door, his arm slung over my hips, pinning me in place.

He made me come quickly; fast flicks of his tongues followed by slow, hard presses that had fireworks exploding behind my eyes. I screamed as my body detonated under his touch, my orgasm fast and intense and then I was lifted from the floor.

"I'm sorry sweetheart but this is gonna be hard and fast, I *need* you," he grunted as he put me on the bed. I heard him pulling at his clothes, then my legs were spread as wide as they could go and he was shoving himself inside me in swift, brutal, punishing thrusts that made my eyes roll back in my head. I fisted the sheets, moaning and thrashing my head as each powerful pulse of his hips hit a new part of me that I hadn't discovered.

"Oh my God, yesss," I moaned. His arms went under my ass, tilting my hips and I babbled like a mad woman as he panted over me.

"Goddamn it's so good," he huffed, amazement in his

voice and I would have smiled if I wasn't busy moaning over what this man was doing to me. "I'll never get enough," he added.

My body began readying for another peak that I thought was impossible. I felt it rolling through me like a wave, slowly building in intensity. He kissed my neck, laved his tongue over my skin and I tangled my fingers in his hair, holding him to me. He worked his way up to my ear and his hot breaths over my sensitive lobe had shivers wracking me.

"Scream for me, sweetheart," he whispered. And like he cast a spell on me, my body tightened and that wave crashed into the shore. I screamed, the sound muffled at the end as he clamped a hand over my mouth. I bit down on his fingers as my body continued pulsing and I heard his curse as he shuddered on top of me and filled me up.

After a while I tapped his hand and he removed it from my mouth and rolled to his side, pulling me with him. I tucked my head into the crook of his neck and he stroked my spine.

"I panicked. Although I wanted you to scream for me, I didn't want all your sisters and Leo barging in to see what the noise was," he chuckled.

I giggled sleepily. "No one's ever made me scream like that before." I nipped at his pec.

He groaned and tightened his grip around me. "You say the sweetest things." We lay in silence, both of us drifting into sleep. When I awoke later with a start it was because he was crying out.

"No, don't touch me!" he shouted, writhing in the bed, the sheets tangled around him.

"Jack?" I asked, confused and sleepy.

"I'm sorry!" he shouted.

"Jack? Are you okay?" I shook him but he didn't

respond. I got up and padded over to the light and flicked it on and he lay in bed, asleep but sweat poured from him and his brow was pinched, his lip wobbling.

"Charlie, don't leave me here alone. Please come back!" he wailed, and my heart beat faster, my eyes filling with tears at the pain in his voice.

I settled next to him and stroked his damp brow, shushing gently.

"I didn't mean to hurt her, I'm sorry Charlie!" he called out again and tears sprang to my eyes. He was stuck in a nightmare. We'd never spoken about the history between us other than some mentions of Daddy visiting him in prison but we never talked about my mother. She hung between us like a ghost that we both ignored.

Now she was front and center, demanding attention.

"It's okay," I soothed but I didn't know which of us I was soothing. Eventually he settled and the little whimpers that fell from his lips tore me in two.

There was a scratching at the door followed by a low whine from Teddy and I got up and let him into the room. He bounded straight over to Jack and rested his head on the edge of the mattress, just staring at Jack, and the sight almost broke my heart.

Jack never gave any signs that what happened still affected him, or if he did, he hid it well. But it was in his dreams that this strong, gentle and unbreakable man was tortured by his actions and memories.

He slowly began to settle, and I laid myself over his damp body, needing connection and some comfort for all the emotions this brought up for me too. Would this be our future? Our ghosts lingering between us, jumping out and scaring us when we thought everything would be fine?

Did we even have a future?

My mind kept me awake all night, locked on conflicting thoughts of me, Jack, and our lives. When the sun rose in the morning, I kissed his forehead and leaving him in Teddy's capable paws, I snuck back home. It was the weekend so I knew I wouldn't be seeing him in an hour to work on the ranch. I got back into my own bed and tried to sleep. I dozed for a little while but awoke when my phone beeped.

Jack: Where'd you go?

I smiled sadly.

Kat: You snored.

Jack: Then I'll buy you the prettiest ear plugs you've ever seen.

Jack: I'll make 'em pink, to match your cowgirl boots and Stetson.

I snorted at his silliness. But the idea of him doing something as small as buying ear plugs for me made me wonder if he saw this as more than it was.

"He's just joking," I muttered to myself before burrowing further under the duvet, trying to hide from all the thoughts running round my brain.

CHAPTER TWENTY-FOUR

Jack

One moment everything was fine.

Then the next I had that horrible sinking feeling that you got when you went to school and all your friends didn't like you for some stupid reason.

The anxiety churned in my gut and it made me desperate for her. I tried to tell myself to take it easy, let her come to me but I worried that if I did that, she'd never come to me again.

I knew Kat liked me, I could see it in the way she looked at me, the way she was when we were intimate. I didn't have anything to compare us to, but it was pretty darn amazing and I didn't *want* to be able to compare us to anyone else.

There were a ton of issues between us and maybe it

was naïve of me but I felt like we could make it work.

The day I woke up after she'd left in the night, I wasn't meant to be helping out at the ranch but I knew those two dipshit charlatans would be back for their money so I watched and waited. I knew she could handle herself, hell she handled *everything* herself, didn't need help from anyone. But I wanted to be there for her, to protect her in any way she would let me.

I worked outside, making a new bookshelf for the cabin. I wanted to place one on either side of the crumbling hearth that I desperately needed to fix, preferably by winter. But carpentry was still new to me, let alone brickwork.

I lost myself in stripping and sanding the reclaimed wood, measuring the planks, slotting them together, and hammering the nails in. I felt at peace when I created something with my hands. I was able to pour my focus into it and all my thoughts and doubts disappeared.

When I heard a vehicle pull up to the house, I put my tools down and came up to the side of the porch, watching as Martin, with his creepy bodyguard, spoke to Kat. She oozed confidence and power, she was the boss here and she was *letting* them have their money. I was so proud of her for not taking any shit and settling what she needed to.

She handed over the stacks of cash she'd pulled together, I guess she hadn't needed my help at the cattle market yesterday either. Martin leaned in to say something to her but he was already too close for comfort, let alone when he got in her personal space. My instincts roared to life and I cleared my throat, making my presence known.

Kat's stare flicked to me, her brow dipped and she shook her head sharply. I nodded back in understanding.

She had this.

Finally Martin and his bozo left. "All paid off?" I asked.

Kat turned to me, tugging on her blonde hair that hung in two long braids. "Yep."

She moved like she was going to go inside the house.

"You avoiding me?" The words shot from me before I could stop them.

She slowly turned on her heel. "Yep."

I smiled despite myself. "Why?"

She glanced inside the house then came over to me. "Because, I don't know what my thoughts are right now."

I tugged the end of her braid. "Why do you need to have thoughts?" She cocked her head at me, frowning and I back tracked. "I didn't mean it quite like that. What I mean is, have all the thoughts you want but maybe you're putting too much pressure on those thoughts."

She puckered her lips like she was lost in thought. "So you want easy breezy thoughts?"

I smiled at her words. "Yeah?"

She laughed lightly, then her expression sobered. She put a hand on my chest, "I just don't know if I can do that."

The door to the porch opened and Kat leapt back, her hand dropping from my chest. I tried not to feel hurt at the way she reacted to us getting caught by one of her sisters.

Maddy appeared and looked back and forth between us and I smiled at her, waving.

"Hey Jack," she waved back. She told Kat that Tilly was staying with a friend tonight and then went back inside the house.

Kat gestured towards the door. "I should go."

"Okay, yeah I've got a shift at the bar in a little bit.

Maybe see you later?"

She smirked at me. "Maybe."

Heat filled my chest and I suddenly felt like things would be okay.

I put my tools away, dragged the planks of wood back inside the cabin in case it rained that night. I took Teddy for a long walk and he brought back three different sticks which I did not allow him to bring inside the cabin. Then I showered and left for The Lonely Bison.

My shift went by fast. I was eager to finish and get back to the cabin and maybe Kat. There was less hostility from some patrons than there usually was so that was a plus. They must be getting used to me. More women tried to give me their numbers but I wasn't interested. Not a single one of them held a candle to Kat.

"Hey, you mentioned before that you like carpentry?" Max asked as we closed up.

"Yeah, still pretty new to it but I love it," I replied.

"Are you taking commissions?"

His question took me by surprise. "Uh, not yet but I could, if it's something pretty simple? I'm still learning."

"The stage at the bar has a couple of damaged panels that need replacing and I've got no clue what I'm doing. It's not much but obviously I'll pay you for it."

I nearly refused the money but honestly I needed it. Yeah the bar shifts and tips were helping but wood was pricey and my hobby was getting expensive. If I wanted this to be a viable business I needed to keep practicing, which meant more wood and more tools.

"Yeah, okay, that sounds doable. Let's catch up on what wood you're thinking, and I can cost it out for you."

Max nodded. "Great, I'll let you know. See you tomorrow."

I practically ran back to the cabin, excited to plan this

project even though it was tiny and didn't need real planning as such. I was just *excited* about having a prospect.

The main house was dark and quiet. I figured I wouldn't be seeing Kat tonight after all and I tried not to let my disappointment smother me.

I entered the cabin and normally Teddy would greet me but he didn't show.

"Teddy Bear?" I called out, glancing around the living room and little kitchenette. I heard a low woof come from the bedroom so I pushed the door open and flicked on the light and there was my dog, snuggled up with my woman.

Kat sat in the middle of the bed, her long legs crossed, that Stetson on her head, her pink cowgirl boots on her feet and not wearing anything else. I couldn't speak, practically choked on my tongue at the amazing sight of her.

"Well? Can you get over here? I'm freezing," she shivered.

"I just need a minute, sweetheart," I said, my tongue heavy and clumsy in my mouth. My cock pulsed, growing harder the longer I stared at her, committing the sight to memory.

"Minute's up," she huffed, pulling the covers back and maneuvering to get under them.

"Not so fast," I said. "Come on Ted, time for you to go, the adults are going to play."

He left reluctantly and I couldn't blame him, I hated it when I wasn't around her either. "You still cold sweetheart?" I asked, pulling my t-shirt off and shrugging out of my jeans.

She eyed me, her stare running over my body, lingering here and there and she ran her tongue over her lip like she could taste me. "I'm warming up now."

I made a noise in the back of my throat, something between a groan and a growl and I advanced on her.

I was going to make her so happy she waited for me.

*

"Psst, August!" I hissed, peeking at her around the door of the stables. Her strawberry blonde hair whipped over her shoulder as she stood up, pushing her glasses further up her nose as she looked around.

I waved, as discreetly as possible, trying not to draw Kat and Tate's attention. Tate was back for another vet visit with the horses and cattle so that meant Kat was distracted.

August smiled softly when she saw me and scurried over.

"Morning Jack, what's up?" she asked sweetly.

"Good morning. I need a favor," I replied, gesturing for her to follow me. August was the one I knew would help me. As far as I was aware, none of the sisters knew that me and Kat had a thing going on, just some suspicions on Daisy's part. For the last month we'd been so careful in our sneaking around to make sure we weren't spotted by anyone. It still hurt like a sonofabitch to keep hiding what we were doing. I understood why, but I wanted to scream it from the rooftops that Kat was mine.

I remembered the time I bumped into August at the library all those months ago and the books she was carrying. She was a romantic at heart and she would be the best person to help me.

"Have you got a picnic basket?"

Her mouth quirked up on one side. "Why do you need

one of those?"

I shrugged. "For a picnic."

She nodded slowly, staring at me with her amber eyes, the sun making them shine brightly with curiosity.

I rolled my eyes. "For a picnic date."

She glanced over her shoulder back towards the stables. "For anyone in particular?"

I squirmed on the spot. I didn't want to tell, I wanted to respect Kat's wishes of keeping our affair quiet but it would help to have at least one sister on side. "Maybe. It's a surprise picnic date though so don't tell her."

August squealed and clapped her hands together. "I know just what we need, come with me!" She grabbed my hand and dragged me back towards the main house. August pulled me into the kitchen and dug around in various cupboards, rummaged in the sideboard for a few bits, and presented me with a wicker picnic basket, checkered blanket and napkins, and a matching set of dishes and utensils.

"This was my mother's," August said, presenting them to me. I hesitated and August smiled softly. "I think she'd be very happy for you to take them and put them to use. Mom was a big romantic, and she and Daddy always used to have picnics. It's okay Jack, take them."

I reluctantly took them, the weight of them light in my hand but heavy in my heart.

"Thank you, August, I appreciate this."

"No sweat," August winked. "Make sure you pack some apricots."

I wrinkled my nose. "Apricots?"

"They were Mom's favorite, and Kat's."

"Ah, great, thanks for the intel."

"Have a great date, can't wait to hear all about it!" she said, then she was gone and I was left in the kitchen on my own.

I glanced at the pictures on the sideboard, the ones of Charlie and Sherry, Sherry and the girls. Seeing the pictures of Sherry and how similar she looked to all the girls now was uncanny. They were like carbon copies, just with different shades of hair. My heart lurched as usual at the thought of Sherry and the life cut short by my reckless actions. But I felt like I was slowly making it up to her and Charlie here, working off my debt and looking out for the girls any way I could.

I laughed at the picture of Charlie and Sherry, she was slung over his shoulder, her mouth open in laughter and he had a mischievous twinkle in his eye. My eyes filled with tears as I stared, sad they weren't here but at least now they were together.

I heard a noise and then Leo came into the kitchen.

"Howdy partner."

"Hey man, how's it going?" I asked, putting the picture back, trying and failing to hide the basket behind me.

"Good. You've not seen Mads, have you?" he asked, looking around distractedly.

"Isn't she on shift?"

"I thought so but she's not at the station."

"Out on a call?" I offered.

"Yeah…maybe. Anyway, when's our next date night?"

I chuckled. "Whenever you like, honey bun."

"Cool, I'll check my schedule and drop you a note. Gotta get to training, I'll catch ya later," he said, and then he was gone, and I was saved a round of questioning over the basket.

I headed back to the cabin and hid the basket just in case Kat came over later. I was planning on taking her for a ride tomorrow to one of the more secluded pastures so we could have some alone time. It was great getting to spend all day with her and nights too, but we didn't get to go out and do anything like other couples did and I was craving some normalcy.

I went back to work, fixing and rehanging one of the stable doors. I had more confidence in my abilities now. I could fix pretty much anything, that included the stage at the bar that Max had requested. He'd paid me well for it and that led to buying more tools. I was trying more ambitious projects now and working with reclaimed wood from some of the older, dilapidated structures in town. I'd been sneakily working on restoring the Adirondack chairs for Kat. I'd seen how much she sat in the one on the porch and it looked seconds from crumbling to pieces. I figured she'd be devastated if anything happened to them.

The day's work ended and I headed back to the cabin to shower, shoved some food in my face, and gave Teddy some love before heading out to the bar for my shift. The evening was half gone when I heard a familiar laugh and looked up, my stare racing over the crowd for her.

There she was.

My chest did this weird fluttery thing as I watched her laughing with August over something. Her head thrown back, blonde hair flowing around her. I watched her talk, the way she moved her hands, how animated her face was when she was excited and felt a grin settle on my lips.

"Hey, Jack!" Someone clicked their fingers in front of my face. I blinked and turned towards the owner of the fingers and saw Daisy glaring at me. "She ain't for you, better get that through your head, now."

I bit my tongue to stop the retort that would reveal that she *was* for me, was currently *with* me.

It hurt that Daisy was the only sister who hadn't

softened towards me, except every now and then it was like she wanted to but held herself back.

I pasted a smile on my face. "What can I get you?"

"Three lemon drops." She continued staring at me, God, was I sweating? This woman was slightly terrifying. I racked up the glasses and poured the shots.

"How much?" she asked.

"On the house."

Her eyes narrowed at me. "What's the catch?"

I shrugged. "No catch."

She continued staring at me but picked up the shots and as she walked away, I called after her, "I will make you like me."

She scoffed and shook her head before stomping off, but she didn't say anything back, so I counted that as a win. The crowd grew heavy and I lost sight of Kat for a while until my phone buzzed in my back pocket.

Kat: There's a real sexy man in the bar tonight.

Jealousy snapped through me before I realized what she was doing.

Jack: Oh yeah? Where?

Kat: Behind the bar. Every time he turns around, I catch a glimpse of his perfect ass.

I snorted and I think I even blushed, I hadn't had a compliment in a long time. I glanced up looking for her, and like the crowd knew what I wanted, it parted and there she was. All alone.

Jack: Perfect huh?

I watched as she read my reply, she looked up and met my eye and nodded nice and slow. I couldn't fight my smile.

Jack: How perfect?

I watched as she typed and then raised an eyebrow at me. I grabbed my glass of water and took a sip as I read her response.

Kat: Perfect enough that I want to bite it, right now.

Kat: Quickie?

I choked on my water, droplets spraying and wiped a hand over my mouth.

Kat: That was sexy.

I smiled and shook my head at this devil woman.

Jack: Max's office?

Kat: See you in five…

Max was busy chatting it up with the band in between their set so I served another customer and snuck off to the office. I barely had the door shut before she was on me.

Her tongue plundered my mouth, leaving the tart taste of lemons behind and I was desperate for more.

She reached down and grabbed two handfuls of my *perfect* ass and squeezed, pulling me against her. I moaned into her mouth and tilted her head, needing deeper access. I kneaded her fantastic breasts and she moaned right back.

A noise outside had us pulling apart, our breaths panting, pulses pounding and bodies aching for each other. I put my finger to her damp, swollen mouth. "Be naked in my bed when I get home," I growled.

She nipped my finger before snaking her tongue out and swirling it around the digit. My eyes were so transfixed on what she was doing that I didn't realize she was unzipping my pants and her hand was wrapping around my hard dick until it was too late. She squeezed and my breath evacuated my lungs.

"Katarina…" I warned but she gave me a sassy look and slowly slid to her knees.

"I've watched you behind the bar all night, getting hit on by other women and I just want to remind you that you belong to me," she purred, pulling my cock out and swiping her tongue over the thick head. I didn't move as I watched her lapping at me, her tongue swirling, her lips puckered around me as she swallowed me down. My head tilted back, hitting the door with a thunk as she worked me. She squeezed my balls gently and my eyes flew open, needing to watch her.

She hummed and the vibrations had my control snapping. My hands tangled in her hair and then I started thrusting, fucking her mouth as hard as I could. She gagged a little and I eased off but not much, she drove me wild and I couldn't control myself. She looked so damn good on her knees, looking up at me with wide eyes as she swallowed down everything I gave her.

When my orgasm high faded, I looked down and found her placing gentle kisses to my thighs before tucking me back into my pants. I pulled her to her feet, kissing her mouth gently and smoothing down the hair I had fisted.

"You're amazing."

She lifted one shoulder casually. "I know."

I barked out a laugh. "I mean it. When I get home, you, naked, bed."

She kissed me one more time. "Can't wait."

And then she slipped out of the office and I had a moment to collect myself. My heart was still pounding erratically but I sensed it had more to do with the feelings she stirred in me than anything else.

Although I hadn't had the opportunity to meet a lot of women, I didn't want to. Not even one of them held a candle to Kat. None of them enthralled me the way she did and never would. It would always be her. I could spend an eternity with her and it would never be enough. And when the time came to say goodbye, I'd fight and scream at the unfairness of it all that I only had a lifetime and not forever.

CHAPTER TWENTY-FIVE

Katarina

Jack woke me up.

Not for sexy time but again with nightmares. I figured he didn't know he had them but it was the fourth time now I'd witnessed them and they were unbearable to see. I tried to soothe him and some nights it worked, some nights he just had to pull himself out of them. But I saw how torn up inside he was about what happened.

Obviously, I didn't think he was inhuman and that the accident hadn't affected him. But now his guilt was right in front of my face all the time, it was clear he hadn't forgiven himself or moved on. Maybe he couldn't, being here at the ranch.

I soothed him until he settled but I was awake by then. Something had been plaguing me, not about saving the ranch, I felt like I'd bought some time now that Martin and his goon were paid off. No one else had come sniffing around yet, but I knew it would only be a matter of time and still, I couldn't figure out what to do and instead buried my head in the sand.

But nope, I'd been stressing because Tilly's sixteenth birthday was creeping closer and I still hadn't found a decent pair of cowgirl boots. I wanted to carry on my father's tradition with her. It was hard enough that he wasn't here to get them for her, and she would be the only sister who hadn't had hers bought by him, so I needed to find a good pair. The best pair, the *right* pair. But so far, they eluded me.

I scoured the internet until the sun came up and Jack stirred next to me. He wrapped an arm around me, pulling himself closer and placing kisses down my arm.

"Morning, sweetheart," he said, his voice rough from sleep and my body woke up, ready for round four. I didn't know when I'd become so desperate for him, only that I could have him all day, every day and it wouldn't be enough. "What ya looking at? Stuff for the ranch?"

I shook my head. "No. When each of us turned sixteen, Daddy bought us a pair of cowgirl boots. Only he died before he could get any for Tilly. Her birthday is coming up and I want to get her some, but I can't find the right pair."

"Want me to look for you?"

I prickled. "No, I can manage on my own."

"I didn't say you couldn't, I just wanted to offer my help in searching."

I sighed. "Sorry, I just feel like I should be the one to do it."

He was silent for a moment but continued stroking my arm. "You put a lot on your shoulders," he said after a while.

"Do I?"

"Why don't you let me help? With the ranch? With this? Or let your sisters if you don't want my help."

I dropped my phone in my lap. "Why are you pushing this?"

He sat up, rubbing sleep from his eyes which made his pec flex in a mouthwatering way. "I just hate seeing how much falls to you, just because you're the oldest. The girls are all old enough to share some of the burden. I could talk to them for you and—"

I tore my gaze away from his bare chest. "But I don't want to burden them. They can go about their lives and not worry. That's what I would prefer, that's what Daddy would prefer."

"I don't think Charlie would want you so stressed and worried," he replied, carefully.

I scoffed. "How would you know?"

The silence between us was heavy and I was annoyed. Annoyed that I'd snapped, that he'd pushed it and tried to get involved. That he acted like he knew my father better than I did. Hell, maybe he did.

His expression softened. "I don't want to fight with you. I just wanted to help."

"I appreciate that but please don't. We're not a couple, you don't need to help me."

He opened his mouth to argue but my face must have stopped him. I got out of bed. "I'm just cranky, I didn't sleep well," I said.

"I'm sorry. Why don't you go and get some sleep and then I'll catch up with you later? There's something I want to show you," he said. The excitement in his voice had me nodding. I grabbed my clothes and dressed in silence. An awkwardness hung between us and I didn't know how to make it go away. I couldn't look at him, didn't want to see the hurt in his eyes.

"I'll see you later," I said and headed for the door. He grabbed my arm and pulled me back to him, his navy eyes heavy-lidded. He pressed a kiss to my lips, soft and heartbreakingly gentle. "See you later, sweetheart."

My heart did the weird pitter-patter it had been doing recently when I was around him. I kissed him back and then left before I took off my clothes and let him worship me again.

The morning sun was low and already scorching. Summer was coming to an end and it had been glorious spending my days in the pasture and my nights in Jack's arms. Even though I had the problem of the ranch hanging over me, I'd felt better than I had in…forever.

I rounded the house, ready to climb the porch but bumped into someone.

"Where are you sneaking back from?" Daisy accused, looking behind me.

"Nowhere," I folded my arms over my chest. "Where are *you* sneaking back from?"

She copied my stance. "Nowhere."

We stared each other down, no end to our stubbornness. Something about Daisy seemed off, there was a tension to her that she usually didn't have and a sharp glint in her eye that told me to back off.

"If you're coming back from Jack's, I'm going to have a lot to say about it."

My throat dried. "Like what?"

"Like, you shouldn't be fucking our mother's killer."

My mouth floundered as I struggled for words. "I thought you were warming to him?"

She shrugged. "I might have been but that doesn't change what he did. And for you to pursue this and think you'll have some kind of relationship is crazy. Mom would be ashamed."

I gasped at her words, unable to believe what she said. She barged past me and up the stairs, stomping with fury. Daisy had always had a sharp tongue but today her words were cruel, which wasn't like her.

I went inside after her but instead of speaking, I just went straight to my room. It was too late to try and go back to bed, I was all riled up and needed to expend my energy. I headed out to the stables and saddled Chester.

We sailed across the pasture, into the forest and I pushed him hard. I could tell he enjoyed it, he seemed to relish the challenge of leaping over fallen trees and turning around sharp bends. His nostrils flared as he breathed hard and even let out an excited whinny.

I rode away from my problems, away from the ranch that I didn't know how to help and couldn't even fathom why I wasn't thinking about it. I rode away from the question of me and Jack, unsure how to answer it. I didn't want to end what we were doing but Daisy's words were bugging me.

I rode until my thoughts were obliterated and all I could see was nature as it passed by me and Chester in a blur. Eventually Chester began to slow, worn out, so I pulled him over near the lake and tethered him by the water. He had a drink and a poke around in the dirt with his hoof while I watched the still water.

I contemplated life and the situation with the ranch and why I had such a damn block against what to do to fix it.

"Daddy wouldn't have ignored it. He would have fixed it," I said to Chester who snuffled close to me. He looked at me and I'm sure he raised one eyebrow.

"Okay, okay, maybe you're right, he did get us into this mess in the first place. And now I've got to pick up the pieces, but I don't have enough cattle left to sell and...I don't want to."

Chester flicked his tail and I buried my head in my hands. "Am I really talking to the horse?" I groaned. I heard rustling from behind me.

"Well, sometimes it's good to talk to someone who won't talk back."

I spun around and there was Jack, sauntering towards me, leading Pickles by her reins. My heart did that silly pitter-patter thing and I breathed a sigh of relief at seeing him.

"How did you know I was here?"

He tethered Pickles next to Chester and came and sat behind me. He put his legs on either side of mine and I sank back into the cradle of his body. "Saw you take off," he murmured, his lips against my temple.

"Shit, you wanted to show me something, didn't you?"

He chuckled. "I did. But this is good too. I just wanted time with you, away from everyone else."

We sat in silence. He stroked my arms and continued resting his stubbled jaw against my temple. We watched the water, the still silent lake with birds tweeting all around, and a serenity enveloped me.

"Wanna tell me what you're riding away from?" he whispered, like he didn't want to break the peace and quiet, and I appreciated it.

I paused. I didn't want him to think I couldn't handle it on my own. I hated admitting I needed help and wasn't strong enough to look after the ranch despite all the years of practice I had doing it.

He squeezed my arms, kneading my biceps. "Hey, you

can trust me. I care about you and want to help, any way I can."

I turned my face and buried it in his neck. "I hate admitting this, but I don't have the slightest clue what to do."

"About?"

"The ranch. There's so much debt and yeah, I paid off some but I don't know what to do with the rest. It's an eye-watering amount of money. My brain won't give me any ideas and I feel useless because I've spent years looking after this place with Daddy, and now I don't have the slightest idea what the hell to do and there's no one to guide me and I don't have the confidence to do it alone and I'm a complete failure." I sighed deeply once the words were out, like my body purged them.

He placed a soft kiss to my temple that felt too damn good, too damn *right*. "Thank you for sharing that with me. Firstly, you're amazing."

I snorted and tried to push him away but he shackled me to him. "You are," he reiterated. "You might have experience with the ranch, which I see every day by the way, but that doesn't mean you should know how to do *everything*. Doesn't mean you should know how to run the business side of things."

"I know but—"

"I wasn't finished, sweetheart," he admonished and damn if my lady parts didn't enjoy the stern tone of his voice.

"Sorry. Please continue," I said, smirking and squirming back into his neck.

"You're the best rancher I've seen. The way you know what's happening all the time, you know the schedules and you spot problems and solve them before they become a real issue. You can spot when an asshole bison is causing mischief. You've got a great relationship with the animals, the girls, Tate and well, me. I really look up to you when we're out there in the pastures. You're amazing, but you can't do it all."

I bristled at his words and as if he knew I would, he stroked my arms again and softened his voice. "Why don't you tell your sisters, let them in and let them help you? Let me help you?"

I shook my head. "They've been through so much recently and I don't want to worry them with this. I didn't get a choice about coming back here and looking after them and the ranch and Daddy, but they have choices. They have lives to live and I won't tether them here out of obligation or guilt."

He was quiet for a moment. "What would you do if you weren't here?"

I shrugged, I hated talking about what could have been. "I don't know, business or something. But I wasn't even doing that well at that. Which is why I feel ridiculous and embarrassed that I can't fix the ranch. It's like I've got a block."

"A block?"

"Yes, a damn stupid block and I need to unblock it before we lose the whole damn place!"

I felt his muscles tighten like he was tense. He took a breath, started speaking then paused. "Do you think you have a block because you weren't planning on doing this without Charlie?"

It was like he flicked a switch.

Everything fell into place: why I couldn't focus on the ranch and think about what to do. Because I didn't want to. I hadn't planned on doing this on my own. Me and Daddy had always talked about me taking over while he was still around to coach me through it. We'd had it all figured out. I would spend years learning from him until he was too tired to teach me. I'd looked forward to the day he could be proud of me but that day would never come.

Tears sprang to my eyes and I buried my face in my hands as I sobbed. "He left me. He left me to do it all on my own and I'm not ready," I cried. Jack put his arms around me and rocked us back and forth, shushing me gently and apologizing.

"I'm sorry sweetheart, I didn't mean to make you cry."

"But you're right. I didn't even realize that was why, but it is! He died and abandoned me, and I didn't have a chance to do this with him."

I cried a little longer, like the floodgates had opened and nothing was shutting them, and when I finally quieted something else occurred to me. "How did you know that's what it was?" I asked softly.

I felt Jack shrug behind me. "Because that's how I feel too."

I pulled away and looked at him, his blue eyes swimming with unshed tears, sorrow emanating from him. "What do you mean?"

Jack brushed my hair behind my ears, smiling sadly. "He always talked about what we were going to do when I was free. How we were going to do this and do that. He's the one who got me focusing on my future. Who nurtured the idea of exploring carpentry and promised me a future here at the ranch together. He got me dreaming again." He looked away at the river, pausing and trying to harness his emotions. "But I just didn't envision having to do this without him and I felt so damn lost."

"You did?" I breathed.

"I did," he replied, brushing a leaf off my shoulder. "Until you. You put me to work, didn't take shit, gave me a routine, and a reason to keep going. Made me start thinking about what to do with my time, made me want other things and brought me back to life…" he trailed off and heat entered his eyes that my body immediately reciprocated. "But I understand that initial panic of being left alone to figure it all out for yourself when you were relying on the one person in this whole world who could have helped you."

"Damn," I said.

"Yep," he chuckled. "We're two of a kind."

I looked deep into his eyes. "Thank you. Really. I wouldn't have figured that out for myself."

His thumb stroked over my jaw. "Yes you would, it just might have taken a bit longer but you would have. I told you, you're amazing."

I ducked my head as heat flushed my cheeks. "You know…" I cleared my throat, the words getting stuck. "You…you are too."

"Yeah?" he said, sitting up straighter.

"Yeah. You're a hard worker, you have an instinct about the animals that not many people do. We work well together and you're a man of many talents…" I trailed off, my meaning clear.

"Would any of those talents be bedroom-related?" He quirked a brow at me.

I tried not to smile. "Maybe."

"I think we should practice those talents right now," The low rumble of his words had me shivering. But my stomach chose that moment to growl, loudly.

"You're hungry?"

I nodded.

"Good thing I packed a picnic," he said, nodding his head towards the basket strapped to the back of Pickles.

My eyes widened. "You did?"

His cheeks flushed and he rubbed at the back of his neck, resting his elbow on one propped knee. "I wanted to have a date, my first date actually."

"Your first?"

"Yes, you've taken a few of my firsts now."

"Yes, I have," I replied smugly. "But now so have you. This would be my first official date too."

"Well, what do you know. Anyway let's get to it, I wanna eat," he said and pulled me closer.

"Then get the basket of food?" I frowned at him, confused.

He pressed a kiss to the corner of my mouth, his voice deep when he spoke. "That wasn't what I meant…"

"Ohhh…" Understanding dawned. "Yay for me."

CHAPTER TWENTY-SIX

Katarina

I woke up Monday morning rejuvenated.
Not just from the sleep and orgasms Jack provided. But I felt like I had turned a corner with the ranch. Jack had helped me uncover what my block was. Now I just needed to figure out how to move past it. I knew it wouldn't happen overnight but now that I recognized it, I could fix it.

I poured myself a cup of coffee and waved Tilly off to school. She was still sulking and mad at me for imposing a curfew on her, but she'd get over it. Daisy also avoided me like she was still pissed over the other morning when really, I felt like I was the one who should be pissed.

Jack came to the door, looking gorgeous in his denim jeans and blue lumberjack shirt that made his eyes shine even brighter. His boots though, looked like they were getting worse by the day. I opened the door and stepped out, closing it behind me.

"God, it kills me not to kiss you good morning," he murmured, his eyes filled with longing.

"It kills me too when you show up here looking like that." I ran my eyes over him, lingering here and there.

He glanced down at himself. "I'm fully clothed?"

"I don't know who you're fooling dressing like that, it's like you want me to throw myself at you."

He groaned. "Don't talk like that, please."

I laughed. "I'm not the one out here dressed like I'm just asking for it."

His eyes widened. "Are you for real? It's a lumberjack shirt?"

"You know exactly what you're doing," I teased.

He laughed and shook his head, blushing adorably. "I have somewhere I need to go and I kinda need you to take me, if that's okay?"

The uncertainty in his eyes as he asked me for a favor nearly ruined me. "Of course, when do you need to go?"

He shrugged one shoulder. "Not until this afternoon. So, where do you want me today?"

"I need you to take the lead as I've got some work to do in the office. There's not a huge amount to do, just sorting out the horses and checking on the cattle, making sure that asshole bison hasn't done any more damage to our fences."

He shook his head, smiling softly. "I feel like you need to let it go. Bert didn't mean anything by it."

I jabbed my finger at Jack. "He did, and he knows he did. You'll see. Anyway, is that okay?"

"Of course, go kick some business ass," he cheered.

I laughed and shook my head, winking at him before I headed back into the house. I went into the kitchen to top up my coffee and found Daisy, Maddy and August huddled together whispering and when they saw me, they hushed.

"Everything okay?" I asked.

Daisy glared at me and flounced out of the room.

"What is with her these days?" I asked, jerking my thumb in the direction she'd left. It couldn't be about Jack surely, or maybe it was. That nagging feeling pricked at me again. What were we doing with our relationship, situationship, whatever-ship it was.

"She's just cranky as usual," August said and then left, dragging Maddy out with her.

"Got another shift, see ya!" Maddy called over her shoulder.

I shook my head and refilled my cup before shutting myself in Daddy's office. I sat down in the chair, surveying the desk and papers that I'd semi tidied. Instead of dread, this time I felt empowered. "It's my turn now, Daddy. Hopefully you'll still find a way to show me the ropes."

*

"You love going for a drive, don't you?" I asked, glancing over at Jack. His eyes were closed in bliss as the breeze came in through the open window of the truck. The afternoon sun bathed him in a warm glow, highlighting the gold streaks in his brown hair. He looked like he was in his element.

He nodded, eyes remaining shut. "I do. I just can't do it anymore."

I flicked my eyes over to him again before turning them back on the road. "I'm sorry."

Apprehension emanated from him, rolling over us both. "Why are *you* sorry?"

"Because you've had something you loved taken away from you too," I spoke softly, almost afraid to voice the words.

The more time I'd spent with Jack, the more I'd come to see the man he was. His entire family had abandoned him, he'd been incarcerated for almost all his young life, and was only just tasting freedom now. He paused to enjoy the little things and did so much for other people. I watched him with the girls, spending time with Tilly and watching silly videos, talking to August about her books, trying to win Daisy over, and interrogating Maddy about her job and Leo.

He was a good man. I know what he did but now I was starting to see it the way my father had; he was a kid who made a mistake. Sure, it was a big one but he paid the price. And he kept paying it.

"Just over here, on the right," he said, snapping me out of my thoughts. I pulled the truck over, parking in front of a row of storefronts.

"What are we doing here?" I asked, getting out of the truck and coming over to him. He stepped up onto the porch, pausing in front of Larry's Leathers.

"I thought we could look for some boots for Tilly," he said, taking my hand and pulling me inside the store.

I paused over the sweetness. He knew I was concerned about it and was trying to help me any way he could. "But I've already looked in here," I sputtered, stepping through the door, a bell tinkling and signaling our arrival.

"Yeah, but you've not looked *with me*." He waggled his

eyebrows and I tried not to smirk. "Also, I need some myself." He lifted a foot and wiggled it, the sole of his boot flapping. I snorted and pushed him away, but he gripped my hand tight, pulling me past the rows of chaps, jackets, and hats to the boots section.

"What about these?" he asked, pointing to a pair of black cowgirl boots with a pink flourish stitched into the leather. They were lovely but they weren't Tilly. I opened my mouth to answer when Larry, the owner came from out the back, rushing towards us.

"Hello Katarina, back again! I was jus—" he broke off when he saw Jack. His demeanor changed, his expression shuttered and lips pursed in disapproval when he spotted our hands linked. "I see you've brought a friend."

"Hi Larry, yes we thought we'd try again for some boots for Tilly, and Jack needs some too."

Larry's stare roved over Jack, his lip curling. "I'm happy to help out with young Tilly's boots."

When he didn't say anymore I reiterated, "And some for Jack."

"I don't think we have any boots suitable for him," Larry said sharply.

I frowned, looking around. "Are you kidding, there's hundreds of boots here."

"And I don't believe any of them will fit *him*."

Jack's grip tightened in my hand and he stiffened next to me. I assessed the way Larry was staring at him, anger and disdain pulsing from the old man. He had known my mother; she had come in here all the time to get things for us. I guess he'd not forgotten what had happened and who was responsible like I had. I glanced at Jack who refused to meet my eyes and decided it was about time someone started showing up for him.

"Then I guess we don't need anything from here," I

announced, my voice wavering.

Jack tugged my arm. "It's fine Kat, I'll wait outside."

I spun to face him, the look of defeat on his face devastating me.

"No." I turned back to Larry. "Have the day you deserve!" I said and spun on my heel, marching out of the store, dragging Jack behind me. I muttered all sorts of insults under my breath about Larry as I got into the truck and it wasn't until I realized Jack was still on the sidewalk that I stopped.

I rolled down the window. "What are you doing?"

His hands were tucked into the pockets of his jeans, his biceps flexing from clenching his fists. "I think I'll walk back to the ranch. That way no one will see us together."

Anger flared in me. "Get in the truck, Jack, we're not going back to the ranch."

"Kat, it's fine. I get it, you don't need to be seen with me and—"

"Get in the damn truck, Jack," I insisted. With a sigh, he did as he was told, my lip quirked up. "Good boy."

"Jesus, Kat," he groaned, clicking his seatbelt in.

I reversed out onto the main road and headed out of town. We rode in silence but it wasn't the blissful silence from only ten minutes earlier.

"Where are we going?"

"Next town over to look at the boot store there. I'm not giving Larry our hard-earned money, even if it is tradition to get the boots from him."

"Kat, no. Come on, don't break tradition for me. Just go back and look at boots for Tilly. I'll wait in the truck."

I didn't reply, just kept driving and I could tell he wanted to protest but he didn't say anything more. The drive was about thirty minutes and when we were almost there, I turned to him. "Is it always like that?"

He didn't look at me, just stared out the window and I looked back to the road. "Yep."

"I'm sorry you're treated like that."

He turned to me, his expression fierce. "Do not apologize to me, Kat."

I took his hand and brought his knuckles to my lips and then placed his hand on my thigh for the rest of the journey. I pulled off the highway and drove through the sleepy town of Haven, our closest neighbors. I didn't come here often, only when I couldn't get something in our town, and it was a nice change of scenery. The layout was similar to Reverence, same strip through the middle of town where all the stores and bars were.

I pulled up outside Carl's Leather Goods Store and Jack followed me silently as we headed towards the building that looked exactly the same as Larry's Leathers. Another bell tinkled as we entered. We must have looked a real pair, both trudging in with sour pusses and a tension between us that was palpable.

"Well, it's not everyday I seen a fine-looking couple like you in my store." An elderly man with a paunch and Stetson came over. "I'm Carl, nice to meet you."

I found myself smiling, tension easing. "Nice to meet you too, Carl. I'm Kat and this is Jack," I pointed at the grumpy man beside me. "We're looking for some boots for him and while you two gentlemen get to know each other, I'll browse the ladies'."

I abandoned Jack, knowing that if I was still around he wouldn't shake off his funk. He needed someone like Carl to tease him out of it. I peeked at them over a row of boots I was browsing and watched as Carl held out a couple of types of boots to Jack and they talked about styles. After a moment, I heard Carl's loud guffaw and looked up to find Jack smiling while Carl dropped a matching black Stetson on his head. Damn he looked good dressed up like a cowboy.

I rummaged through the ladies' boots and although there were some great options, I just couldn't find what I was looking for.

Eventually I gave up and went back to Jack and Carl to find that Carl had talked Jack into buying a hat and two pairs of boots. A nice, sturdy black pair and a deep brown pair.

"For dancing," Carl winked at me, and I giggled.

"You find what you needed for Tills?" Jack asked softly, placing a hand on my lower back as we stood at the cash register.

I shook my head. "Some nice ones but not *the* boots."

"I'm sorry sweetheart," he said, leaning forward and dropping a kiss on my head. I closed my eyes, tilting my head up into his lips. As we were leaving the store, Jack paused by the window display.

"Did you see these?" He pointed at a pair of boots in the window. "You think Tilly would like these?"

I looked down and saw a pair of powder blue boots with a white chunky heel and white stitching up the calves. I tried to keep the smile from my face. "Do *you* think she would like these?" I asked, knowing full well they were damn near perfect.

He scrubbed the back of his neck. "I think so. I mean, as soon as I saw 'em I thought…they're cute but not too girly, like Tilly."

I eyed him and a flush spread over his cheeks and neck. "Yeah, I guess you're right."

"If you think she won't like them we'll keep looking," he rushed out.

"No, I think you're right. They're perfect for Tilly." I

leaned over and grabbed them, inspecting them and checking the size. It must have been fate because they were a size six, perfect for Tilly's little feet. "Great find, Jack."

Jack smiled adorably, glowing under the praise and mumbled something I couldn't quite make out. I paid for the boots and grabbed Jack's hand, tugging him outside.

I stored our purchases in the truck and then dragged him down to the ice cream parlor a few stores down. That was one thing our little town was missing that Haven had, a damn good ice cream parlor. Gertie made the best ice cream and I took out my phone and snapped a picture of the store front and sent it to her with a *wish you were here* caption. I'd barely heard from her recently and missed her so much.

I bought a couple of ice cream cones. Predictably, Jack protested but I insisted as a way to say thank you. I wouldn't have spotted those boots if it wasn't for him. We sat on a little bench that faced the road and watched the slow traffic.

"What did you want to be when you grew up?" I asked.

Jack swiped his tongue over his triple chocolate swirl and I fought to keep the filthy images from my mind of what that tongue could do. "I didn't really want to do anything except get away from my folks."

"What were they like?"

He shrugged, biting into the cone. "Drunk, angry, young. And disappointed in me. Nothing at all like Charlie was, or how I imagine Sherry would have been."

When he mentioned my mom's name, it didn't hurt. I just became sad that Jack had never known a loving family the way we had. "I'm sorry they were like that. You must have had a tough upbringing."

He shrugged again. "No tougher than anyone else."

I squinted at him in the late afternoon sun. "Why do you do that?"

"Do what?"

"You diminish your struggles."

He was silent for a while. "I guess I don't want to focus on them. I just want to focus on the future which is so damn bright, I have to shield my eyes. Why would I want to look back at the dismal gray of my past?"

"It's bright, huh?" I smiled at him.

He looked at me, really looked at me. "It sure is." He smiled and then stole an ice-cold kiss from me.

We finished our ice cream and headed back to the truck and drove home in silence, our hands clasped on the arm rest between us, and Jack back to his blissful state.

We'd had an afternoon out from the ranch together and although it got off to a rocky start, it had been so wholesome that I'd be lying if I said I wasn't picturing how it could always be like this.

CHAPTER TWENTY-SEVEN

Katarina

The following day I was out hustling again, at a different bank trying to get another loan.

If I could clear everything and owe a bank rather than shady businessmen, then it would give me some breathing room to plan.

I had one or two ideas starting to filter through to me now that I'd realized why I was blocked. I couldn't picture doing this without Daddy, but I was going to have to start tackling it on my own. The block was cracking and ideas were slipping through. Nothing concrete yet but the suggestion of something, maybe to do with riding lessons, renting out one of the pastures seasonally, stuff like that.

I didn't get laughed out of this bank. They needed a bit more from me and I had a follow-up meeting in a couple of weeks, which I needed to do some prep for but I left in better spirits. I made it home a little later than anticipated after stopping by Mom's bench and having a chat with her.

I'd left Jack in charge all day, trusting him with the ranch and annoyingly, I missed him. I was eager to get back and see him but when I arrived home, I found all my sisters around the kitchen table, looking solemn.

"Everything okay?" I asked, glancing at each of them nervously.

"We need to talk," Daisy said, the first thing she'd said to me for a couple of days since our spat the other morning. Maddy stood up and pulled a chair out for me and I frowned at her before slowly sliding into the seat.

"We know about the debt," August spoke softly. Each one of them met my stare with concern and pity, and heat flushed my cheeks, my pride prickling.

"How—"

"It doesn't matter," Daisy interrupted.

"The important thing is, we're not mad you kept it from us, we just want to help," Maddy added.

"I was thinking I could start riding lessons for kids and adults. I bet there's a load who would love to learn," August said, her eyes bright.

"But—" I began, my anxiety flaring at the thought of them swooping in to save me. Frustrated at the fact that I'd buried my head in the sand for so long that they'd had to step in.

"I have an idea too. Raleigh Ranch is some fancy ass spa retreat thing but there aren't any true cowboy Dude ranches in the area, so we could be the first and bring in some tourism. That way we can put them to work and save on staffing there. Jack could help build it and—"

I cut Daisy off. "Jack?" Since when would Daisy *ever* suggest working with Jack? Unless…dread filled me. "Did Jack tell you about the debt? Did he put you up to this?"

Daisy shook her head. "No."

A rushing sound filled my ears as I replayed my conversation with him. The one where I opened up to him, trusted him with the affairs of the ranch, and my feelings of inadequacy. How little I'd been doing to fix everything.

"You've done a great job but…" Maddy trailed off, looking to the others and the *but* twisted in my gut like a knife.

"The debt's been paid," Daisy spoke quietly.

"What!" I shouted, leaping up. I glanced around the table but none of them would meet my gaze. Humiliation crawled through me, the flush creeping up my neck to rest on my cheeks.

"H…how?" I stuttered, clamping my mouth shut as my stomach churned with sickness.

"It doesn't matter," Daisy said.

"Daisy!"

"It's all paid. We just need to focus on making money now so we can—"

"You don't need to focus on anything, that's my job!" I snapped. I'd never raised my voice to my sisters and the room went silent. I couldn't look at their disappointed faces a moment longer so I left the kitchen and ran upstairs to my room to escape.

I struggled to catch my breath as all my inaction caught up with me. I'd prided myself on being able to handle things here, setting good examples, and yet I'd done fuck-all for weeks, *months* even since Daddy passed.

My sisters had been forced to take action when I wanted them to remain removed from the issues here, all because I couldn't handle my shit. I was meant to be the leader. Daddy had left it all to me and I'd let the girls down. I'd let *him* down.

There was a soft knock on my door. "Kat?" August called softly.

"Leave me alone, please!" I called back. I was too hurt, too embarrassed and emotional to have a rational conversation about this. There was a beat before I heard August's footsteps pad away.

You've done a great job but...

The debt's been paid...

We're not mad you kept it from us...

Their words played over and over in my brain until I couldn't take it anymore and got into bed. I needed sleep, I needed this night to be over.

I slept fitfully, bad dreams of the ranch being repossessed, and the girls being kicked out on the streets tormented me.

In the morning, I awoke. My eyes were stinging from lack of sleep. I dressed slowly, my enthusiasm for a hard day's work waning. It was only just getting light but I wanted to get out and start work, the labor would force me to focus on something other than my miserable failings.

I worked hard baling hay, tidying the stables up, and then saddled Chester to ride out to the pasture and check the fence line. But my thoughts wouldn't leave me. How I felt ambushed by my sisters, and their disappointed expressions. But how did they know there were issues to begin with? I didn't want to think it could be him, but it was the only way that made sense.

"Jack," I hissed, remembering what he said the day

before about his *bright future*. He told them, he must have. How else would they know? The timing couldn't be denied, I just happened to tell him everything and the next day I'm confronted by my sisters? Rage filled my veins at my own stupidity, letting him in and trusting him after all the red flags I so casually ignored.

Like he knew I was thinking of him, he appeared at the mouth of the pasture. And when he spotted me, he urged Pickles on.

"Here you are," he said when he rode up to me, flashing me that big smile that made my stomach twist. Oh, how stupid I'd been. He played me to get what he wanted. Whether that was the cabin, the ranch or a contract to develop it or God knows what. He swung down off the horse and jogged over, leaning in to kiss me but I jerked away.

He frowned. "Everything okay?"

"You tell me."

He cocked his head to the side. "Sweetheart, what's going on?"

"Sweetheart," I scoffed. "I'm surprised you're not lording your victory." Had he always been after the ranch? He'd come here straight out of prison, maybe he knew about the deed after all. Then he bumped into me and realized he wasn't going to get his hands on the place.

Until I handed it right to him.

He looked around, confused. "Wh-what victory, what do you mean?"

I glanced away. Of course he would play dumb. "The girls. You won. Whatever it is you wanted, you got it."

He reached for me. "Won? I don't understand."

I stepped back. "I trusted you; I can't believe I opened up to you, and told you everything only for you to go and immediately tell the girls. For what? So you could talk them into a guest ranch that *you* get to build? Haven't you done enough to us? You're so calculated and cruel that you just had to take it one step further?"

His expression shuttered. "I don't know what you're talking about."

"Yes, you do, you know exactly what you did!" I shouted.

"I haven't told anyone *anything* you've said to me. Those are conversations between us," he dipped his voice lower, softening it. "They mean something to me and I would never do that to you. Do you really think I would betray you like that?"

The earnest look in his eyes, imploring me, had me faltering. I shrugged. "I don't know."

He reared back. "You really don't know me by now?"

I just stared at him, wanting to believe him but I'd already fallen for his schtick once. When I didn't reply, he shook his head and kicked at the grass.

"Will you ever see me as anyone but the man who took your mom away from you?" His tone was filled with despair, the words rasped from him.

I bristled, folding my arms over my chest. "Why are you bringing that up?"

"Because I need to know if you can ever forgive me?"

"Do you need my forgiveness?"

"Of course I do! I need to know that you can forgive me so we can move forward!" His voice raised, startling the birds pecking at the grass and they flew off with a disgruntled caw. He scrubbed a frustrated hand over his jaw.

I watched the emotions fly over his face and thought of his nightmares. This wasn't about me, not really. "I think you need to forgive yourself."

He whipped back to face me. "You don't, do you?" he

challenged.

"You think it's that easy?" I snarled. "A few orgasms and sweet words and what, all is forgiven?"

"Of course not, but I thought this was more than *orgasms and sweet words*. I thought this was serious, I thought this could be forever!" he shouted. His admission startled me but before I could process the words or react, he continued. "You think it's easy for me to picture our wedding day and know the reason your mom isn't going to be there is because of me? Like with all those amazing women back at the ranch? You think it doesn't break my *soul* to look each one of them in the eye and see the sorrow and know that it was *me* that put it there?"

"Jack—" I began but he kept going.

"So many times I nearly left and walked away, finding it too hard to face you all each day. But I didn't. I stayed because I owe you, I owe you all everything I've got and always will. I owed it to Charlie." His chest heaved with emotion and the release of all the words he'd been keeping inside.

His expression slipped into a blank mask. "But hey, if this is all just *orgasms and sweet words* then I guess that makes it real easy to walk away, don't it?"

He spun and stalked away, the ground practically shaking under his bootheels. He gripped Pickles' reins and lifted himself into the saddle with a grace I still admired. He tugged the reins and flexed his heels, urging Pickles to move and then he was tearing back across the pasture.

CHAPTER TWENTY-EIGHT

Jack

I somehow made it through the rest of the day, my rage and hurt keeping me going.

Her words played over in my mind. I should have known she wouldn't forgive me for the accident, that I was getting in over my head and too attached. I was dreaming of a life with her when I never really knew for sure how she felt about me, about us. How could I expect her to shack up with me after everything?

The ache in my chest didn't dull, even as I pressed my fist into the flesh, willing it to lessen. "My first heartbreak at the age of thirty," I snorted without humor.

I didn't see her again for the rest of the day, which was just as well. I didn't think I could look at her without begging her to love me.

It was ridiculous how gone I was for that woman. The

moment she stood up for me at Larry's Leathers, apologizing for how others treat me, then kissing my knuckles, I fell in love. Hell, I didn't fall, I plummeted. And landed with a sharp, jolting agony that I couldn't shy away from. What a fool I'd turned out to be.

I finished up for the day and headed back to the cabin for a long, miserable night alone. I paused when I saw all the Cartwright sisters gathered on the porch, glancing between themselves with worried expressions.

I detoured. "Everything okay, ladies?" I asked, stopping at the steps to the porch.

"We're worried about Kat. We haven't seen her since last night," Maddy said.

My stomach clenched at the mention of her name. I scrubbed the back of my neck. "She was in the south pasture a few hours ago."

"You haven't seen her since?"

I shook my head.

Daisy narrowed her eyes. "I thought you were working with her?"

I met her hard stare. "I was. But now I'm not. What's going on?"

"We may have…ambushed her last night," August said.

"Right…What about?"

"I found out about the debt on the ranch and that she'd been keeping it from us," Daisy replied, accusation in her tone.

The last thing I wanted was to start another fight, especially with Daisy who, frankly, scared me as much as Kat did. But I didn't like the way this sounded. "Do you own the ranch?" I asked her, raising an eyebrow.

"No, do you?" she snapped back.

"No, none of us do!" I yelled, not afraid to support my

woman, even against her own sisters. "Kat owns the ranch which means it's Kat's business."

"But we all live here, she should have said something," Tilly piped up, peeking out from behind August.

"Which is why she wanted to protect you from worrying about it. The last thing you need to be concerned about is losing your home. She's been working hard to get things in order and make sure none of you are impacted after everything that's happened lately. She was looking out for all of you," I growled, staring at each one in turn. "How did you find out?"

Daisy sniffed. "Well, I eavesdropped when those two bozos turned up demanding money and did some digging. I have my sources."

"Didn't expect you to be her biggest supporter," Maddy said, arching a brow at me, a small smile on her face.

"Sounds like someone has to be if you four are sneaking around behind her back and doubting her."

"I hope you're supporting her from a purely platonic standpoint?" Daisy shot back.

"It's none of your business what we are." *Damn these nosy women.* "But it's not something you need to be concerned about anymore," I added, looking off into the distance.

"Oh no," August moaned, her brows dipping in. "What happened?"

I picked at a bit of wood sticking out from the porch. "Hell if I know, although I expect it's fallout from whatever happened last night."

"Daisy!" Maddy growled and flicked Daisy on the nose.

"Ow! What was that for?"

"You started this whole thing and now you've ruined

299

their relationship!"

"Good!"

"No, not good! You can't mess around with people's lives just because you don't agree with what they're doing. I bet Kat thinks your *source* was Jack."

I zeroed in on Daisy. "Who is your source?"

Daisy whirled on me. "It doesn't matter and it's not anyone's business."

"Just like what's going on financially with the ranch isn't yours," I added and had the satisfaction of watching her expression fall. "Just…" I floundered. "Be careful with whoever it is, and let me know if you ever need help dealing with them."

Daisy's expression softened slightly before her trademark resting face slipped back into place. Deciding I was done with the Cartwright sisters for the day, I waved goodbye and went back to the cabin.

I sat on the couch, and tried to work through my thoughts as I hugged Teddy who was ecstatic about spending so much time together.

I figured that Kat had assumed I'd spilled the beans to her sisters then she felt cornered so attacked me. My chest ached at the idea of my strong, proud woman feeling like everyone thought she wasn't handling shit. If I ever needed someone to handle shit for me, I would pick her. She'd thought she wasn't doing a good job, but she was. She'd kept this place running smoothly and tackled every problem that arose, planning a funeral, becoming a guardian, fending off debt collectors, managing without ranch hands and even an asshole bison. She was too hard on herself, and I could only imagine the knock to her pride this had caused.

But she'd hurt me too.

She'd thought so little of me that she assumed it was

me who betrayed her confidence. For my own nefarious purposes, whatever those would be. She didn't trust that I was a man of my word and all I wanted was to make things right with her family. She didn't trust my actions, my hard work and my perseverance with her.

I'd been abandoned plenty in my life, I just wanted someone to show up for me. I wanted family and I'd stupidly thought I could find it here with these women, who owed me nothing.

I wanted to leave, to run away just like I'd told Kat. Only I had no idea where to go, I wasn't exactly flush with cash and…

"Now I have you," I said, ruffling Teddy's fur. I stroked the sides of his face. "Where shall we go, boy?" I asked. He barked and leapt off the couch and stood by the door. "You wanna go right now?" I laughed. He barked again so I got up and opened the door. A walk might be good for clearing my head.

I closed the cabin door behind me and looked out at the sky. The sun was setting, giving the sky that gorgeous pinky orange glow that I missed looking at when I was in prison. Teddy's bark distracted me and he charged off. I jogged after him and saw him run around the side of the house to the porch.

"Teddy, no!" I called.

I rounded the porch after him and saw Kat being huddled by her sisters. Teddy ran over to her and sat at her feet. She glanced down at him and stroked his head before she looked around for me.

Clearing my throat, I ordered, "Come on, boy." I wanted to get out of here and not have to face her. Turns out she wanted the same thing. As soon as she saw me, she brushed past her sisters and went into the house.

"Teddy, come on!" I called again, anger lacing my

voice. Daisy looked at me then her stare followed Kat into the house and frowned.

Teddy eventually found his way back to me but the joy was gone. I trudged along after him as we went on a twilight walk. He investigated all the bushes and trees. Stuck his nose in fallen hollow tree stumps and scared a sleepy squirrel or two. He was having the time of his life while I was lost in thoughts of Kat.

I shook my head, willing the thoughts away. But they stayed, even as we went back to the cabin, as I tried to sleep later that night, as me and Kat avoided each other for the rest of the week, and as I made it through my weekend shifts at the bar.

She wouldn't leave my brain. She was embedded in my DNA, wouldn't leave me alone and I couldn't take much more.

Love sucked.

*

The following week on a random evening, there was a knock on the cabin door. Hope flared to life inside me and I ignored it, knowing it wouldn't be Kat but still being disappointed when I opened the door and saw Daisy standing there.

"Are you lost?" I sighed.

She pursed her lips. "It's taken a lot for me to come here, don't make me regret it."

I tipped my head in acknowledgement and stepped to the side to let her come in, confused as to why she was here. She looked around the cabin, poked through my bookshelf, peered into the bedroom before getting comfortable on my couch with my dog.

"Please, make yourself at home."

"I will," she replied, turning a full force smile on me.

"To what do I owe the…pleasure?" I tucked my hands into the pockets of my navy sweatpants and leaned against the fireplace.

"I've been hard on you," she stated.

"I wouldn't say that."

She laughed and it made me laugh too which felt good, a welcome release.

"I've found it hard having you here, even harder to see you and Kat developing…something. I can only imagine how hard it must have been for her to put aside our issues and start seeing you, and I wasn't very supportive of that."

My throat closed at the mention of her name.

"I inadvertently fucked everything up for you two and I can't really fix it. But I can help with the ranch. I have an idea to make this a guest ranch and I would like you to help me make a 3D model of the plans so I can present it to Kat."

Whatever I'd been expecting when she came in, it wasn't any of this. I got the feeling she didn't want to have some gushy conversation or share feelings. It seemed like her acknowledgement of her feelings was also essentially the closest to an apology I was going to get. But I didn't need one. I was just glad she was comfortable enough to be in my presence and that she sought my help, to do something for Kat. To *support* Kat.

Also, the idea of having something to create with my hands was exciting. I'd had no inspiration with my woodwork recently and hadn't touched any of my tools, too busy moping around. The thought of creating something that would help the ranch was invigorating.

I pushed off from the fireplace and grabbed my toolbox. "Then let's get to work."

CHAPTER TWENTY-NINE

Katarina

I'd fucked up.

I knew I had. It only took me a couple of hours after Jack left me in the pasture to know I'd fucked up completely, but I had no clue how to fix it. I'd let my hurt from my sisters and my own inadequacies consume me.

When I'd locked eyes with him that same night on the porch, the hurt that shone in the blue depths had devastated me. I'd run from it, too scared to face it. My sisters had tried to talk to me and apologize but I hadn't let them. It wasn't about them. I was upset with myself.

The weeks had gone by, and I'd had to work side by side with him, seeing the hurt expression on his face whenever I dared to look at him. But he no longer looked at me, he avoided me.

And yet I knew that I could ask him to do anything, and he still would, and that made my heart ache even more.

I wanted to ask him to forgive me. I wanted to ask him to hug me and kiss me and call me sweetheart again. Because now that I'd heard him call me that, I wanted to hear it for the rest of my life.

But I wouldn't. I wanted him to choose it, not give it to me because I demanded it. He'd had so many choices and decisions taken from him in the last twelve years and I wouldn't take any more.

I'd misjudged him completely. He'd done nothing but help and support me, and at the first inkling that something was amiss, I'd leapt to conclusions and flung hurtful accusations instead of trusting that he would never do that to me. I knew it deep down, but I'd let my pain cloud my judgment and I didn't know how to fix it.

I missed him so much. Missed his arms around me, his soft hair under my fingertips. His words of encouragement and his belief in me. His strong muscles as he worked beside me, his rough hands calloused from hard work. His care for the animals, and for my sisters too. I'd seen how he'd developed a relationship with each of them. The other day, I even saw him and Tilly go off for a ride together and I was *jealous*. Jealous that my little sister had a good man to bond with and look up to when I should only be grateful.

Some nights I sat on the porch, just desperate for a glimpse of him passing by. I couldn't bring myself to sit in my father's office and watch him. Too many memories tried to claim me. I just needed to figure out a way to get to him.

I was sitting there now, in a newly refurbished

Adirondack chair that I knew was down to him and his big, loving heart, waiting for him to come home from the bar. My eyes caught the pair of headlights coming down the gravel road towards the house. I assumed it was Leo arriving so didn't pay too much attention until I realized it was a little pink classic Volkswagen Beetle.

My heart leapt into my throat, I was out of the chair before the car door opened. A head popped out. Wild black curls appeared. The same ones I'd spent my teenage years braiding and playing with. Then her curves came into view, and I couldn't believe it. She was here. She was home.

I was on the porch steps running to her by the time she was closing the car door and then we faced each other. My wide eyes latched onto the bruise surrounding one of her piercing blue eyes. Traveling down to her plump lip, swollen and split.

"Gertie…" I shook my head, my throat clogging with tears. My best friend's lovely face was marred by a battered appearance. She seemed to shrink under my stare, a far cry from the vibrant life and soul of Reverence she'd been as a teenager.

She stared at me a little longer and that plump, swollen lip wobbled. I sobbed as I grabbed her and crushed her to me.

"I'll kill him," I hissed. "I'll cut his fucking dick off and force-feed it to him."

Gertie sob-laughed, I eventually pulled back and looked her over. My vibrant, beautiful best friend was hardly recognizable. But I'd never been happier to see her. I gently touched the spot next to her black eye. "Tell me he's rotting in jail?"

Gertie shrugged. "Not exactly, he's got friends in high places. But I'm free and here."

"I'm so glad you're home," I said, pulling her into another hug, unable to believe she was standing in front of me. "I've missed you so much."

"I've missed you too, Kitty Kat," she sighed, sinking into my embrace.

"Are you home for good, Flirty Gertie?"

She laughed, the sound rusty. "I sure am."

"You staying at your mom's house?"

She pulled back tossing her hair over her shoulder then flinching. "No room, I just need to buy some time until I can figure something out. Can I stay with you?"

"Don't even ask. Redemption has always been your home."

She looked up at me, tears filling her eyes. "Thank you."

"Come on, let's get you inside. You have any stuff?"

She shook her head sadly, her curls flying around her. "No, I just grabbed my purse and left."

"No problem, we've got five women in this house. If we ain't got clothes, we ain't got shit!"

Gertie laughed, a full bellied laugh. She almost sounded like her old self. I took her inside and gave her some towels and she showered as I dug out some clothes, then I left her to it. I poured two big ass glasses of wine and went back out to the porch. She emerged after a while and gratefully accepted the wine.

"Start from the beginning," I said.

She slumped down into the chair beside me and proceeded to tell me all about Shithead Gary. My blood ran cold and I had to keep my emotions in check so she could get through it all but she did and once she had, it was like a weight was lifted from her shoulders.

"You can stay as long as you need to. Stay forever, please?" I begged.

She laughed and patted my knee. "I'm home for good, don't you worry about that." She turned her sad eyes on me and nibbled her lip. "I'm sorry I've been so distant. After everything you've gone through with Charlie, I've been so shit."

I held up my hands, my wine sloshing. "Don't! You clearly had your own stuff going on."

She nodded. "I had, but I could have still messaged more. I'm so sorry." We hugged, I gripped her tightly before we pulled away again. She sniffed and blinked rapidly to fend off tears. "Now, tell me about the ranch. Do I still need to kick Jack's ass?"

I sighed and downed my glass of wine. "No, you need to kick mine."

She narrowed her eyes but she held up a finger before getting up and going inside. She returned with the bottle of wine and topped our glasses back up before tucking her feet under her. "Continue."

I told her everything about the ranch, Jack, my sisters and the debt and my uselessness at dealing with anything, purging it all out to her. I was mid-*I'm so shit* when she interrupted.

"Hold up. Now I know you're not talking about my girl like that. You've had a lot of shit recently. Your dad *died*, that's a lot all on its own. For your mom's killer to turn up, you to take on everything at the ranch and actually keep it fucking running, is a huge success. Do not put yourself down."

I opened my mouth to argue but she cut me off again. "No! Okay, so you got a little bit blocked about how to make money, but I'm not surprised after everything. There is nothing wrong with that, and needing time to suddenly become this savvy businesswoman who saves the ranch? Damn girl, grant yourself some grace!" There was a pause as we stared at each other. "But at least you were getting dicked down," she snorted.

I spat my wine out. "Oh, I was getting *really* dicked down. God he was so good. I miss him." I dropped my head in my hands, wine sloshed onto the wooden porch. "I fucked it up and I can't stop thinking about him. I'm always looking for him, I need to be around him, even if he ignores me. The satisfaction I get just being in his presence is intense. And he's so good with the ranch, the girls and the animals *and* he's got such talent with wood."

"I'll bet," Gertie joked.

I rolled my eyes. "I meant woodwork not *wood*. But I hurt him and I don't know how to fix it."

"Tell him." She sat up straight. "Say, *Jack, I fucked up and I love you*. It's that simple."

My cheeks heated when she said the word love. But the more I thought about it, the more this icky feeling that had been plaguing me for weeks became clear. I *did* love him.

"Oh shit," I said.

"Epiphany!" she guffawed. "You love him *sssoooo* much!"

"You're slurring."

"*You're* slurring, my speech is impeccable," she shot back.

Gertie looked so proud of herself that I burst out laughing. After a while I could see her eyes drifting closed and I helped her upstairs to my bed.

I took the couch that night and I paced around the living room, thinking about her and her stupid woman-beating shithead of a soon-to-be-ex-husband. I thought about the ranch and Jack and eventually I gave up and went into my father's study.

I lingered by the window in the dark and looked out.

Jack's cabin was dark and my mind whispered cruel scenarios. *He's out with another woman. He's already moved on from you. You didn't mean anything to him.*

When the lights came on inside the cabin, I released the breath I hadn't realized I'd been holding. He wandered into the little kitchenette shirtless, just in his sweatpants, and my heart leapt into my throat. I took in the curves of his body. The smooth thick skin that covered his muscles and I ached to run my tongue over it again. I moaned softly in the dark and like he heard me, he turned and looked out the window, staring straight at me.

It was dark, I knew he couldn't see me, but I also knew he knew I was there. If history had taught me anything, he always knew I was watching him. I waited, seeing what he would do. I needed a sign that he missed me, that he was aching with our separation too.

But he turned away and the lights in the cabin went out and my hope died with them.

*

The next morning, I woke with a crick in my neck and a fucked-up back from the couch. I sat up and rubbed the sleep from my eyes before stumbling into the kitchen in dire need of coffee. I heard a loud sound and instantly smiled as I recognized Gertie's laugh.

My bestie was home.

I went into the kitchen, and she was there at the table, with my sisters crowded around her and Leo watching from his place next to the sink. He spotted me and held out a mug of coffee.

"I know lots of good stretches to help work out the kinks from a night on that evil couch," he offered.

"Thanks," I replied, accepting the coffee.

Leo moved closer to me and raised his mug to his lips. "Is there someone we need to fuck up?" he murmured, flicking his stare to Gertie. Her bruises looked just as bad today as they had last night and would probably take a few days to die down. I should have warned my sisters as it was a startling sight.

"Yes, we do indeed. No one messes with our Gertie."

Leo grunted and clinked my mug with his. "I'm on it," he said, then moved away and put an arm around Gertie's shoulders, always the protector of our little group. I caught the way Maddy's stare lingered on the arm Leo slung around Gertie before her eyes flicked to mine then away again.

After a while, Gertie broke away and came over. She had her wild hair piled up on her head, a few curls spilling out from the messy knot but her eyes were bright and clear. She had on one of my dresses that struggled to contain her generous curves and the lilac cowgirl boots that Daddy had bought her for her sixteenth birthday. She looked amazing.

"How'd you sleep?" I asked, hugging her.

"Like a log. How I've missed that Redemption Ranch air," she sighed.

"It was probably all the wine," I added.

"Definitely the wine," she agreed with a smirk. "What's the plan for today?"

My brows shot up. "You wanna help out?"

She shrugged. "Sure, I need to earn my keep if I'm staying here."

"No Gerts, you don't."

"Well, I want to. I love this place so put me to work, boss." She mock-saluted me.

I took Gertie with me to the stables and immediately

bumped into Jack coming out of them. I rebounded off the wide wall of his chest and teetered on my feet. He gripped my arm and tugged me forward to stop me from falling. The heat rippled all the way up my arm and had me fighting a shiver, but when I lifted my stare to his face, he wouldn't look at me.

"Sorry," I mumbled. He didn't say anything, just ducked around me and out of sight. His black Stetson perched on his head, his brown hair curling out from under it. A pair of blue Wranglers molded to his hips and his boots clomping as he walked away. He looked every inch a true cowboy and the sight was something to behold.

"Oh dang," Gertie whispered when he walked away. "Check out those muscles." I glared at her and she held up her hands in surrender. "Sorry, they just took me by surprise, that's all."

"You and me both," I sighed. I tugged her into the stables and she started cleaning the stalls while I fed the horses.

I was inspecting her work when Tate came in.

"Morning Katarina," he said, his deep voice echoing around the stables. Gertie stiffened and a small smile split her face before she slowly turned to face him.

He did a double take, his forehead puckering. "Gertrude."

"Hey Tatey," she waved at him.

I watched as his eyes roved her face, taking in her injuries and his mouth pulled into a tight line. He stomped over to her and gripped her chin, raising her face to the light and inspecting her wounds, a low growl emanating from him.

My eyes widened in shock at Tate's movements. His face twisted into a mask of anger, unlike anything I'd seen from him before.

"Was it him?" he uttered, his voice dangerously low. Gertie gave the slightest shake of her head.

"Then who did this?" he demanded. I was ready to step in and save her from being abused by yet another man, when a small smile unfurled from her lips as she stared at him.

"No one, sugar," Gertie replied.

He stroked his thumb over her chin before releasing her, his hand fisting and knuckles blanching. "Are you...well?" His voice was strained and harsh, but his face had slipped back to its usual calm, blank expression.

Gertie dipped her head. "I am, are you?"

Like whatever spell he was under was broken, he glanced around, seeing me standing there, gazing at him in shock. "Excuse me," he said in lieu of answering her and stalked from the stables.

"What the hell was that?" I said, looking at Gertie who was staring after him. "He's never acted like that before!"

"He always was a little strange. He was just concerned, Kitty Kat. Is he still living in the same house?"

I nodded. "Yep, he's still there. So if you had moved back into your mom's place, you'd have been neighbors again."

Gertie sighed. "Great."

Tate never reappeared but it wasn't an issue, he was only checking up on one of the horses. If I saw the medication wasn't working, I could call him.

Other than briefly introducing himself to Gertie, I didn't see Jack for the rest of the day and I was like a junkie needing a fix. I was twitchy and nervous just wanting to be around him.

I sulked through the afternoon and when it was dinnertime, Gertie insisted on helping me cook but quickly got frustrated.

"Kitty Kat, you are no use to me if you're pining like that."

"Hmm?" I lifted my head from where I was peeling potatoes but all I'd done was peel so much it was just all potato shavings and no potato.

Gertie nudged me with her rounded hip and flicked a dish towel at me. "Go and talk to him."

I shook my head. "I can't."

"No, you *won't*. There's a difference."

I met her disapproving stare, my stomach twisting when I locked onto the bruising again, horrified at what Shithead Gary had done to my best friend.

"You know, I don't remember you being this much of a chicken," Gertie goaded.

I gave her a withering stare. "I'm not fifteen anymore, that won't work on me."

She smirked. "Sorry, all I heard was *bawk bawk bawk…*"

I chucked a handful of potato peelings at her. "You're unbearable."

She ducked and laughed. "That's why you love me. Now *go*." She chased me out of the kitchen and then the next thing I knew, I was on the small porch of the cabin, smoothing my hands over my jeans and fluffing my hair.

I raised a trembling hand and knocked.

CHAPTER THIRTY

Jack

The knock on the door had me throwing a blanket over the diorama I was making.

Daisy had already been by this afternoon to see how it was shaping up, so I doubted it was her. I wanted it to be Kat but I also didn't know what I would say to her. It was probably Leo wanting another guys' night, but I wasn't in a sociable mood.

I was stunned when I opened the door and saw Kat on the other side. She looked at me with wide eyes, her expression so open and hopeful. She was wringing her hands together and I realized she was nervous. I'd never seen her nervous before. Her long blonde hair hung over one shoulder in a thick braid and her white sundress contrasted beautifully against the deep tan she'd gotten from all our work in the sun.

I knew her feet were tucked into those damn pink cowgirl boots but I don't think I could have kept my hands to myself if I'd looked down and seen them. I kept my stare straight ahead and locked on hers.

"Everything okay, Katarina?" I asked, concerned that she actually needed my help and wasn't just here to talk or for anything else.

"Are you alone?" she asked, peering behind me.

I frowned. "Yes?" I must have imagined the look of relief that flitted across her face before she smoothed her expression.

"Can I come in?"

I stepped back to let her pass, her floral scent drifting on the breeze behind her and making a beeline for my nostrils. I cleared my throat, willing myself to pull it together but I just wanted to grab her, bury my face in her neck and take a deep inhale.

I closed the door and she looked around the room and I panicked she would spot the diorama and want to know what it was so I stood on the opposite side of the room to make her face me.

"What's up?" I folded my arms over my chest.

Her eyes latched onto the action before she swallowed loudly and met my stare. "I, uh, wanted to apologize."

"No apology necessary," I replied curtly.

"Jack, please let me?" Her brows dipped in, pleading with me and I was helpless to resist, I nodded. "I'm so sorry I blamed you for telling my sisters about the problems with the ranch. I shouldn't have doubted you. I know you wouldn't do that, hell I realized it right away, but I just couldn't face you. I was a coward, and I let things fester and I'm sorry."

She twisted her hands together again and spoke softly. Each one of her words was like a soothing balm to my tattered pride and aching soul. I felt the weight lift from my chest, pleased that she knew my character and knew I wouldn't have done that to her, *couldn't* have done that to her.

"Do you..." she began. "Do you think we could pick up where we left off?"

God, I wanted to, I did. But that fight in the pasture had highlighted more than one issue between us. She was right. I hadn't forgiven myself for what happened to her mother and I didn't think I could. It would always loom between us, like a dark presence, and I didn't want that to bleed into any good times we would have, even if it killed me to stay away from her.

I scrubbed a hand along my jaw, my heart pounding as I said the words that tasted so foul. "I don't think that's a good idea."

"Oh..." Her expression smoothed but the light in her eyes dimmed, and I hated myself for doing that. I didn't say any more, couldn't, because all I would do was drag her into my arms and beg her to love me, beg her to tell me that it would all be okay, and we would have a happy life together.

But it was just wishful thinking.

She stared at me, and my heart cracked and shattered into pieces the longer I had to look at her. I saw the tears form and they wrecked me. She ducked her head, staring at her hands and a moment later, a tear fell. My hands gripped my biceps to stop myself from reaching for her.

"Kat..." I rasped, my throat hoarse from all the words, the emotion I was holding back.

"Okay well, like I said, I'm really sorry and I hope we can continue to work together," she said, her voice wobbly and then she was hurrying out the door.

The cabin was silent, empty. I seethed at myself, at the

unfairness of life for putting this beautiful, perfect, wonderful woman in front of me, so close yet so out of reach.

"Fuck!" I shouted, stepping forward and swinging my hand, knocking the diorama to the floor. My skin vibrated with anger. I needed a release. I needed a drink but I didn't do that anymore and I wouldn't again, which left nowhere for the anger to go.

I paced up and down, stomping my feet against the creaking floorboards. I went for a run, hoping the exercise would tire me so my anger would dull but it remained, sizzling away and only growing worse.

When I got back to the cabin there was a woman on my porch, leaning against the side, one leg cocked, the foot resting against the wall. I'd only met her today, she was Kat's best friend which meant she was someone I wanted to get on with but judging by the look on her face, I was already an enemy.

"What the fuck do you think you're doing?" She spoke softly but there was a lethal edge to her voice. "You fuck with that woman in there," she pointed towards the house. "And you fuck with me."

"Listen, Gertie, you don't understand—"

She poked my shoulder, her face coming into the light and I spotted the bruise around her eye and the cut on her lip. She'd clearly been through her own version of hell recently.

"No asshole, *you* don't understand. My girl just came out here to put her heart on the line and I'm guessing from her tears, you didn't take care of that heart, did you?" she spat.

The knowledge that Kat was so upset tore me up inside. "It's for the best."

Gertie snorted. "Says who?"

"Says me!"

"I call bullshit. What's your ish?"

"My ish?"

"Your issue? We've all got them, what's yours?"

She had a lot of balls for someone so tiny. "That's none of your business." I brushed past her, careful not to hurt her and went into the cabin. Teddy barked like a madman when he saw Gertie and although I tried to shut the door, she hip-checked it and busted her way in. She cooed to Teddy who immediately quieted and rolled over, showing her his belly.

"I've never seen her like this, Jack. You're special. And I've only known you one day but the way you were trudging around the ranch like someone stole your favorite toy tells me she's special to you too. So help me understand why you're not having make up sex right now?"

I rubbed my hands over my face, still damp with sweat from the run that didn't help at all. "It's complicated."

"Uncomplicate it for me. My beauty may be bruised but I've still got brains, I can figure it out."

I snorted, she was a pistol all right, and I found myself admiring her guts. "I can't be with her, it wouldn't work so it's best we end things now."

"Why?"

"Because I killed her mother!"

Gertie shrugged. "And?"

I gaped at her, my eyes and mouth as wide as each other at her nonchalance. She rolled her eyes and bent down to rub Teddy's belly. "Look, what happened, happened. No one can change it but it's already damaged everyone enough. You're going to let it stop you both from being happy? It's clear she's forgiven you for it, seems like the whole family has."

"I can't forgive myself."

"Ah, I see. Survivor's guilt?"

I shot her a weak smile. "I just call it guilt."

She straightened and stepped over Teddy and the shattered diorama but didn't spare it a glance. "Have you ever done anything about it?"

I shook my head. "Like what?"

She threw her hands up, exasperated. "I don't know, like try and move on? Go to therapy and work through it?"

I looked away from her bright, penetrating stare. She was annoying me now, asking me questions and acting like everything was so damn easy.

"Imma take that as a no?" she pressed.

I huffed out a breath. "No."

"Well, Mr. Smarty Pants, why don't you start there and do it fast, before she sees you're not willing to fight for her and finds someone who is." With that, she gave me a once over and shook her head before she stomped out of the cabin.

When she was gone I slumped down onto the couch. Teddy immediately got onto my lap and peered up at me panting, his tongue lolling out the side of his mouth. I stroked his head and found myself relaxing. Teddy was a bit like a therapy dog, he calmed me and gave me a sense of purpose.

Thinking about Gertie's words and Teddy's influence, maybe I should look into therapy. I scoffed at the thought but my brain refused to let it go. I clearly wasn't getting very far dealing with it on my own. But is that because I didn't want to? I got to live my life, I got to have fun and go out and work hard and love, and Sherry didn't get to do any of that. Because of me. Making myself feel shit was a way to punish myself for what happened, and I felt like I should be punished, it was only fair.

But what if you've been punished enough? A tiny voice piped up, a voice that sounded a little bit like Kat. Maybe I'd been so busy focusing on the need to punish myself even after my sentence ended that I hadn't taken a step back to see if I *should* be doing that.

I glanced down at Teddy, then at the ruined diorama of the new guest ranch. Hope sprung to life at the possibility of this project. "Maybe it's time I start living for me?" I said to Teddy. He barked in agreement.

I pulled my phone out of my pocket and opened up Google and proceeded to search for *therapists near you*. Once that was done and I had a couple of places to call, I stood up and picked up the diorama and began to rebuild.

CHAPTER THIRTY-ONE

Katarina

It had been two weeks since I'd run from the cabin, blinded by tears.

There was still an awkward tension between me and Jack, but we managed to work together which was the important thing. I didn't know what I would have done if he had quit the ranch. I knew he felt bound here but there really wasn't anything stopping him from leaving except his honor.

Some days it hurt to be so near him. I felt like if he looked at me, I'd shatter, but I held myself together. Gertie held me together. I didn't know what I'd do without her right now.

She'd given me a stern talking to. That woman had a

way with words. She'd told me to stop being so stubborn about letting my sisters help out with the ranch. She'd reminded me that it was their home too and they had a right to have a say in what happened here. She was right, Gertie was always right. I'd been blinded by my need to prove myself and lead them now that our father was gone.

But a good leader listens to others. And that was what I was doing today. The girls wanted to have a family meeting so there we were all sitting around the table, Leo hovering over by the sideboard with Gertie.

"Okay, let's hear it, get all the ideas out," I said, looking around at their excited faces.

August put her hand up. "Can I go first?"

"Of course."

"Um, I would love to do horse riding lessons here. Maybe do some school visits for the children with learning difficulties. We actually have some very calm horses who wouldn't be startled by some of the loud noises or sudden movements that the kids might make and it would be a great way for them to interact with animals."

I was touched that she had come up with something so thoughtful. There was a local school for children who had learning and behavioral challenges, and there wasn't a lot around Reverence for them to experience.

"I think that's a great idea, August. Let's take a look at what we need to do that: insurance, health and safety, and so on."

August beamed at me and nodded, beginning to scribble furiously in the notebook she'd brought. I looked around the table and everyone was smiling except Daisy who was peering towards the door and glancing at her watch.

"Who's next?"

"I wanna do a fundraiser for the fire station," Maddy said, and Leo pushed off from the sideboard and stood behind Maddy, placing his hands on her shoulders in support.

"Tell me about it, what do you picture?" I said.

"We could have a demonstration from the team, have competitions like who can put the uniform and equipment on the quickest, that kind of stuff."

"You could make it a fundraising fair and get local business owners in to show off their products, have food vendors and play games." I tapped my chin thoughtfully. "The vendors would donate a percentage of their profits in exchange for the visibility."

"You could auction off some of the guys, ooh and do a Hotties with a Hose calendar!" Tilly piped up and I wasn't sure how I felt about my almost sixteen-year-old sister thinking like that, but I didn't want to stifle anyone's creativity.

"We could make the calendar exclusive to the fair, like a 'when it's gone, it's gone' type of thing. That way it would bring in more fairgoers and make people spend more money to support the station, the ranch and local vendors?" I added. My head began spinning with ideas. "We can host weddings, team-building days, survival trips!" I shouted each one out, unable to stop the flow.

"Yes!" Gertie shouted, clapping her hands together and whooping. "There she is, now you're thinking like the badass businesswoman I know you are!"

I laughed, shaking my head but my cheeks flushed with pleasure knowing she had my back. The excitement in the room escalated and the ideas were thrown around faster than August could write.

I glanced around at the enthusiastic chatter, amazed at

how we'd worked together to come up with some exciting events and ways to support not just the ranch but local causes too. I was annoyed at myself again for shutting the girls out when they had so much to offer.

When everyone finally died down, I turned to Daisy. "Did you have something you wanted to share?" There was still tension between us. It was strange because I felt like she was avoiding me and keeping something from me, I just didn't know what. I had a feeling it had to do with the debt on the ranch and how it mysteriously got paid but when I'd pressed her on it, she had remained tight-lipped and snippy.

"Yes, but I just need—" She was interrupted by a knock on the front door. "Ah, there's my assistant now." She got up and left the room.

When she reappeared she was followed by Jack, looking delicious in his black jeans and forest green sweatshirt that hugged his broad chest and made me want to snuggle up against him. He was carrying something big under a blanket and Daisy was helping him maneuver through the kitchen and he placed it on the table in front of us.

He raised his eyes to meet mine and my breath caught in my throat at the soft smile he gave me. I almost cried. Missing him was a constant ache in my chest. I wanted him so much, wanted to tell him I loved him and throw myself at him but instead I just offered him a small smile in return.

"Hi," he said.

"Hi," I replied, like I was a lovestruck teenager when actually I was a lovestruck thirty-something.

Daisy cleared her throat, distracting us and Jack rubbed his hands together before pulling the blanket off whatever sat in the middle of the table.

"Ta da!" Daisy cheered and I stared at the wooden 3D diorama in front of me.

"What's this?" I asked.

"It's the new Redemption Guest Ranch!" Daisy flourished, waving her hands over the model *oohing* and *ahhing* like she was an assistant on a shopping channel.

I looked at Jack who had taken a place by Gertie at the sideboard. "Did you make this?"

He nodded. I looked at the model, at how carefully crafted it was, gorgeously varnished, the detail of the woodwork was intricate, immaculate. "It's beautiful," I breathed.

"Thank you," he replied, twin spots of pink appearing on his cheeks. I'd seen a couple of the pieces he'd crafted before, the bookcase and coffee table which were lovely but this was so much more complex and detailed. He was truly talented.

"This is what it could look like," Daisy began, gesturing at a section of tiny cottages. "This is where we would have the guest cabins, surrounded by trees for privacy but close enough to the pasture and stables that they can experience the ranch to the fullest. Each one comes with a hot tub so they can gaze up at the stars at night. Then we have a fishing area down by the lake where we can also do some water sports and activities. We can get our hands on some dirt bikes and ATVs and take them through the trails up towards the mountains. Then horse riding, and we can run a kids' activity club during the summer months which will appeal to locals as well as vacationers."

I stared at Daisy, amazed at what she'd pulled together and the thought she'd put into it. I knew she'd done marketing and event planning in college and had excellent grades, but once again, I was blown away by her ability.

"This is incredible," I said, shaking my head in disbelief as I looked down at the model. I turned to Jack. "And you'll build it?"

He stood up straight and rubbed the back of his neck like he did when he felt uncomfortable. "Oh I, uh, I think you'll need to hire someone to do it. I'm not good enough to—"

"Then you'll help until you're ready," I interrupted. "What's this?" I pointed to a little wooden figure in the treeline.

Jack's lip quirked. "It's an asshole bison."

My mind drifted back to that day when we worked together to fix the fence, to the almost-kiss that started it all. His eyes heated and goosebumps dotted my skin before he flicked his stare away.

The girls began chattering about all the exciting things we could do and the energy in the room lifted yet again.

"Thank you, all of you. I couldn't ask for a better family. I think, together, we're going to do something amazing with Redemption Ranch and I can't thank you enough." My voice became choked with emotion. "Daddy would be so proud." Once I said that, all bets were off and there wasn't a dry eye in the kitchen.

Eventually everyone dispersed into their groups. August was taking me through her notes when I saw Jack slip away. "Perfect, that's perfect, thank you," I said, patting her hand. "Just give me a minute?"

I left the kitchen and went out the door, but Jack was already gone.

"Go after him," Gertie said from behind me.

I faced her. "He doesn't want me."

"He does, he's just an idiot. You think he would have spent all that time making that diorama if he didn't care?" She pushed me towards the door. "Try one more time, for me."

I sighed. "Fine, but you're going to be in so much trouble if I come back crying again. Make extra ice cream just in case."

Gertie waved me off and pushed me out the door. The air outside was chilly, summer was ending and fall was on the way. I couldn't wait to watch the leaves change color on the trees. Fall was stunning at the ranch.

I reluctantly trudged over to the cabin and knocked once. I blew out a breath, squeezing my eyes shut and praying for a sign that things would work out.

"Hey," I said when Jack opened the door.

"Hey." He stepped back to let me inside and Teddy immediately leapt at me, yipping excitedly and I laughed as I fended off his excited licks.

"Teddy, relax," Jack chuckled, taking him from me and shutting him in the bedroom. "Damn dog," he muttered when he came back.

"You love it really," I teased, trying to lighten the mood.

"I do," he nodded. We faced each other, not knowing how to start. I just stared at him, at the soft brown hair that fell across his forehead. His bright eyes had lost some of the wariness they usually held and, in general, he seemed less reserved than normal.

"Thank you for working with Daisy on the model," I said.

"I need you to know, I didn't do it so I could help build the guest ranch. That wasn't my intention."

"No, I know. But I want you to put your stamp on this place."

He quirked a brow at me. "You do?"

"Of course. You're so talented and hell, this is your home. You're part of Redemption, you should be able to have input in what happens here too. Daddy would have wanted that. You're family."

A slow smile spread across his kissable lips. "I am?"

I nodded. "Once you've broken down Daisy's defenses, you're in," I joked.

"You have that much faith in me?"

"I do. I know we'll need contractors to do some of the other foundation work but I want you to help build it."

He stepped closer and I tensed, waiting to see what he would do, but he stepped back and I tried not to feel disappointed.

He cleared his throat. "Thank you, that means a lot."

"You're welcome."

He continued to stare at me, fists clenching and unclenching. There was an intensity radiating off of him that I didn't understand. But when he didn't do anything else, I began to feel like I was taking up space in his cabin.

"I'd better go." I headed towards the door and he followed behind, reaching around me to open in. "Goodnight Jack," I said, trying to keep the sadness out of my voice.

He growled, actually growled. "Fuck it."

Then he slammed the door shut and the next thing I knew, I was being pushed up against it and his lips were crashing into mine. My body melted against him, like I'd been holding myself together for too long, just waiting for the next time he touched me, and now I surrendered.

He ate at my mouth, his hand coming up to cup my jaw, angling my head for deeper contact and he rumbled low in his throat when our tongues teased each other.

My hands were up under his sweatshirt, my nails dragging down his skin, pulling him closer in a frenzy. I needed to feel him everywhere. I'd been without him for so long that I was starved for him.

He pulled his mouth away, trailing kisses over my face, cheeks, eyes, and back to my lips. Then they trekked down my neck and back up to my ear. "I can't stay away from you," he murmured.

"Then don't." I sighed blissfully as his hands cupped my ass, lifting me, and my legs wrapped around him, feeling his hardness right where I needed him. "Don't leave me again, please," I pleaded, pulling his sweatshirt over his head.

His hands made quick work of the buttons on my shirt and then we were skin to skin, both of us sighing at the contact. He walked us towards the bedroom door, managing to kick Teddy out and shut us in and never once moving his lips from mine.

He lay me down on the bed and pulled back. His eyes wide and hot on me, his hair spiky from where I'd tugged at the strands. His stare roved over my face before he lowered himself to his forearms, stroking my hair and touching his nose to mine. "So beautiful, sweetheart," he whispered and I nearly sobbed.

I writhed against him and he grunted as he worked our pants off. Then his hands were spreading me open and tracing slick circles over me. He pulled back to watch my face as he worked me, taking me higher and higher and my eyes fluttered closed right as I was about to fall.

"Stay with me," he said. "Stay right here."

I opened my eyes as my climax slammed into me, watching him, the intensity in his stare, the *love*. I whimpered, my body shuddering and clenching but he wasn't inside me.

"Now, Jack," I sobbed and then a moment later he was filling me up. So thick and perfect.

He hooked an arm under one of my knees, bringing it up and hitting me deeper. My eyes flew wide as he pounded into me and grunted with each thrust. His muscles flexed as he worked and our skin slid together, damp with sweat. He tilted my hips, hitting that spot inside me that had me crying out as another peak loomed.

"Come for me, sweetheart," he begged, pressing a wet kiss to my lips. The endearment, the plea, the pleasure, it all built and then I was thrashing under him as I came again, muscles squeezing him tight.

"I love you," slipped out but I didn't care. I meant it, I truly did. And then he was shuddering over me, pressing kisses all over my face as he moaned through his release. He rested his forehead on mine, panting.

"Did you mean it?"

I nodded. "Yes, not great timing but I meant it."

His eyes squeezed shut. "I love you, too."

My heart skipped a beat. "You do?"

"I do, so much I can hardly bear it," he groaned, then kissed me again, rolling us so he could hug me tight.

"But..." I trailed off.

"I know, I know. I was an idiot." He pulled back, brushing my hair off my forehead and stroking the strands. "I thought our history and issues would sink us and I didn't think I could survive the heartache. Then Gertie talked some sense into me—"

"Gertie?" I asked, startled.

"She's a great friend and a tiny, scary woman," he nodded solemnly.

I laughed. "That she is."

"I decided to start seeing a therapist because you were right. I'll never understand how you can forgive me, I'm just beyond grateful you can. But I haven't forgiven myself and don't know if that's possible. I was punishing myself but I was also exhausted from fighting it. I've been going to therapy to try and work on living with it all."

I stroked over his face, his stubble grazing against my hand. "How's it going?"

He turned his head and pressed a kiss to my palm. "It's hard, it's still early days and there's a lot of work to do but I can't stay away from you anymore. It's been too hard, and call me selfish, but I don't want to."

"I don't want you to, either."

"I don't know what I did to deserve you but I'm so grateful. I love you so damn much, you're the most amazing woman."

"You're not too bad yourself," I replied, and he barked out a laugh.

There was a whining and a scratching at the door and Jack sighed before throwing the blanket off us and striding to open it. I watched the way his ass flexed and his thighs moved, obsessed with every single part of him. Then Teddy was running into the room and launching himself at me.

"Even my damn dog loves you so much," Jack grumbled, coming back to bed.

"And I love him too," I smiled. "But not as much as I love you."

EPILOGUE

Jack

Six Months Later...

"Ouch!" I grunted, stumbling over something and trying to right myself.

"Oops, sorry!" Kat sang as she pulled me along. I was blindfolded and my life was in her hands. Normally, I would completely trust her but right now, I was having second thoughts.

"Where are we going?" I grumbled, annoyed that I wasn't home with her naked and moving under me. I was impatient. I hadn't been able to get my hands on her properly for days and I was getting cranky about it.

The construction was beginning on the guest ranch. We'd had another anonymous influx of cash which enabled us to get started on some of the basics. There were plans under way to raise more money to build the rest. Between Daisy's proposals and Kat's business acumen, money was starting to roll in.

Events were being held and one of the pastures rented out for various occasions. There were even talks of a movie being shot on the property, apparently it was the perfect location with the Tetons in the background. August's horse-riding lessons were going well and she was so caring with the kids, it was wonderful to watch.

Me and Tilly went for a ride every Sunday morning and I enjoyed being someone for her to look up to and I'd given her advice on her future, and she actually listened. She was planning on going to college in the next couple of years and was looking at what to do to apply for scholarships.

I was working with my hands and experimenting with my craft and learning more skills. I loved losing myself in creating and building something lasting at the ranch.

Me, Leo, Max and even Tate had been hanging out more, and it was amazing to have friendships where you ribbed the shit out of each other but still supported one another.

My therapy was going well, some sessions were tough, and some were more healing than others. There was a lot of guilt to work through and some days I wanted to give up, but I kept going. Rome wasn't built in a day and it would take a long time to heal, but with Kat, the guys, and the Cartwright sisters by my side, I would get there.

Life was damn near perfect right now.

"You'll see," Kat teased.

I could tell we were outside but I didn't know where. I could hear traffic and noise, and then she let me go. "Wait here."

"Oh yeah, I'm really gonna run off right now," I

grumbled.

She leaned up, pressing her body against me, stirring my blood. "I love it when you're cranky like this," she murmured before swiping her tongue across my lips.

I groaned when she pulled away, desperate for her to put her tongue right back where it was.

"If you're good for the next two hours, I promise to drive you wild later, how does that sound?"

"Like fucking perfection," I growled, my cock already hardening in my jeans.

She tapped her hand against it. "You might wanna get rid of that."

"I can think of a few ways," I replied and she tsked. I snorted, trying to think of things to get my blood cooling. When it eventually worked, she praised me and it almost got me going again.

"Okay, we're ready," she said, grabbing my hands and pulling me forward.

"Who's we?" I darted my head side-to-side, desperate to work out what was going on but I couldn't. Then the blindfold was pulled from my eyes and I blinked, trying to focus.

"SURPRISE!"

I was stunned to see we were at The Lonely Bison. The bar was decorated with balloons and streamers and party poppers were being let off. I glanced around, seeing the Cartwrights, Leo, Max, Gertie and Tate with little party hats on and tears damn near filled my eyes.

"Happy birthday, sweetheart," Kat murmured, pressing a kiss to my lips before slipping a hat on my head.

"I…" didn't know what to say. Emotion overwhelmed me. Obviously you don't celebrate your birthday in prison and I hadn't wanted to after what happened on my eighteenth birthday. It wasn't a day to celebrate anymore, it was a day to remember when I made a shitty choice and Sherry lost her life. The pain didn't hurt as much as usual though, and I could thank my therapist for that, for all the work we'd done and continued to do.

"It's fine, we're all fine," Kat added, and I looked over her shoulder meeting Maddy, Daisy, August and Tilly's stares but they all just smiled brightly at me. The love flowing from them broke me and a tear leaked out. I brushed it away and they raced forward and hugged me.

I would never be more grateful to have people in my life than right at this moment. I'd lost my family but I'd found a new one, and this family was the best damn one I could ever be blessed with.

When they pulled away, I was smiling and I searched for those blue eyes I was so enamored with. Kat was standing off to the side, letting me have my moment, and I stormed towards her, dragged her against me and dipped her back, slamming my lips into hers.

"Thank you, sweetheart," I whispered when we pulled apart, male satisfaction roaring through me at the glazed look in her eyes.

"You're welcome. Now let's celebrate," she said, handing me a root beer. I glanced around and saw that we had the place to ourselves, I could relax and just enjoy the company. I chatted with Max, challenged Maddy to an arm wrestle, beat Daisy at pool, and danced with August.

I slipped away, pressing a kiss to Kat's hair while she chatted with Leo and Gertie, and went over to the bar. As I approached, I spotted Tilly talking to Max and he was gesturing like he was agitated.

"You need to move on, Princess," Max said, and Tilly looked at him like he'd just told her Santa wasn't real.

"Everything okay here?" I said, eyeing them both.

"Sure thing. Someone just needs to get it into her thick skull that she's a *child* and get over this pathetic little crush of hers," Max snarled. Tilly gasped, then promptly burst into tears and ran off.

"Give me a reason not to deck you right here for that," I warned Max.

He spun and faced me, his eyes narrowed. "You think I wanted to do that? She's been hanging around for months and it's got to stop. I was cruel because being nice hasn't worked. It's your birthday, I don't wanna fight with you. I didn't wanna be a dick but she needed it. Now she can hate me and move on and stop staring at me with hearts in her goddamn eyes!" Max shouted, slamming the dish towel down on the bar and storming off.

I shook my head, deciding to deal with this drama another day. Max had a point but I just hated seeing little Tills hurting after everything she'd been through.

I went over to Kat and Leo who were now joined by Daisy. "I think someone needs to check on Tilly," I said.

"I'll go," Leo volunteered. "This one is too drunk," he pointed to Daisy. "And this one needs a night off from parenting," he pointed to Kat.

"Appreciate you," Daisy called after him.

"Damn, you are drunk," he teased.

"Hush up, Rodeo Clown!"

"Now that your inhibitions are lowered, are you going to reveal to me who cleared the debt and gave us some money to start our plans?" Kat asked, staring intently at Daisy.

Daisy nibbled her lip before she sighed. "It's Raleigh."

"Duke? No!" Kat gasped.

"Yeah, and?" Daisy grew defensive. "You went to him for help too!"

"Yeah, but not for money! Oh Daze, what have you

done? You know there's no such thing as a gift with him!""

"It wasn't a gift," Daisy hedged.

"What did you agree to?" I asked, wondering how nervous I should be about what Daisy had gotten herself into.

"Do we owe him back? With interest? Does he get a say in what happens to the ranch?" Kat was panicking and I put a hand on her lower back, rubbing it gently to soothe her.

"No, nothing like that. *We* don't owe him anything." Daisy picked at the label on her bottle.

"Daze, what did *you* agree to?"

"Nothing that I can't handle okay, let's drop it. It's this big lug's birthday so let's celebrate. Race you to the bull!" she shouted and charged down to the mechanical bull, knocking Gertie aside to get to it.

I looked at Kat whose face said it all. "Stop worrying,' I told her. 'She's not an idiot. If she says she can handle it, she can handle it. They're grown adults, you need to stop mothering them at some point."

She stomped her foot like a teenager. "I don't want to!"

"Well you need to. Focus on me instead," I teased.

I pulled her over to the bull and watched as Gertie and Daisy took turns trying to stay on the longest, with neither of them doing very well. Leo reappeared and said he was going to take Tilly home.

Then it was finally time for us all to leave and Kat drove us back in the truck. I sat in the front, closing my eyes and enjoying the drive. Every now and then she took me out in the truck, knowing how much I loved it. She offered to let me drive around the ranch, but I didn't want to. My ban was for life, and it would stay that way.

"I'm just gonna make sure everyone is put to bed, then I'll come down," Kat said, herding the girls into the house.

"Be quick, please. I want my birthday present," I said against her mouth. She groaned and shoved me off before shouting at the girls to get their butts upstairs.

I headed to the cabin, fending off an excited Teddy as he greeted me. I fussed over him before putting him in his new, hand-crafted doggie bed.

I was tidying up the kitchenette when I felt that telltale prickle. I looked up, through the window and towards the house.

Smirking, I stalked over to the window and crooked my finger, knowing she was watching me. She mostly stayed with me in the cabin but sometimes when she had lots of work, she would stay at the main house. But she'd watch me. Every so often I put on a show for her but not tonight, tonight I needed her here.

My phone buzzed and I pulled it out.

Kat: Coming now.

Typing out my reply and sending it, I looked up at the house and saw the light shine in the window. Satisfaction flared inside knowing she was there watching me.

She met me at the door and I carried her into the bedroom. Before I could rid her of her clothes, she stopped me. "Your present," she declared, holding out a little box.

I glanced down at it, sealed with blue ribbons, touched. "You didn't have to get me anything, you're more than enough."

"Well I didn't get you something, I made it."

I tore the box open and on a bed of blue tissue paper, was a little wooden heart with our initials etched into it. The wood had a few dings in it, like she had caught it while carving the heart, and seeing she'd done this herself, touched me more than words could say.

"You made this?" I asked, staring at it in awe. She nodded. "No one's ever done anything like this for me."

"I know," she smiled. "But now they have."

I tackled her to the mattress, raining kisses over her until she was breathless and begging, and then I made love to her again and again until we were both finally sated.

"Love me forever?" she mumbled, her voice drowsy with sleep, one arm slung over my chest.

I smiled against her hair, trailing my fingers lazily up and down her bare back. "I'll do anything you ask me to, sweetheart."

"Good," she snuffled.

That night, I couldn't sleep. Not from nightmares or bad thoughts, just my mind playing over the last few hours. The love, the joy, the family I'd found.

"Thank you, Charlie," I whispered, not wanting to wake Kat. I thanked him for showing me the way, forever grateful to him for showing up for me, for giving me a family, and getting me to consider my future.

And forever grateful that I made my way to Redemption Ranch...

The End.

Cowgirls Do It Better

Want more tales of our cowgirls on Redemption Ranch?

Then keep your eyes peeled for:

Cowgirls Do It Better Volume Two: Revelry – Tate & Gertie's story coming September 2025…

ALSO BY LILA DAWES

Citrus Pines Series:

Come and visit the fictional small town of Citrus Pines, Tennessee, that's full of broody, sexy, muscley men and the sassy, independent women who bring them to their knees…

Book One: It's Only Love

Book Two: Color of Love

Book Three: Sweet Surrender

Book Four: Love Me Good

Book Five: Take A Chance

ACKNOWLEDGEMENTS

Thank you so much to every reader who has taken a chance on my new series. If you had asked me in December 2023 if I would ever write a western, cowboy/girl series, I would have laughed and told you I knew less about ranching than I did about rocket science.

But then I heard a song. Just one line in a song and the whole damn series was born. The kicker? I can't even remember the song, haha!

Huge thanks to my cover designer; the wonderful Loni at The Whiskey Ginger. I'm so grateful to work with you and love our shared passion of badass women, vintage art and ranching. I'd been thinking about the cover for a year before I found you and my God, it was worth the wait, it's absolutely stunning – *heart eyes emoji*…

Massive thank you to my critique partners in crime, Mimi Flood, Anna P and Anna Lindgren; for all your endless feedback and support. You're all lifesavers and I enjoy every second of our half hour voice notes.

A big, big thank you to my amazing beta readers, Jessi, Natalie and Emma. Your love for these two kept me going through all the doubts and imposter syndrome; I still look back at your comments now when I need a boost; I'm truly grateful.

And finally to my fabulous editor, Caron Allan – thank you for fixing all those commas and removing all my 'ing' words!

ABOUT THE AUTHOR

This section used to read that Lila was a thirty-something living in Derbyshire, England with her parents – but not anymore!

She finally managed to buy a house – so now she lives on her own, in her own chaos with too many plants that she can't keep alive, candles that she refuses to light and is probably pondering over whether to get one cat or five.

She has a completely ~~un~~healthy obsession with Henry Cavill, LOVES talking all things romance and firmly believes that enemies to lovers is the ultimate trope and will fight anyone who says otherwise. If you disagree; feel free to drop into her DMs to have a long, heated debate before you ultimately agree that she's right, ha!

Lila loves connecting with readers so feel free to get in touch and sign up to her newsletter for monthly updates including firsthand news on her books, giveaways and freebies and a monthly Henry.

Website: http://www.liladawesauthor.com

Newsletter Signup: http://www.liladawesauthor.com

Instagram: @liladawesromance

Tiktok: @liladawesauthor

Facebook: https://www.facebook.com/lila.dawes.7/

Cowgirls Do It Better: Redemption

Printed in Dunstable, United Kingdom